More praise for
DO UNTO OTHERS

"Jeff Abbott's Jordan Poteet is a genuine hero, fighting insidious enemies in a humorous yet touching tale of small-town warfare. A carefully considered plot, clearly drawn characters, and Abbott's irresistible Southern voice combine to create an exciting new entry in mystery fiction."
—DEBORAH ADAMS

"Small hometowns are like the old feather ticks that lay on your grandmother's bed: you sink down into soft familiarity, but you wake up feeling smothered. Jeff Abbott clearly knows all about small towns—and his first novel plays comfort against claustrophobia as tangled bloodlines lead to bloody tangles in Mirabeau, Texas. A promising debut and a fine new author I shall watch with interest."
—MARGARET MARON

"Jeff Abbott is a major new talent, Jordan Poteet a refreshing and delightful new series character, and *Do Unto Others* a powerhouse debut. One can only hope that this is but the first in a long line of adventures for Jordy Poteet."
—SUSAN ROGERS COOPER

DO UNTO OTHERS

Jeff Abbott

BALLANTINE BOOKS • NEW YORK

Copyright © 1994 by Jeff Abbott

All rights reserved under International and Pan-American Copyright Conventions. Published in the United States of America by
Ballantine Books, a division of Random House, Inc., New York,
and simultaneously in Canada by Random House of Canada Limited, Toronto.

Library of Congress Catalog Card Number: 94-94420

ISBN: 345-38948-4

Manufactured in the United States of America

First Edition: November 1994

10 9 8 7 6 5 4 3 2 1

In loving memory of Jeffie Hagle
Grandmother, Teacher, Friend

ACKNOWLEDGMENTS

SEVERAL PEOPLE CONTRIBUTED TO THIS BOOK and I'd like to thank them: my family and friends for their support; my editor, Joe Blades, for his enthusiasm and thoughtful suggestions; my agent, Nancy Yost, for her hard work; Dr. Robert Power for medical information; Karen Bell of the Smithville, Texas Public Library; Chief Lee Nusbaum of the Smithville Police Department; and, finally, the members of The Black Shoes Writers' Group: Barbara Burnett Smith, Jan Grape, and Susan Rogers Cooper. The friendship, encouragement, and criticism of these three writers has made all the difference to me.

CHAPTER ONE

IT WAS REALLY RUDE OF BETA HARCHER TO argue with me right before she got killed. Downright inconsiderate if you want my opinion. The woman acted like she had a toll-free line to Jesus, so you'd think she would have had forewarning of her fate. Plus she went on her tirade in front of folks, which caused me all sorts of grief later. Fortunately I'm not a man to complain about the lack of trump cards that life deals you.

The day she died was a typically humid, sunny spring day in central Texas. I'd been running an errand and I was in a cussing mood when I got back to the library. You see, coming back from the pharmacy, where I'd bought Mama's medicine, I'd tripped over a damn baseball bat some kid had left in the small ballpark next to the library—and I'd nearly planted my face in the grass. I picked up the bat, looking around for a batless kid, but didn't see the owner. I figured whatever little Billy Joe or Bobby Jack had lost his equipment would come wailing about it soon enough, so I took the bat inside.

The Mirabeau public library was its usual hub of activity. Shelves of dusty, unread books made a place scintillate. I walked in, nodded to some of the regulars, winked at a couple of the pretty ladies, and dumped the bat into my little office behind the checkout counter. I surveyed the library.

In Mirabeau three's literally a crowd, so we had ourselves a horde that morning. Old men sat in the periodical section, slowly scanning the papers and frowning over progress. A couple of book-minded youths from the high school fed their spring break reading habits in the science-fiction section. In the most distant corner of the library, the gossipy ladies of the Eula Mae Quiff Literary Society (led by the one and only Eula Mae herself) quietly pretended to discuss the latest offerings in romance literature while chatting about their neighbors. All in all, a quiet group, idling away several hours in the coolness of the books and avoiding the smothering spring humidity.

I'm not usually found at the checkout counter, but since I didn't have a staff I didn't have much choice. The last chief librarian, the much-loved Miss Eugenia Pollard, had died three months earlier; and her staff had departed for greener pastures. One had taken a job as chief librarian in nearby Bavary; the other had gone off to be a country singer in Houston. I, of course, was the one left warbling the blues—although their departures had left the job available for me. My assistant, Candace Tully, was only half-time and was at a dentist's appointment this afternoon.

The only advantage was I didn't have a staff continually pointing out how everything had been done under the golden touch of Miss Eugenia. My own library experience had been ten years earlier, working part-time in college at the Fondren Library at Rice University; so I'd brought a certain . . . flexibility to the work. *Flexible* meaning that I often didn't know what the hell I was doing and just rolled with the punches.

Fending off my desire for a cigarette with a wad of Juicy Fruit gum, I sat behind the counter and unfolded my many folders. One was of résumés and applications for my unfilled staff; one was a grant request I was working on to the U.S. Department of Education to get money for a literacy program; another folder held the layout for our monthly newsletter (much of it devoted to children's activities); and the last contained a request from the mayor (my boss) to take a look at the Library Rules and Policy, since Miss Eugenia hadn't updated that particular document since Reconstruction. I attacked the résumés first; the sooner I got help, the much less stressful my days would be.

It was the Juicy Fruit that caused the commotion. Beta Harcher resented folks sinning right in front of her. And since I was chewing gum and not reading religious literature, I raised Beta's ire.

I knew she was standing there for a full minute, waiting for me to look at her, so I kept my eyes lowered.

It didn't work.

"Mr. Poteet!" she snapped, not bothering to modulate her voice. That irritates me. After all, it is a library. I try to keep the noise down, even if most of my patrons are hard of hearing. I'm a librarian now (although not by training, and my respect for the profession has grown by leaps and bounds).

I looked up at her. She was in her early forties—but carrying all the sins and worries of her neighbors had aged her. Once she might have had a delicate, doll-like face; now lines of worry and pinched anger marred her forehead and cheeks. Shots of gray streaked her thick dark hair. I'd wondered what kind of body might be lurking below her frumpy clothes. It was hard to tell beneath the dark, shapeless jackets and the Bible she constantly clutched to her bosom. Her blue eyes gleamed with shiny, repressed indignation. I suspected her righteousness was going to be all over me like white on rice.

I popped my gum and picked up the book stamp, as though I expected Beta to actually check out a book instead of lighting a bonfire underneath one. I saw the hardback novel Beta held in her quavering hand.

"Goodness, Miz Harcher." I smiled my public relations smile. "I didn't know you liked English literature."

"This isn't literature, mister. This book is obscene."

"*Women in Love* by D. H. Lawrence? Oh, Miz Harcher, that's a classic." I gently tried to take the book from her hands, but she wouldn't let go. She didn't want to miss a chance to wrestle with Satan.

"Classic smut, you mean." She slapped a familiar piece of paper on the counter. The last sixteen times she'd done this, I'd sighed. Now I fumed.

"What's this?" I asked, all innocence.

"Another Request for Reconsideration of Material." Beta smiled. I glanced at the form; she had filled one out for Lawrence's *Women in Love*. Just as she had for books by Mark Twain, Jay McInerney, Raymond Chandler, Nathaniel Hawthorne, Alice Walker, and others.

We're open-minded folks in the New South, no matter what the media might have you believe. If you object to something in the Mirabeau library, you can fill out one of these requests for reconsideration. We didn't get them often; at least we hadn't until Beta went on her empty-the-shelves campaign. I scanned her latest report, written in her creepy thin handwriting; no, she admitted she hadn't read the whole book ("it liked to make me gag, so I couldn't finish the Godless trash"); her estimation of the main idea of the material was innovative ("promote sex outside of marriage"); and in her judgment the book would have a deleterious effect on the youth of Mirabeau ("it's liable to make them want to fornicate before they get halfway through").

I leaned back in my chair. I'd had enough of this harassment.

"Look, Miz Harcher . . ."

"I know my rights, Jordan Poteet. Talking to you isn't going to satisfy my complaint. You got to call a meeting of the Materials Review Committee."

I groaned. If someone files a request, and I can't resolve the problem, I have to call a meeting of the MRC, which consists of me (naturally), the chairman of the library board, and another member of the board. Beta had demanded sixteen meetings thus far and hadn't gotten one book off the shelves. I decided to try polite reason with her.

"Miz Harcher, no one considers Lawrence obscene these days. Why, you can go to the big universities in Austin and College Station and they teach him there."

This academic recommendation didn't sway Beta Harcher. She ripped open the book to a passage of dire sin she'd marked with her bony, blame-pointing finger. She lectured me like she was calling fire down to the pulpit.

"Not to mention that the title itself suggests unnatural acts, but listen to this: 'The thought of love, marriage, and children, and a life lived together, in the horrible privacy of domestic and'—here she puckered her sour face—'connubial satisfaction, was repulsive.' " She glared at me. "This book is antifamily."

I sighed. Miz Harcher hadn't consulted Noah Webster on what connubial meant, but it sounded decadent enough to warrant her attention.

Her harangue riveted everybody. I could see Old Man Renfro and my other elderly regulars look up from their reading. Eula Mae Quiff and her groupies watched, more interested in local passions than those described in the bodice rippers they discussed. Gaston Leach stuck his head out from behind the science-fiction stack, ogling the scene through his bottle-thick lenses. Ruth Wills, a local nurse, glanced up from the card catalog.

Biggest crowd in the Mirabeau library in three days. Beta loved an audience. I'd seen her poking around the shelves the past couple of days, sniffing out depravity, and now she'd made her move.

"And you know chewing gum's not allowed in the library, Jordy Poteet!" Beta Harcher added, taking on all transgressions in her immediate vicinity.

"I'm trying to quit smoking," I explained, hoping for a little mercy. "And as the librarian, I allow what I like in this library." I tried to puff out a bubble to piss her off, but Juicy Fruit's not built for blowing.

"The city council might argue with that." Beta shook the offending volume of Lawrence in my face.

"If the city councilors want to fire me, they can. *Women in Love* is not obscene, Miz Harcher."

She pulled out her big censorship gun. "Oh, really, Mr. Poteet? I think the God-fearing folks of Mirabeau'd like to know what else goes on in this book." She leaned her face close to mine and I could smell her unpleasant breath. Probably chewing brimstone as a mint.

"Men. Wrestling in the nude together." She enunciated the words carefully, making sure I understood their import.

"Yes, the two men in the book wrestle. It shows their friendship," I explained patiently. "They don't have sex." My twentieth-century Brit Lit professor surely would've found Beta a challenging pupil. "Why don't you really read the book, Miz Harcher? You might find it interesting."

"I don't have time for such smut."

"No," I said, knowing that folks were watching, "but you do have time to come in here, make a scene, disturb the other patrons, and in general make a nuisance of yourself."

"I don't appreciate your tone, Jordy Poteet." She set her lips tightly, glaring at me.

"And I don't appreciate yours, Miz Harcher." I had grown tired of her stunts since my victory over her two months ago at a library board meeting. I stood, hoping to look tough at my height of six feet two. I didn't think it'd work; I've been told repeatedly that my blond hair and green eyes make me look too boyish to scare anyone but infants. "I'll remind you that you were thrown off the library board because of your censorship stance. If you don't want to read the book, don't read it. No one is hog-tying you down and forcing you to read Mr. Lawrence. But don't expect you can come into this library and dictate to others what's available to them. This tactic of continually filing complaints—"

"This trash undermines people's souls."

"Good God, Miz—"

"Don't you take our Lord's name in vain!" she shrieked. You could have heard a page turn in the silence, but no one in the library was reading anymore. Not with Beta's soul-saving floor show playing.

"Hardly anyone checks out that book." I lowered my voice rather than lowering myself to her level. "Very few souls are at risk." I hated all the eyes that were suddenly on me. I'd felt that way ever since I'd come home to Mirabeau and I still wasn't comfortable with it. I can't stand pity. "Maybe we can step into my office and discuss this Request for Reconsideration."

I considered that a perfectly reasonable suggestion. So I was awfully surprised when she slapped me. With *Women in Love*.

She belted that book right across my face. Not a love tap, but an honest-to-God blow. And Jesus made that woman strong. My head whipped around and the ceiling lights flared in my eyes. I felt my lip split and there was a wetness on my nose that I was sure was blood. The carpet felt rough against my hands and I realized I was kneeling on the floor, knocked clear out of my chair. I saw my wad of gum stuck on my office door. I glanced up at Beta Harcher; she smiled, as pleased with herself as a child with a new toy. Her eyes were two shiny pebbles, cold and stony.

Screams erupted from the Eula Mae Quiffers. Gaston Leach ducked back into the space operas and fantasy novels. Old Man Renfro creaked out of his chair, arthritically trying to hurry to my defense. Ruth Wills beat him to it. She ran over and grabbed Beta's arm.

"Let me go!" Beta squawked, as though Ruth were a demon wresting her from the Lord's work.

Ruth pulled the book from Beta's clutches and tossed it on the counter. "I think you'd better go, Bait-Eye. You've caused enough trouble."

The look Beta gave Ruth Wills held pure venom. "You watch your mouth, missy. You're a sinner, too. You have no right—"

"You've just assaulted Mr. Poteet," Ruth interrupted coolly. "In front of witnesses." I like Ruth; she's one of Mirabeau's nicest residents. She's also a lovely brunette with a figure a boy could doze against and die happy. "He could press charges against you, and no one here would blame him."

"You better leave, Beta." Eula Mae Quiff herself had come up behind them, keeping the younger Ruth as a buffer between her and our local zealot. Eula Mae is fond of bead necklaces and she nervously fingered one of the several around her throat as she watched Beta.

"That smut he's offering our young's no better than that trash you write, Eula Mae," Beta snarled. "All that sex—and women living independently from God's plan."

"My fans judge it otherwise," Eula Mae sniffed. She swirled her colorful, robelike dress to emphasize her point. I thought she might take a bow.

"God's the final judge." Beta stared down at me like a dog eyeing a pork chop. "I'll close this pit of lies. God will help me."

"Beta, stop it!" An unexpected ally had appeared: Tamma Hufnagel, the Baptist minister's wife. She had come up behind Eula Mae. Beta was one of their flock but Tamma's young face looked pained. "This is not the way to conduct our Lord's work—"

"Hush!" Beta ordered. Poor Tamma clammed up abruptly.

Back on my feet, I grabbed a tissue and wiped the blood from my nose and mouth. I poked at my nose experimentally; it didn't shift into a new shape, so I decided it wasn't broken. I was still in shock that this woman had whacked me. She looked so harmless until she opened her ornery mouth. Why couldn't she have assaulted me with a nice thin book—say *Of Mice and Men*?

"No, the final judge is over in the courthouse." I reached for the phone. "You get out and lay off the library, or I'll call Junebug Moncrief and have your God-fearing self hauled into jail." I couldn't resist, and I should've. "You think St. Peter'll be impressed with your having a record when you approach those pearly gates? He might just put you on the down elevator."

"You're burning in hell, not me," Beta announced, pulling away from Ruth's grasp. She straightened with righteous dignity. "I'll leave, although I'm not afraid to go to jail. I have the Lord's work to do today." She cast a baleful eye over the stunned, silent faces in the library. "Y'all remember that. I have the Lord's work to do."

I wondered if I was the only one on Beta's holy hit list. I leaned across the counter and jabbed my finger in her face, tempting her to take a bite. "Fine, you poor misguided woman. Go make trouble for someone else. This may be a public facility, but you are damned unwelcome here. If you bother me, or anyone at the library again, I will press charges."

"You can't punish me. You judge me not. Though God is judging *you*." Her voice hardened, and it amazes me still that there could be so much spite in that frumpy form. "He's judging you, Mr. Know-It-All Jordy Poteet. That's why your mother is the way she is—"

"You shut up!" I yelled. "Get out!" Dead silence in the stacks. Those dark, deadened eyes stared into mine. I fought back a sudden, primitive urge to spit in her face. Yes, I do have a bad temper and Beta saw she'd gone too far. She didn't flinch away, but Ruth hustled her out into the spring heat. I could hear Beta protesting the whole way, threatening Ruth with various fundamentalist punishments. I could only imagine what special levels of Gehenna she reserved for me.

I slumped into my chair. My hands shook. I was ten years younger and a foot taller than Beta Harcher, but her words rattled me more than her punch. I admit it: I could've throttled her—just for a moment—when she made that crack about my mother. Whack me with books all you like, but leave my family alone.

The bleeding stopped, but I kept dabbing my nostrils with the tissue. The blue-haired crowd headed straight for me, gabbing with their henhouse tongues. The Eula Mae Quiffers examined me carefully and, assured that I was okay, offered their opinions on Beta.

"She's addled," said one lady.

"Poor dear just takes the Bible too literally," opined a more pious woman who had not been battered with a book recently.

"I can't believe she struck you," added another, disappointed that my nose was intact.

"What a bitch," Eula Mae commented. She's the closest thing to a celebrity Mirabeau has—a romance novelist known to her fans by the nom de plume Jocelyn Lushe. I have nothing against romances—I could probably use one in my life—but Eula Mae gets inordinate amounts of local adoration for her prose. I can only take so many heaving bosoms and smoldering loins per page, and Eula Mae isn't big on setting limits.

Mousy Tamma Hufnagel watched me carefully. "Miz Harcher's upset about being kicked off the library board, Jordy. She's just awful tetchy about civic morals. She means well."

"No, she doesn't, Mrs. Hufnagel," I answered. "She's a lunatic and they're usually not concerned with the public good." I watched Ruth come back into the library, without Beta. "I could just kill that old biddy."

"Don't you listen to Beta Harcher, Jordy." Dorcas Witherspoon, one of my mother's friends, took my hand. "She's a bitter fool. She's unhappy, so she wants everyone to be that way. We don't care if you keep smutty books. You know all I read here is the Houston paper for 'Hints from Heloise.' "

"Please, ladies, I'm fine," I assured them. I sighed. "I guess Mrs. Hufnagel's right; Beta's just mad she got kicked off the library board. She'll just find someone else in Mirabeau to terrorize."

That, unfortunately, didn't happen. The good Lord decided, I suppose, that He needed Beta Harcher at His right hand a far sight earlier than any of us reckoned.

The rest of the afternoon passed without divine retribution for keeping D. H. Lawrence on the library shelves. At six I closed up and drove past the well-kept homes and fake antique light posts on Bluebonnet Street. Mirabeau is Texas old, founded in 1841 during the Republic days, but I figure the powers that be don't think it looks quaint enough for antique buyers and city folks looking to move to the country. So they've started adding Dickensian touches such as Victorian light posts and wrought-iron benches on the major streets in town. We natives try not to mind.

It doesn't take more than ten minutes to get anywhere in Mirabeau, and getting home takes me all of two minutes. I veered left onto Lee Street, drove down a block to Blossom Street, and stared up at the neat, two-story frame house I'd grown up in and recently returned to. Did it look smaller, or was it that I was just bigger and wiser? I couldn't tell.

I went inside and found my mother walking in circles around the cozy living room. She does that more and more now, shuffling along in her slippers and robe. I suppose it's a nice room to orbit. Mama just has to navigate a wicker sofa and an oval, polished wood coffee table with a fan of *Southern Living* back issues spread across it. Normally I would have steered Mama to a chair and told her to sit down, but I had a throbbing headache. This was not the life I'd ever planned on coming home to. So I sat down and watched Mama for a few minutes. She was intent on some journey of her own and she made for good quiet company.

Our quality time together didn't last long. "You're not being much help, Jordy, letting her do that," my sister Arlene muttered as she walked in from the kitchen. I could smell the wonderful aroma of black-eyed peas and chicken-fried steaks. Sister (I never call her Arlene unless I'm really mad at her) flared me a look as hot as her skillets. She took Mama's arm and aimed her toward a chair. Mama, a lock of her blondish-gray hair straying into her face, sat unprotestingly and looked at me as though unsure of who I was. "Jordy," she announced finally, in the same tone she'd used to reproach me for mouthing off as a youngster.

That was a relief. In her mind for the past two days I'd been her long-dead brother Walter, and it was nice to be back among the living.

"Eula Mae called and told me what happened at the library," Sister said with That Tone. She gawked at my busted lip. So much for my three minutes of peace, which was my daily allowance at home.

"I guess you'd like to get fired from that library," Sister observed archly, going back into the kitchen with a toss of her blonde hair. I can always count on Sister for loving support. "That way you could just go back to Boston and your precious little publishing job, and never mind Mama."

My throat tightened. I'm still not used to Mama. It's hard to go away from home, leaving your mother full and vital and smart, and return to find her mind eroding like a clay bank on a flooded creek.

I got up and followed Sister into the kitchen. "Why are you pissed today? You have a fight with Bubba?" Bubba Jasper owned a truck stop called The Near End on Highway 71, where Sister cooked God's food like chicken-fried steaks, enchiladas, and pecan pies. She worked from eight at night till four in the morning, came home, and slept till ten when I went to the library. She hated that schedule, and I wasn't that crazy about it either, but it kept one of us at home most of the time. I took care of Mama at night; Sister handled her during the day. I suspected Bubba gladly gave Sister that shift to discourage competing suitors. Bubba needed any advantage he could muster.

"Never mind Bubba." Sister's rosebud mouth pouted. She poked at the simmering black-eyed peas with a stained wooden spoon. She was so pretty when we were kids; I'd been jealous of Sister's popularity in school. I'd spent most of my academic career in the Mirabeau public schools as "Arlene Poteet's little brother." It wasn't a bad label. Having a popular sister helped no end in the date department.

"What's wrong?" I asked.

"I—I think you resent me, Jordy. You haven't been much help with Mama this past week."

I had a reply ready (as usual with Sister) but I stopped. She really looked sad, staring down into the warming vegetables. She'd pulled her thick blonde hair back from her face and it made her look older and tired. Her features were still striking, with high cheekbones and clear green eyes. "I think you resent me 'cause I brought you back here."

"You didn't bring me back, Sister. I chose to come back."

"No, you didn't. We've been playing this guilt game long enough. I made you feel guilty about being up North, and now you won't let me put Mama in a nursing home." Sister looked up from her bare feet.

"No, I won't put Mama in a home." I hoped we wouldn't have this argument again. "I'm not going through what we went through with Papaw again." I set my teeth. I remember walking out of my grandfather's nursing-home room while he sobbed as we left him. Just the memory makes my heart clench.

"You had—or have—the money to put Mama in a good place, and she won't know the difference. Her mind is going, Jordy. Yesterday she thought I was Aunt Sally visiting from Houston. She kept asking if I was going to vote for Harry Truman."

I always try to find the bright side of bad times. "At least she knows it's an election year." I bit down on my swollen lip as soon as I said it, surprised at myself.

Sister wasn't amused. "Sometimes she doesn't even

remember Mark, and that's hard for him. Her own grandchild."

"The money isn't the issue, Sister."

"Yes, it is. You have it and I don't. That's how it is, Jordy, and has been for years."

"And you accuse me of resenting you? Listen to yourself."

She shrugged. "Maybe I do resent you. Mr. Big Book Editor, living up North and making money to burn." She shook her head and laughed her drawly little giggle that annoyed me when we were growing up. "You're really using that fancy college degree, aren't you? Stacking books back at the Mirabeau library."

"Look, running a library's not easy. You know that was the only job I could find here connected with books . . ."

"You care more about books than you do me!" she snapped. "God! I have my own life to live and I have Mark to raise. You could give me the money and keep Mama from being such a godawful burden to me."

"Yes, I could, I suppose. But I won't. I won't have Mama in a home. She needs us, not strangers in uniforms."

"It's not your choice to ruin my life and Mark's, too."

"It's my money," I answered, not adding that there wasn't a lot of my money left. "I'm sorry you feel this way. You don't have to help with Mama. I'll move her into a place of my own and get daytime help while I'm at the library. You don't have to have a damn thing to do with her."

"And let you have all that moral superiority? Let people here think I don't care about Mama as much as you do? Forget it." Public opinion in Mirabeau still mattered to Sister. Left over from her cheerleader days, I'm sure.

"Then quit complaining." I spoke more sharply than I intended, but the strain of quarreling with her showed.

"Dinner'll be ready in about ten minutes." Sister went into her monotone. "Please set the table."

"All right." I didn't want to argue any more. I set the table quickly and haphazardly, flinging the silverware and plates down like I was dealing cards.

Sister twitched at the noise, but didn't look up from the cream gravy she stirred. "Would you please go find Mark?" I turned and went.

I stumbled out the front door into the fading spring sunshine. The evening was still warm and hazy with moisture. Spring had been rainy. Mirabeau is the lush, dark, deep green that always surprises folks who've based their visions of Texas on John Wayne movies that were shot in dusty, brown Arizona. The oak trees, pregnant with leaves, shook in the twilight breeze above my head. The crepe myrtles were short explosions of pink, scattering their blossoms on the air.

I leaned against my blue and gray Chevy Blazer and looked out down Lee Street, across front yards that were maintained like badges of honor. Yards—whether front or back—usually aren't divided by fences in Mirabeau, and the residential streets don't have curbs. The grass just goes straight into the neighbors' yards and into the street. When I was little this whole neighborhood was my playground, but now I felt like I was trespassing. What was I doing here? I'd bolted at age eighteen, swearing to never come back. Twelve years later and here I was. I scanned the street. My nephew Mark was down a few houses, talking with a neighbor's kid.

"Mark! Supper time!"

He waved back, almost begrudgingly. Maybe Sister was right. Was I controlling her and Mark's life by insisting that we take care of Mama at home? I didn't feel in control; Mama's disease was. It dictated and governed every aspect of our lives. I'd given up a life I'd loved, being a social sciences editor for a prestigious textbook publisher in Boston. I'd acquired authors, negotiated contracts, planned marketing campaigns to storm college campuses nationwide. It had been decent money and a lot of fun. Now, I was back at my life's square one because I didn't want my mother in a nursing home. Logical, aren't I?

I couldn't blame Sister for being mad. If she blamed Mama's condition for running her life, she thought I was making it worse. She'd wanted money to put Mama in a nursing home over in La Grange. She didn't have the money, hadn't had anything except Mark since her rodeo smitten husband had abandoned her five years ago and headed to parts unknown. I had headed for parts unimaginable (New England), but Sister'd had my phone number.

I stood in the carport, staring at the modest house I'd grown up in. It was built at the turn of the century and had belonged to my father's uncle who died widowed and childless. Two stories, white, with plenty of blue-shuttered windows across the front to let in light and maybe neighbors' peering eyes. The porch was wood and held two white wicker chairs that should've held Mama and Daddy. Sister and I sat there and moped these days.

We hadn't kept up the house as Daddy had; it had been his pride and joy, but we took the house for granted. Mark trimmed the yard and tended the flower beds, but the house needed a paint job, especially across the front porch. I knew I should get it taken care of, but I was wary of spending money in front of Sister. Every cent I wasted on other expenses was a cent that could help lift the burden of our mother from our shoulders. If only Daddy had been as thoughtful about insurance as he was about lawn care.

The average yearly cost of nursing home care in this

country is thirty thousand bucks. It tends to be one of those facts you don't bother with till your mother's walking in circles, drooling on her chin, and thinking you're her long dead brother Walter. My investments and savings couldn't bear that assault.

Part of me didn't want Mama in a home, and the other part of me didn't want my savings flying away so quickly. I couldn't tell Sister my financial woes. She thought my college education resulted in an instantly swollen bank account. She wouldn't believe me if I told her I didn't have the money to keep Mama in a home for years of Alzheimer's. Contrary to popular belief, publishing is not a gold mine.

Mark swaggered up to me like only a thirteen-year-old can. He doesn't even have the grace to look like a Poteet—not that it's his fault. He's tall and rangy like us, but that's about it. Where Sister and I are fair-haired and green-eyed like both our parents, Mark is dark and just looks like trouble. He's the spitting image of his daddy, the aforementioned rider from responsibility. Even wearing silvery round glasses, he looks like a rebel. I never managed that in my youth.

"I hate to interrupt your cramped social schedule, but supper's on," I said. Usually I tease Mark, but arguing with Sister had soured my mood.

Mark surveyed me with eyes older than the rest of him. "You and Mom have been fighting over Mamaw again."

"What are you, psychic?" I put my arm around his shoulder and steered him toward the house.

"I don't know why you two just don't accept Mamaw for how she is. She ain't getting better."

"Isn't," I automatically corrected. We walked into the living room, where Mama sat chatting chirpily with shadows.

Mark waved his arms in front of her face. "No one's here, Mamaw. Nobody but us."

She looked at him, hurt. Turning her face away, she pressed the back of her hand to her pinched mouth.

I took Mark by the arm and shuffled him into the kitchen. "Must you argue with her?" He's a good kid, but I wondered if the strain of our difficult domestic situation was wearing on him.

"Nothin' to argue about with Mamaw. An argument takes two people armed with opinions or facts. Mamaw's lacking both."

"Don't be disrespectful, Mark."

Mark smacked his chewing gum in a most impertinent teenage fashion. I do wonder where he gets it. "You know, Uncle Jordy, I don't see disrespect in facing up to Mamaw going out of her head."

I opened the fridge, got out a pitcher of iced tea, and slammed the door. "You're too young to understand. Mama's not exactly going out of her head." Who was I kidding? I was mad at Mark for saying exactly what I thought.

"I think there's going to be a vacancy sign hung up real soon," Mark muttered as Sister came back in. Needless to say, the rest of the meal did not go well. Little family squabbles over the sanity of the clan matriarch do not make for carefree dinner conversation. Mark huffed off to his room to read; as I said, the boy is not entirely without redeeming features. Sister pouted again and left for The Near End and the company of Bubba. And I sat watching TV with Mama. I think the vapid sitcom made as much sense to her as it did to me. I started reading an old copy of Eudora Welty's short stories, disturbed only by Mama's occasional giggle-along with the laugh track, as automatic and sad as a last breath.

It was ten o'clock and I was putting on the news

from Channel 36 out of Austin when the phone rang and my life turned left.

"Jordy." It was Sister. "How's Mama?"

"Fine," I answered. Sister thinks she takes better care of Mama than I do.

"Did you give her her Haldol?" Sister asked, and I slapped my forehead. Crap! I'd gotten the prescription filled and my confrontation with Beta Harcher had driven the pills right out of my mind. I glanced over at Mama; she looked wide awake. Our family doctor prescribed Haldol for her restless nights, so common in Alzheimer's patients.

"Um, yeah, just about to give it to her," I fibbed. I'd left the pills in my office at the library. Well, Sister didn't need to know about my slight dereliction of duty. I could run down to the library and be back, with Sister none the wiser.

"Okay. I'll see you in the morning then." There was the barest hint of reconciliation in her voice.

"Fine. Bye." I hung up. Mama was watching the television and had turned the volume to a murmur, the way she liked it now. I went to the stairs in the entryway and called up to Mark.

"I'm heading off to the library for a second. I'll be right back. Come down and sit with Mama, please."

As I went out the door, I heard the shuffle of his feet as he descended the stairs.

I got in my Blazer and headed down Lee Street, driving past Mirabeau's little city park. I could have turned onto Bluebonnet then, but a bit of curiosity as to what was going on in town steered me past the park toward Mayne Street (spelled that way because some founding mother didn't want Mirabeau to copy every other small town in America). It had been the same growing up here—the hope that something fascinating might be go-

ing on if you just went around town to find it. The night
had cooled some, but the air felt wet with unfallen
spring rain. Distant thunder rumbled faintly, toward
Austin and the Hill Country. I scanned the clouded skies
for lightning, but the night was dark and still.

There's no long drive around Mirabeau. If you head
north of Mayne, you get the lovely quiet neighborhoods I
grew up in. If you head south of Mayne, you go through
the small business district. Stores stand in sturdy brick
buildings that have survived tornado, flood, and modern
architecture—and proudly have their dates of dedication
carved in the crests on their highest (usually third) floors.
Past the business district is a small railroad yard, and beyond are the mix of trailer parks, ramshackle shacks, and
small but tidy homes that make up the poor part of town.
The railway also divides Mirabeau by color, an unofficial
segregation marked by the nightly whistle of the train.
Complete your circle and you run smack dab into a gentle
curve of the Colorado River, where Mirabeau and its few
thousand souls sit. The Colorado was swollen with spring
rain and with my window down, I could smell the faint
but pungent odors of muddy river and decay.

Mayne was as dead as a street could be. A scattering
of cars squatted at Hubbard's Grocery and some high-
school kids sat on the back of a pickup truck in the
Dairy Queen parking lot, watching the world not go by.
I sighed and made a left onto Loeber Street, away from
the business district. I wasn't missing anything by not
going straight to the library and then straight home.
This wasn't Boston.

The library was at the intersection of Loeber and
Bluebonnet and sat dark and solid in the night. We're
lucky in Mirabeau; the library is a handsome building,
built only ten years ago, made of solid brick and native
granite from the Hill Country, modern materials shaped

into old-style architecture. The words PUBLIC LIBRARY CITY OF MIRABEAU were carved into granite above the front doors, and at night a light shone on the words like a beacon of knowledge. Beautiful, ancient live oaks stood guardian around the building.

I pulled the Blazer up to the entrance. The library doesn't rate a parking lot. You have to park either on Loeber or Bluebonnet, or in the little lot next to the small softball field, or maybe in the little, tatty apartment complex that's down Loeber. As we never have a crowd, we never have a parking problem.

I fumbled for my keys, unlocked the door, and threw on the lights. Same old place, I thought. I walked past the dedication plaque, past the new, neon-colored posters my assistant Candace had hung to encourage kids in the summer reading program, past the new-arrivals bin, to the checkout counter. I opened my office door, turned on the light, and found Mama's pills in my desk drawer. Pocketing them, I turned off my office light and closed the door.

I paused—and to this day I don't know why. Something was wrong. A prickle ran along my neck like a ghost's fingernail. I looked across the wide doors and the stacks of books. There was only the gentle hum of automatic air-conditioning, comforting to any modern Texan. I wandered from the checkout counter to the children's section, glancing around like a determined shopper at the bargain mall. Everything seemed in place.

It felt like someone was watching me. I took a deep shuddering breath. I was being silly; a long day with Beta Harcher and my mother had gotten to me. I looked around again, shrugged off my exhaustion, turned out the lights, and locked up. I got into my car and drove up Bluebonnet, back to my mind-numbed mother and my sarcastic nephew.

And the next morning, all holy hell broke loose.

CHAPTER TWO

THERE ARE SO MANY IFS IN THIS WORLD. IF I hadn't forgotten Mama's pills, if I hadn't fought with Beta Harcher the day before, if Beta had never found her own personal Jesus. . . . And the biggest if of all: if Mama had never gotten sick and brought me home to all this rotten lying, deceit, and death. But there's really no point in articulating your ifs even once. I learned that the hard way.

I got to the library about 9:45 A.M., parking per my custom right in front. I always want the city council to know that I'm on the job. They're functional illiterates but they might wander by the library by mistake.

My assistant Candace Tully arrived as I did, pulling her teal Mercedes up behind my Blazer. Candace is a real piece of work. She's Mirabeau's youngest professional volunteer and everyone's just real worried that she hasn't gotten married yet. Her daddy owns five banks in central Texas and her mama owns six, so Candace is not one for regular, gainful employment. Aside from her part-time library work, she serves the Mirabeau Historical Society, the various county Daughter associations (of the Republic of Texas, the Confederacy, and the American Revolution), and has actually been sighted escorting elderly ladies across the street. Everyone admires Candace Tully and she's been a constant pain in my butt since I got the chief librarian job. Candace was on a husband-hunting safari and I was big game. If she wasn't so cute, ignoring her would be easy as pie.

Candace sidled up to me as if we were in a smoky bar and I had the last cigarette. Today she was sporting a navy silk blouse, cream-colored pants, and a colorful paisley scarf pinned to her shoulder with a fetching drape. She looked real nice. I wasn't nearly as appealing in faded jeans, cowboy boots (an old pair I'd hardly ever worn living in Massachusetts), and a blue chambray shirt. I got out of the car, and Candace nearly strained her neck looking up at me; maybe she's five-foot-three on a hot day. She brushed her brown hair out of her blue eyes and examined me critically.

"I heard about your little encounter with Beta Harcher," she said severely, "and I can't believe she'd wallop you." She patted my bruised cheek.

I shrugged. "Not a big deal, really."

"I wish I'd been there to punch her lights out." Candace grimaced, digging in her purse for her library keys.

I peered down into the chaos. "You got Mace in there I can borrow in case she comes back?"

Candace grinned. "I imagine you took care of yourself."

"Didn't need to. All the ladies came to my defense."

Her eyes flashed up at me. She's a looker, but she tries too hard. And dating a co-worker is a recipe for disaster.

"I'll bet they did," Candace retorted.

I couldn't resist teasing her. "Especially Ruth Wills. She must've worked in an asylum once. She manhandled ol' Beta."

"Hmmph. I hope her bedside manner's better than

that," Candace muttered, then shot me a look to imply I best not know anything about Ruth Wills and beds.

Candace plied me with questions as we opened up the library and went about our usual chores. She checked the after-hours drop for any returned books and I went to the back room to brew some coffee. We can't drink beverages out on the library floor, so we keep a little fridge with Cokes and a Mr. Coffee in a back storage room. I usually manage to sneak a cup to my office and I've seen Candace sip a Diet Dr. Pepper, then hide the can in her file cabinet at the checkout counter. We're fairly hardened criminals at the library.

I walked in front of the checkout counter, past the children's section, and past the stairs that went up to the public room that civic groups sometimes used for their meetings. I thought of my feeling of unease last night when I was alone in the stacks and decided I was being silly.

My complacency lasted all of the four seconds it took to reach the storage room. My eyes registered muddy footprints on the carpet near the back door and I frowned, wondering what idiot had tracked in mud. I opened the storage room door and saw Beta Harcher's body lying across the tile floor.

I wanted to yell, but my throat didn't work and instead I just leaned soundlessly against the open door. I could hear Candace humming a favorite Garth Brooks tune of hers, and it sounded as small and as distant as a cricket's hum in a summer night.

I never associated baseball bats with evil. To me, they were just thick sticks of wood, lying in the grass of the backyard. You'd sling a bat over a shoulder and walk down to the weedy field at the elementary school, where for a while you and your friends could forget about schoolwork, parents, and bossy big sisters. Bats were tokens of boyhood and of a game that I never excelled at, but loved to play. They appeared from my closet early in the spring, usually around March when the rains abated, and retired after another season of service when I went back to school. To me, bats represented happiness, an innocence that I had before I left Mirabeau to venture beyond river and highway.

The bat I'd found yesterday and left in my office was next to Beta Harcher's body. I could see one huge bruise, about an inch above the imaginary line between left eye and left ear. From what I was told later, she probably didn't suffer. Her left eye was swollen shut. Her heart must've kept pushing blood into her brain and the pressure of that blood inflated her tissues before she breathed her last susurration of air. I saw blood and hair, but not much of either, on the flared end of the bat. Specks of blood dotted the floor by her head.

My voice asserted itself and I screamed, "Candace!" She came running like a jackrabbit on fire. I felt her arm close around mine and her harsh shudder of air. She pulled me away from the door.

"My God!" Candace gasped. "Miss Harcher! How? What happened?"

"She's dead. I think." I pulled away from Candace, stepped back into the room, and put my fingertips to Beta's neck. Her throat was as cool and still as a winter day.

I leaned back. How—and why—was Beta Harcher dead in my library? I stared at her again, as if expecting her to raise her battered head and provide an answer. The only other item to register in my mind was her clothing; she was wearing a black turtleneck, a black skirt, black pantyhose, and black shoes. She'd always dressed frumpy but now she looked like a New York

Bohemian poet. Tar-black mud caked her shoes, and I saw tracks of mud on the floor.

I turned and grabbed Candace's arm. I pulled her away from the room and headed for the phone at the checkout counter. Dialing 911, I wondered how the hell Beta Harcher had gotten into the library. And that's when I remembered my creepy sensation of being observed last night.

Mirabeau isn't accustomed to murder. Our streets are eerily quiet of violent death. Last year, there'd only been one murder in all of Bonaparte County, and that'd been in the county seat of Bavary. A fight in a pool hall had suddenly turned into a stabbing and a man who didn't speak much English coughed up his life on the smooth green felt of a billiard table. I couldn't remember a murder in town at all until Sister reminded me of when Buell Godkin got stinking drunk and blasted his brother to kingdom come. That'd been years ago.

Women don't die from blows to the head in Mirabeau. They die of seditious disease, of bodies that have weathered years and are simply ready to rest, of the little death that lurks in too many beer bottles, of reckless driving, or maybe of just loneliness when they are left solitary after decades of marriage and their husband lies cold in the ground. Or in my mother's case, they'll die because their minds will eventually vanish and nothing will remain to motivate the breath and the heartbeat, not even life's most secret, sacred memories.

Our chief of police, Junebug Moncrief, arrived quickly with the coroner and an attitude of outrage that such an event had taken place in His Town. Candace was outside directing the ambulance (and moving her Mercedes out of the way) and I was guarding the body. I don't know why, it just seemed the proper thing to do.

I wished for a blanket to cover Beta; one stony blue eye was open and I hated the way it stared blankly at the ceiling, as though pleading with the powers above for kind judgment and resurrection.

Junebug stormed in with one of his officers, nodded sternly at me, and glanced in at the body. "Jesus bitchin' Christ," he said, which I'm sure Miss Harcher would not have appreciated. The other officer, a youngster with cropped red hair, fidgeted sweatily as he loaded film. His eyes darted between the camera and Beta's corpse while his fingers fumbled with the controls. I wanted to assure him she'd hold her pose, but I thought it'd be ungentlemanly.

Junebug waved me off. "Go outside, Jordy, and just sit. Don't let anyone else come in here 'cept the paramedics. I know it's a burden, but don't open your mouth either. Library's closed for today, okay? You and I and Miss Tully'll all talk in a minute."

I nodded wordlessly and went outside, grateful for the scents of wildflowers and fresh air. The air in the library had taken on a dense quality I didn't like.

Candace fretted as she watched the paramedics tumble a portable gurney from the ambulance. She opened the door for the two men and they rushed in.

"They don't have to be in a hurry," I said, and then thought what a rotten comment that was.

"How, Jordy? How did she get in here? Who killed her? Why?" Candace hissed in a whisper, shaking her head in disbelief.

I took Candace's hand and sat down with her on the front step. I told her Junebug said for us to wait outside and he'd come talk to us. She nodded, her normally permanent perkiness blanched away.

The wait was awful. I guess they have to take pictures and examine the body some before they move it and secure the area, whatever that means. I held Candace's hand and thought about all the energy that had been in Beta Harcher, energy enough to make scenes in libraries, whack grown men, and be so sure of her own rightness. All of that life vanished with one solid blow. I felt my breakfast shift uncertainly in my belly. I stuck my face into the next breeze that blew and felt better. It was sad that, meteorologically, this was shaping up to be a fine day.

Folks wandered over to the ambulance, some from homes and some from the small businesses near Bluebonnet. In a town that is populated mostly by senior citizens, you get used to seeing ambulances idling in the road. Losing an elder is of course mourned but not unexpected. However, the library isn't usually where people expire, so there was curiosity.

Old Man Renfro, our most loyal patron, arrived, walking with his cane and dressed as always in a threadbare gray suit. His wrinkled, coffee-colored face frowned as he looked at Candace and me on the steps. We obviously didn't belong there during library hours.

He and others inquired, and I replied that there'd been an accident and the library was closed for the day. I didn't know what else to say. This revelation didn't get anyone to turn on their heels and seek other entertainment. The crowd, about fifteen strong, stood by the ambulance, waiting grimly.

A little Japanese sedan spewed gravel as it screeched to a stop next to Candace's Mercedes. Her hand tightened on mine at the thought of all those little meteors denting her finish. A dapper, short little fellow I knew to be an utter fool jumped from the car and practically skipped to the library. He obviously couldn't wait to see the body. His dark eyes glanced at Candace and me. I didn't raise a hand to stop him. Billy Ray Bummel, the assistant D.A., wouldn't have stopped anyhow. He dashed into the library.

Some indeterminate time later, Junebug, the coroner, and Billy Ray Bummel emerged. The paramedics followed, trundling a blanketed form. Gasps and other expressions of surprise and curiosity arose from the crowd. They sounded like a freakshow audience ogling a particularly ugly mutant. Junebug fixed the group with a stern eye.

"Y'all get! Get going about your business and let us do ours."

A few spectators moved away, but most acted like their feet were mired in mud. "Who is it?" a voice croaked from the crowd.

Junebug leveled his eyes at the offender. "You can read about it in the paper. Now get moving along." He'd put on his reflective sunglasses for the proper authority image and stuck a Stetson back on his brown crewcut. He was bigger and taller than me, with a solidly broad face. I'm sure he'd already thought it'd look good next year on a sheriff's poster. He looked much the same as in high school, except for the slightest of beer guts and a few worry lines creasing his brow.

A second warning sufficed and the crowd ambled apart as the ambulance was loaded and roared off toward the hospital. The lights didn't flare and the siren stayed silent. I felt sick and sad; Beta might've been crazy, but she didn't deserve this.

Junebug took me by the arm. "C'mon, Jordy." His deep voice was raspy from tobacco. "Let's talk inside."

Let me explain about me and Junebug. We'd known each other since first grade. In a small town, when you spend twelve years of school and summers with the same kids, you develop what those TV shrinks call love/hate relationships. It's inevitable. You play with these kids day after day and you can't imagine life without their company. But you're also guaranteed to get plenty mad at each other.

Junebug and I got along fine until high school, when we got all competitive. We competed for sports honors (he usually won), academic honors (I usually won, but Junebug beat me in math), and the same pretty girls, of which we had a finite supply in Mirabeau. Our friendship didn't pick up when I returned to town. I'd been beyond Mirabeau and he'd stuck close. We didn't hang out together, but neither were we sworn enemies. He came to my daddy's funeral and three weeks ago I'd gone to his daddy's funeral. You do that here, even if comforting words to someone you've drifted far away from taste odd in your mouth. Junebug of course isn't his given name. He's Hewett Moncrief, Junior, and everyone knows that a Junior is sometimes saddled as a toddler with being a Junebug. Well, that saddle stuck. His daddy was mean that way.

We sat in the periodical section, the day's Houston and Austin papers still wrapped in their plastic covers, dotted with drops of water from the wet grass.

"You want us to get y'all some coffee?" Junebug offered. "I can't let you go back there to make any, but I'll call over to the diner and get you and Miss Tully some."

I shook my head. I suddenly realized that Candace was not there.

Junebug saw my face. "She's outside. I'll talk to her in a minute." Junebug's voice is always slow and languorous, like he just woke up. I couldn't imagine him yelling at an arrestee; he'd probably thank them once he locked the handcuffs. "I need to ask you some questions."

"Okay," I said blankly, but I stared at the pack in his pocket. "I'd really, really like a cigarette."

"Here. I'm quittin'." He tossed his pack on the table between us and I retrieved an ashtray from my office. It was an ugly misshapen glazed-clay expression of thirteen-year-old angst that Mark had made in an arts class. So much for quitting smoking. I lit and dragged hard, telling myself what a filthy habit it was. Just one. I'd have just one.

Junebug eyed me. "I don't think you're supposed to smoke in here."

"I'm not. But I don't care and you probably don't either right now," I answered. He let it go and began taking my statement.

His first question was simple: what had happened that morning? He wrote down my story in a battered notepad he'd produced from his pocket.

I made my answers short and distinct. I was still in shock over my grisly discovery. Just try finding a corpse in your workplace and see how *you* handle it. Have the body be someone you know. My hands weren't shaking and I was glad of that. My voice shook a little and if Junebug hadn't known me he might not have noticed.

"I suppose that Miz Harcher had a key to the library?" Junebug asked.

"No. She used to have a key, because she was on the library board up until February. She tried to ban some books—real bits of trash like *The Color Purple*, *Huckleberry Finn*, and *The Scarlet Letter*—and the board got fed up with her. They booted her out. She turned in her key and I had the locks changed."

"Y'all always do that when a member leaves the library board?" Junebug raised an eyebrow at me.

"No, of course not. But I felt that, considering the . . .

uh, extremity of her views regarding certain books here, it would be appropriate to limit her access to business hours." God, I sounded like an official report.

"That's interesting. We found a key in her pocket, separate from her key ring." He pulled a plastic bag from a large paper bag next to his feet. "Is this a library key, Jordy?"

"Yeah, looks just like mine." I produced my key from my pocket.

"I wonder how she got this," Junebug said, thinking aloud. He did that back in school and used to drive our teachers nuts.

"I don't know," I answered. "Not from me."

Junebug gnawed at the end of his pen. "I understand you had a little run-in with her yesterday."

My gut churned, as if I'd just narrowly avoided stepping into an elevator shaft. Before I knew it I was sliding my palms down my jeans, drying them of sweat.

"Miz Harcher threw herself a hissy fit in the library over what she considered porn and whacked me upside the head with a book. She left, or rather was shown the door."

"Made some comments, didn't she? About shutting down the library?"

"Look, Junebug, you already seem to know the answer to that question. You've already heard the gossips' version. Yeah, she did just that. How'd you know and what's your point?"

"I have my sources," he said loftily. "And my point is I got a dead woman here. You argued with her just yesterday, Jordy. I have to ask these questions."

My temper decided to make an appearance. It's one of the finer Poteet family traits. "You can't seriously think I killed her, can you? For God's sake!" My voice

sounded alien to me, still deep and drawly, but saying
words I never thought I'd say.

"Jordy, I have to ask. Would you like an attorney
present?"

I swallowed. "You can't think I killed her, Junebug.
That's crazy."

"Do you want an attorney now, or will you answer
further questions?"

I bristled. My Uncle Bid was an attorney, but sum-
moning him might be more unpleasant than being
hauled off to jail. I made myself calm down. "Go
ahead. I have nothing to conceal and I want to cooperate, Junebug."

Junebug sat and stared at me for a full minute. It was
unnerving, but I resolved not to let it bother me. I
pulled my blanket of outraged innocence closer about
me. He pulled a loose page from his notepad. It was
light blue stationery.

"This list mean anything to you?"

He handed me the paper, and I saw his eyes dart to
see if my hands were steady. I willed them to stillness.
The list was written in Beta's spidery handwriting; I
recognized it from the notes she used to send the library
when she was on the board. I tried not to drop the paper
as I reached the end of the list:

> Tamma Hufnagel–Num. 32:23
> Hally Schneider–Prov. 14:9
> Jordan Poteet–Isaiah 5:20
> Eula Mae Quiff–Job 31:35
> Matt Blalock–Matt. 26:21
> Ruth Wills–2 Kings 4:40
> Bob Don Goertz–Judges 5:30
> Anne Poteet–Gen. 3:16

Mama? What the hell was she doing on a list written by some religious zealot who'd been murdered? Names with Bible quotes next to them. What was this list even for? Invitees to a revival meeting? I didn't think so. I took a long draw on my now-stubby cigarette and committed the names and quote numbers to memory as best I could. I used to do that with sales figures on my books at the textbook publishers' before I had to confer with my jerk of a boss, so I had a quick memory.

"The list doesn't mean anything to me," I said. "But I know all these folks. Miz Quiff, Miz Wills, and Mrs. Hufnagel were here yesterday when Beta made her scene. Hally Schneider's family is distant kin to me and they live on my street. Matt Blalock and Bob Don Goertz—well, everyone knows them. And I've no idea what my mother and I are doing there. I don't know what significance the Bible quotes have. She wasn't quoting the Good Book when she was here yesterday. Where'd you find this?"

Junebug narrowed his eyes at me but kept his voice soft and slow. "It was stuffed down her shirt. She'd hidden it there, I guess."

"Or someone planted it," I suggested. "Maybe to confuse the issue."

Junebug appeared unwilling to grant such cleverness to a local murderer. He watched me fish another cigarette from his pack and light it. I resolved to keep the amount smoked to a prime number, to give myself some leeway.

"You ever see that bat before? The one that killed her?"

My stomach sank to somewhere near my ankles, and I'm sure my cigarette shook. "Oh, God, yeah. And I'm sure my prints will be on it, unless the killer wiped it clean. I found it yesterday in the softball lot when I was coming back to the library."

"I see." He jotted on his pad and eyed me like I might make a sudden move.

"And so did everyone else who was in there, Junebug! A roomful of people saw me carrying that stupid bat. I put it in my office."

"Well, Jordy. This is all very interesting. You know what I learned at the police academy?"

I bit back my first reply, which involved mastering how not to leave a piss stain on your pants. Junebug wasn't acting like a childhood friend. I couldn't believe he imagined I had any connection to this.

"That most murders are awful simple. You just got to worry about motive, opportunity, and access to a weapon." He looked up at me with the eyes of a stranger. "Sounds to me like you got all three, buddy."

"Please. The woman hit me with a book, made a spectacle of herself, and stormed off. That's not a motive for murder. Plus, do you honestly think I could kill anybody?"

Junebug didn't answer that question; instead, like a Socratic teacher, he posed me another one. "Did you have any other dealings with Miz Harcher aside from yesterday?"

I looked him dead in the eye.

"Like I said, she got thrown off the library board. She didn't approve of the city council hiring me and she'd been trying to get certain books off the shelf for ages. I had to deal with her through the library board. She lost and I won. So my feud was over with her, as far as I was concerned." A rational thought fought its way through my shock. I stubbed out my cigarette and snatched the list back from Junebug, who didn't look at all pleased.

"The library board," I said. "Ruth Wills and Eula Mae Quiff are both on it. So's Hally Schneider's mother and Tamma Hufnagel's husband. And Bob Don Goertz replaced Miz Harcher when she was taken off."

"What about Matt Blalock?"

"He's not on the board, but I let the county Vietnam vets support group meet here."

"So who all has keys to this place?"

"Well, me, of course. And Candace. The board members: Eula Mae, Ruth, Adam Hufnagel, Janice Schneider, and Bob Don Goertz. Matt Blalock has a key because the vets' group meets after hours on Thursday, which is our short day." I tried unsuccessfully to dredge up more names. "I think that's it."

"Interesting, isn't it?" Junebug's quiet drawl dripped with accusation.

I raised my palms in mock surrender. "I don't know what that list means. She was a crazy, bitter old woman who believed she was doing God's work when all she did was piss folks off. But nobody on that list is a murderer."

Junebug stared back at me with the look he'd used to try to psych me out before basketball tryouts. "There was a dead woman here this morning, and I can't find a single shred of evidence that points to a break-in. She had a key on her. Where'd she get that key or a copy? Narrows the field a tad, don't it?"

"I should tell you," I said, "that I was here last night, around ten, for about three minutes. And something creepy happened."

That brought him forward on his haunches and I explained about forgetting Mama's medicine.

"Did you see or hear anything unusual?"

"No. Nothing. I just came in, got the pills, and left. I can't explain it—but I just had a funny feeling that someone was watching me. I just thought it was nerves."

Junebug judged me with his eyes and scribbled in his notepad. "I want you to come to the station with me, Jordy, and sign a statement. Okay?" His tone was almost friendly again.

"Sure. Let me tell Candace—"

"She'll be at the station. I'll need a statement from her too."

I paused. "So who do you think did it? You have to be pretty damned cold-blooded, killing someone with a baseball bat."

Junebug smiled a know-it-all smile. "Lots of people are cold inside. We just never see it."

I myself felt a little bit frosty and I didn't argue.

"Your mama's keeping you in town for a while, right, Jordy?" Junebug sounded more casual than he meant.

"Yes, she is." My voice was like stone.

"Good. I don't think you should go anywhere till this is all over."

Before we left, I sat in my car, found a gasoline receipt, and scribbled down the list of names and Bible verses. I thought I'd gotten them right. I hoped so.

As I followed Junebug's car the two blocks to the police station at the corner of Loeber and Magnolia, I thought about that list. Why did Beta hide it on her person? She wouldn't have wanted someone to see it, perhaps. And why did the list exist anyway? Why those eight names? I'd give my statement, then get home as quick as I could. Mama kept a Bible at her bedside, although she didn't even look at the pictures anymore. And maybe, if the foggy veil lifted from her mind for a while, she could tell me why Beta Harcher would have her on such a list. That wasn't likely, though.

Providing my statement was easy. I was finished in twenty minutes. Then I waited for Junebug's secretary to type it up. The whole time Billy Ray Bummel looked at me like I was a cross between Jack the Ripper and Joseph Goebbels. (I'm giving Billy Ray far too much credit in knowing criminal history. He probably thinks Jack the Ripper is someone with a gas problem and Joseph Goebbels is a turkey tycoon.) Despite his law degree (undoubtedly granted by one of the finer mail-order institutions), Billy Ray has carried on the fine Bummel tradition of denseness. Education doesn't erase high-quality stupidity like Billy Ray's; it just makes it more dangerous.

Junebug's secretary, Nelda, announced to him that she'd reached Beta's niece in Houston. Junebug got up to take the call. I signed my statement. Billy Ray took the document and examined it critically, as though hoping to spot a confession somewhere in there. His black eyes, larger than most, widened as he caught what looked like a clue. It must have been waving to him. He set his bony, knobby hands on his beer belly and chewed his bottom lip. I've seen cows masticate in the exact same fashion. Cows aren't bright either.

"So you were there last night after ten? Wouldn't surprise me if that's about the time the coroner says Miz Harcher met her dee-mise."

I gave him the withering look that Mama and Sister taught me when I was young. You narrow your eyes, raise your brow, and flare a nostril like there's a rank smell. It's also important to maintain a demeanor of indifference to what the other person's saying. "Excuse me, Billy Ray, but you ought to wait until you have a few more facts before you start making accusations."

"You had the murder weapon. You run the place where she was killed. And you had both opportunity and motive." Billy Ray must've had a pit bull at home for inspiration.

"You're being ridiculous. She had a key. *She* could have let her murderer in."

"I don't think so. And don't fool yourself that knowing Junebug for so long will help you any. I'm watching you, Mr. Jordan Poteet. You're my number one suspect. And I'm gonna nail your skinny ass to the wall." For dramatic effect Billy Ray ran a hand through his rapidly thinning hair. It only took half a second. You think all the sun his head gets would help his brain grow, but his mind isn't fertile ground.

I felt scared and mad at the same time. I didn't want either emotion to show. "You've got my statement. You haven't charged me with anything. May I go?"

Billy Ray smiled officiously and gestured toward the door. "Go on ahead. Be sure and let us know if you intend to leave town."

I walked without hurry to the front door. I didn't look back at Billy Ray. The sunshine was bright and cheery, but my skin was ice-cold. I hadn't killed Beta Harcher, but at least one member of the local authorities considered me guilty as sin. Think about it. Think about being at the top of the list of suspects of bashing in a woman's head, and see if you don't have a bit of trouble swallowing.

Candace's Mercedes was still in the parking lot; she hadn't yet given her statement to Junebug. I considered waiting for her, then imagined her hanging around me like a stray cat behind a restaurant. I didn't want *that* right now. I'd call her later.

First things first. I wanted to talk to Mama and to find me a Bible. I needed to know why Beta Harcher thought of me in connection with a verse from Isaiah.

CHAPTER THREE

IT WAS ABOUT ELEVEN-THIRTY WHEN I reached my house. Nothing seemed different from when I'd left, except that I could smell skunk on the late-morning air. Sometimes the critters wander in town looking for food, get scared, and let fly with their chemical defense. Then they scurry back to the woods. Just like Beta Harcher. Come in, raise a stink, get out of the picture, but leave an an noying reek behind. It was the meanest thought I'd ever had in my life. By the time I got inside, I was sullen with guilt over it.

Mama sat in the den, watching *All My Children* on a whispering TV. Since she'd gotten sick, she couldn't stand loudness, although it never bothered her before. She'd sit for hours, simply watching actors move their lips. I couldn't hear what trauma the pretty blonde on the soap was enduring. I had my own to fret about.

Sister was still in her robe, yawning and reading the Austin newspaper over coffee. She saw my face and bolted to her feet.

I told her quickly what happened. Sister of course was horrified. I spoke in low tones of having discovered the body, so Mama wouldn't hear. I described the list that Junebug had found and produced my copy. I confessed to having forgotten Mama's medicine and going to the library at what now seemed like a mighty inopportune moment. At the end, Sister sank into her chair.

"And so Billy Ray told me I'm the number one suspect. Me! Can you believe the nerve?"

Sister shook her head. "They can't be serious. I mean, Junebug's known you forever. He knows you wouldn't kill a tick, much less Miz Harcher." She stood. "We have to call Uncle Bid."

"There's no need. I haven't been arrested for anything and I'm sure Junebug'll find whoever did this." Plus I didn't want to have any unnecessary contact with Uncle Bid. I've always contended that Uncle Bid should be belled like a leper so you'd know when he's coming. I don't believe there's a more unpleasant old fart of a lawyer in Texas.

I went into the den. Mama watched the TV screen intently as a very quiet argument raged. I switched off the set. Mama kept staring at the screen without changing one muscle in her face.

I knelt before her. "Mama? Look at me."

She turned her face and gave me a shy, uncertain smile.

"How are you today?" I asked gently. I sensed Sister hovering nearby.

"Fine, thank you." Etiquette was no longer a certainty with Mama, but today, at least, she hadn't forgotten her manners.

"Mama, I want you to think. Do you know a lady named Beta Harcher?" I enunciated the name carefully, as though that would help Mama fight through the choking mass of abnormal nerve cells the disease spawned in her brain.

"Who?"

"Beta Harcher."

Mama looked blank. I asked again; she looked blank again.

"Maybe she'll remember later," Sister offered.

"She probably won't remember this conversation later," I snapped. Sister looked wounded and I said, "Sorry. I'm stressed."

I took a deep breath. Try association. "She was real active in the Baptist church, Mama. She's short, dark hair, kind of frumpy. Sort of bossy?"

This complimentary description of Beta didn't penetrate far. "I don't know," Mama said. She looked down into her lap. "I don't know," she repeated, her voice wavering.

"It's okay, Mama. Don't worry. You watch your show now." I stood and switched the TV back on.

"Try again later," Sister suggested.

I leaned down and kissed Mama's cheek. Her hand came up to my head, unexpectedly, and her fingers tangled in my thick hair, so close to the strawberry-blonde color of her own. I held the embrace for a moment, then turned back to Sister.

"Her Bible still up in her room?"

"I think so," Sister answered. "C'mon, Mama, let's have a glass of iced tea."

I left them in the kitchen and bounded up the stairs. In my room I got paper and pen, then walked down the hall. Mama's room was quiet and comfortable, with Irish lace curtains and an antique oak bed that had been her aunt's. Pictures of Sister and me as children, joined by the more recent photos of Mark, dotted the walls. I sat on the quilted bedspread and opened her Bible. It occurred to me that I didn't know which translation of the Bible Beta had used to select these quotes; I could only hope that I got the gist of the meanings from the same verses in Mama's Bible.

I smoothed out the folded list and considered it. Beta had written it, then hidden it. Why?

It was a diverse roster. Each person had a connection with the library, although some were more tenuous than others. I decided to treat it as a list of folks that Beta Harcher had a gripe with. I knew the people on the list weren't her friends and she didn't want us to be. Certain folks and certain verses. There had to be a reason.

Mama and me first. I looked again at the verse next to my name: Isaiah 5:20. I flipped through the Bible till I found it: *Woe unto them that call evil good, and good evil.* I said the words aloud. Did the woman think I had my sensibilities reversed? Considering I kept books in the library that she considered objectionable, I suppose so.

I looked up the quote indicated by Mama's name. Genesis 3:16: *In sorrow thou shalt bring forth children.* I didn't retain much from the Sunday school classes that my parents made me attend, but I did recall that verse referred to Eve's curse of blood and painful childbirth. Good God, what did that have to do with my mother? She'd had two children and plenty of pain in the process due to our large Poteet heads. But why would Beta Harcher write this down? Perhaps Beta considered bearing a heathen like me to be the utmost in maternal agony.

I copied my makeshift list into a notebook and then copied the verses. I started through the rest of the list, writing down each corresponding verse by each name. It made for interesting reading.

I sat back on the bed. The police would surely be talking to these people. Junebug and Billy Ray were probably conducting their own version of the Spanish Inquisition right now. Then I heard Billy Ray's words: *I'm going to nail your skinny ass to the wall.* Maybe their questioning of the others was going to center around me. I had access to the scene; access to the weapon; and I'd fought with the deceased. I shut my eyes, remembering how a libraryful of folks had overheard me say I could've killed Beta. God! Sometimes the police didn't need to look beyond that, if the district attorney thought there was a case. My motive seemed slim to me, but I played devil's advocate. Beta had threatened to close the library. What if the police postulated that I believed her and feared she'd cost me the only job I'd been able to land? Would someone kill for a job? Maybe not, but Junebug might surmise I'd kill for my mother. My position at the library allowed Sister and me to keep Mama at home. It was common knowledge that I'd returned to Mirabeau from a good-paying job up North to keep Mama out of an institution. How far would I go to maintain that arrangement?

I swallowed. I wondered that myself. I knew I wouldn't resort to murder, but I would have fought tooth and nail to keep the library safe from Beta Harcher. I think folks in town, such as the chief of police, knew that too.

And Mama. Why was she on the list? Never mind the library—what if Beta had threatened my mother in some way? If Junebug assumed I could kill once to protect my job, protecting my mother might induce me to a tri-state slaying spree. I sounded paranoid, even to myself.

Mama wasn't going to be much help, I thought. I scanned the names again. Perhaps one of them knew a perfectly logical reason for this list.

The library was closed, and Sister was here until eight tonight. I could ask some questions of my own and maybe find out why Beta Harcher had ended up on the wrong side of batting practice in the library.

* * *

The First Baptist Church of Mirabeau is one of the ugliest buildings that's trying to be pretty that I've ever seen. It's built of beige brick with purplish windows, smeared with white to give the windows a marbled effect. I've seen birdshit that exact color. Even God would call this church ugly. It sat on the corner of Alamo and Heydl Streets on the south side of Mayne.

Like most churches in town (and there aren't many—the Baptists, Catholics, and Methodists have just about everyone covered), First Baptist has an announcement sign, with a black felt background with big white letters that stick into the felt. Each sermon here gets treated like a blockbuster summer movie, at least for its one week of fanfare.

Tamma Hufnagel knelt in front of the announcement board as I pulled up. A box of letters rested in her lap and she was posting the theme for next Sunday's sermon.

I opened my notebook on my lap and reread Tamma's verse, which was Numbers 32:23: *Be sure your sin will find you out.* Whoa! Sounded juicy. I wondered what sin mousy Tamma could have committed in Beta's eyes. Dancing? Playing cards?

I only knew Tamma Hufnagel to say hello, but I did know her husband a sight better. Brother Adam Hufnagel's preaching wasn't exactly fire and brimstone; more like a light grilling. I'm surprised Beta tolerated such slackness on his part. My dealings with Brother Adam on the library board had been polite if distant. He'd been Beta's biggest supporter in her censorship stances but had tried to get her to soften her hysterics. He hadn't fought too hard when Beta got punted from the board; I think he knew it was a losing cause, and he didn't want to put his own position in jeopardy. He was a real smooth talker, who could make you feel like Jesus was just around the corner, so you better run the dustrag over the furniture to get it spiffy for Him.

I got out of the car and approached Tamma Hufnagel. She watched me as I walked toward her. For some reason I felt uneasy. Tamma's pretty in a plain way: reddish brown hair, green eyes, with a slim, almost boyish figure. Her nose is snub-shaped and looks as though it belongs on another face. Her hair, which would have looked better let down, was pulled tightly back into a bun. She wore a plain white polo-style shirt and a denim skirt, long and modest. I guessed she was about my age but was trying to look twenty years older, maybe to catch up with her husband. The only softening of her face was the scattering of girlish freckles across her nose and cheeks. Those freckles were like a memory of summer. I remembered hearing she wasn't a local girl; I'd been told she came from Giddings or one of the other predominantly German and Wendish communities in east-central Texas.

"Hello, Mrs. Hufnagel."

She wiped her mouth with the back of her hand, as a schoolgirl might. "Hello."

"I guess you've heard about Miz Harcher."

She nodded and bit her thin lip for a moment. "Chief Moncrief phoned us. She was a prominent member here, you know. He wanted to know if we knew her next of kin. We gave him her niece's name."

I wasn't expecting such a detailed explanation. "I'm sure you must be very upset."

Her answer was a gesture toward the sermon board. It read MAKING PEA. I was sure more letters were needed.

"You know that I found her in the library?" I wondered just how much Junebug was telling folks and I decided to start with the basics.

She nodded. "He said someone had"—here she swallowed deeply, her thin throat moving like a snake under water—"bashed her head with a baseball bat."

"That's true. You know, Mrs. Hufnagel, I didn't agree with Beta as far as books went, but I'm sorry she's dead. I didn't wish that on her."

"Of course you wouldn't!"

"Who do you think might've killed her?" I asked, and Tamma Hufnagel stood abruptly, the box of plastic letters tumbling from her lap and spilling across the grass. I glanced down wondering if anything interesting was now spelled out on the lawn.

"I don't know!" she gasped. "Why are you asking me?"

"Mrs. Hufnagel, please. I'm asking because you knew her and you knew the people that knew her. She was killed in the library, or at least her body was left there. There must be a reason. It was a terrible shock to me and I just want to know what happened. If she was killed there, it means she was there after hours with someone."

I put my hands on Tamma Hufnagel's arm and she froze. I stared into her face. "Listen to me, Mrs. Hufnagel. Beta had a key. Either she met someone there or someone lured her there. She hated that library and I'd already warned her to stay away. But somehow she got a key." I paused. Tamma Hufnagel stared at the grass, shaking her head.

She knelt by the letter box, carefully pulling her skirt around her legs so I didn't even see a flash of calf. "I've made a mess," she said, and began gathering the letters.

I knelt next to her and helped her pick the little plastic vowels and consonants out of the lawn. I offered a palmful to her; she took the letters from my hand, touching the plastic extrusions on the letters and not me. I thought I'd made her uncomfortable when I touched her. She sorted the letters into the box.

"I don't know who would have wanted to kill her." She shrugged. "Yes, she was difficult sometimes. I think she believed she had been specially touched by the Lord." She looked skyward, but no answer was forthcoming on the accuracy of her statement.

"I really didn't know her well. What was your relationship like with her?" I tried to sound conversational rather than interrogative.

She glanced at me, ran a thin tongue over thin lips, then went back to putting letters into the board. MAKING PEACE W "We got along okay. She was a woman of . . . strong convictions. She had very definite opinions about the church. About God." She searched for a letter in her palm. "And about morality."

"Did you ever disagree with her?"

"Well, of course we did. It is Adam's church, after all." She shrugged. "She liked to be in charge of every thing: the rummage sale, the bake sale, the tent revival in the summer—"

"The book burnings," I added in a miffed tone.

Tamma paused. "You know that Adam and I didn't agree with her about her attitude toward the library. Well, not entirely. We don't approve of every book you keep, but that's neither here nor there. We certainly didn't want to see the place shut down. Remember at the library board meetings, Adam tried for compromise regarding your views and Beta's views."

"I appreciate that, Mrs. Hufnagel." It took every fiber of my being not to disclose what I thought about censorship and her holier-than-thou attitude. I wondered again what sin she'd committed in Beta's eyes. I was tempted to mention the list, but I decided not to. Let Junebug do that.

"I wonder, did you ever see my mother with Miz Harcher?"

"Your mother?" The question surprised her. She gave me a long, cautious look. "No, not that I remember. Your family's not Baptist, are y'all?" There was disapproval in her voice, but I ignored it.

She decided to be forgiving, since my mother was losing her mind. "You know, we have a healing service on Tuesday nights. You could bring your mother and see if Adam could help. And we'll add her to our prayer list."

I didn't know whether to laugh or say thank you. Mama had always taught us that saying thank you was as automatic a response as breathing, even when faced with the impossible. If Adam Hufnagel *could* drive the neurological demons from my mother's mind, I'd drag her down here, let Brother Adam lay hands on her, and dance with a snake in my mouth. I decided on politeness. Medicine hadn't done much yet for Mama; and including her on the prayer list was kind of Tamma. "Thanks. Maybe we will come."

"Prayer heals, Jordy." We were now on first names. "Acts of God do happen here."

"Really?" I asked. "And have they happened to you? Have they made you free of sin?"

Tamma Hufnagel stared at me. There is a look of defiance people who are terrified can muster. And she did. I thought she wasn't used to being challenged. Probably most of Brother Adam's flock wouldn't say boo to her; being the preacher's wife made her untouchable. Her mouth set into a thin frown. "Of course not. We're sinners from birth. Only Jesus offers us a chance at redemption."

"Miz Harcher doesn't seem to have believed much in the redemption side of the equation," I observed dryly. "All I ever heard from her was the judgment, the fire, the eternal damnation. I never heard once about the rewards to follow for good behavior." I paused and realized I needed to keep my tongue in check. Tamma Hufnagel looked at me like I was a pagan dancer for Dionysus, come to town to set up a temple and do a little drunken shimmy. I paused and thought. If she decided I was getting uppity, she might respond the way most fundamentalists do; with a torrent of words to tell you why you're wrong and why they're right.

When she spoke, her voice cut with an unexpected edge. "You nonbelievers think you know everything. Well, you don't."

"I'm not a nonbeliever. I'm a good Episcopalian. And I can't know anything when people don't answer questions," I retorted. "I guess you've got something to hide, Mrs. Hufnagel. I asked you a minute ago if you knew anything about that key Beta Harcher had and you've managed to dance around an answer." Since Baptists don't approve of dancing *period*, I thought the very suggestion of her performing any sort of mental terpsichorean activities would annoy her. I didn't like being rude, but I needed to know what she knew. She'd made Beta's list because of some sin she'd committed, and manners weren't going to prevent my finding out more.

It worked; she looked at me like I was a Vacation Bible School student who'd challenged the existence of God. "For your information, Mr. Smarty Pants, Chief Moncrief called my husband and asked him about his key to the library. When Adam checked, it was gone. He kept it on the same ring that he keeps the church keys on, which are here during the day. It would have been simple for Beta to take Adam's key. So there's that mystery solved." She wore her conviction like a starchy, ill-fitting blouse. "Now will you let me be?"

"Adam's key? I'm sure Junebug found that interesting. And I'm sure he asked you where you and Reverend Hufnagel were last night around ten or so."

She kept the awkward smugness a tad longer. "Of course he did. He wanted to know when Beta could have taken that key. Adam saw her at the church yesterday afternoon around four. He now thinks she might have taken the library key from his office—he said he was talking to Lenny Mauder out in the assembly hall about expanding the parking lot and Beta could've gotten into his office then. I met Adam at the church around six for a meeting, we stayed until seven, then we went home, had dinner, and watched John Wayne on cable. *Rio Bravo*. We were in bed and asleep by ten." She ignored the implicit suggestion that she or her husband could be a suspect. "That meeting at seven was for the Vacation Bible School group to start planning this summer's sessions. It was odd that she didn't show up for the meeting; she'd been adamant about guiding the church's children along a path of rightousness."

Whata horrible concept. Beta shaping young minds. The keen edge still adhered to Tamma's voice and I wondered if she hadn't cared much for Beta herself.

"Who else was there?" I asked.

"You sound like Chief Moncrief. Why all the questions?"

"Why not answer?" I countered. "I'm sure you don't have any secrets."

"Of course not." Flustered, she fumbled in the box for a letter. "It's not a secret at all. I'm just surprised you're curious. The planning committee was me, Beta, and Janice Schneider. This year Janice and I are doing most of the teaching. Beta took on recruitment."

And pity the parent who didn't sign up Junior. "I know what a pain she was on the library board. Did she run you ragged on the Vacation Bible School stuff? Want the kids to light fires under their Curious Georges?"

"Of course not," Tamma said quickly for the second time in a minute. "That's mean of you, Jordy."

I shrugged. "So what else can you tell me about her?"

"Nothing new." Her voice sounded tired and I could tell she wanted to be rid of me. "She could be awfully judgmental at times, but that was her burden. She had a very strong sense of morals. She liked to remind people that there was a definite right and a definite wrong. She'd let them know when they'd failed and what they had to do to make amends. But people don't always"— she paused, looking for words—"cotton to advice."

"May I ask when you last saw Miz Harcher?" I asked, trying to get onto less philosophically slippery rocks.

"Yesterday afternoon, I guess around two. I knew she'd be upset after your little altercation in the library." She glanced over at me. "So I stopped by her house, to see if she was feeling better. She was. She'd found strength in the Bible and was studying it."

Studying it or writing down verses to go alongside names? I wondered.

"We talked for a while and then I left," she continued.

"You didn't see anyone else there, did you? Did she have any other visitors?"

Tamma Hufnagel finished her task and stood, balancing the box of letters so she wouldn't drop it again. She looked me dead in the eye and there was nothing shy, afraid, or mousy about her now. The mask was set like old makeup. "Why, yes, she did. Bob Don Goertz stopped by as I was leaving and seemed rather upset. I gather there was some problem between them. Now, if you'll excuse me, I have to fix Adam some lunch. Goodbye, Jordy." She turned and walked into the ugly church.

I glanced down at the completed board. MAKING PEACE WITH DEATH. What a lovely invitation. The air now felt moist and hot, as the noontime sun began its drumbeat on the town. I sat in my Blazer for a few minutes, running the air conditioner at arctic blast and watching the leafy oak branches sway in the wind. I didn't regard Beta Harcher and Tamma Hufnagel as such bosom buddies; they might have been allies, members of the same church, followers of the same version of God, but maybe they just weren't friends. People who pride themselves on their powers of judging others don't bond well. There's always that withholding of true affection, waiting for a sign of human weakness from one that the other can deliberate on. Clearly Beta Harcher rejoiced in finding people deficient in some way, so she could proclaim what awful sinners they were and how bad they needed God—and her guidance. How do you stay friends with a miserable so-and-so like that?

I pulled away from the First Baptist Church of Mirabeau. Making peace with death. Tamma Hufnagel seemed to have already done that, and right quick.

CHAPTER FOUR

I COULDN'T STAND BOB DON GOERTZ. FORTU-
nately I only knew him from a distance. Bob Don
owned the two biggest car dealerships in Bonaparte
County. If you looked up *charlatan* in the dictionary
you might find a bejeweled and polyestered Bob Don
leering back at you, ready to shake your hand and ar-
range financing for your new or quality pre-owned car.
I'm only a bigot toward car dealers; I've yet to meet
one I like.

He replaced Beta on the town's library board when
she got booted. The Hufnagels liked him, which was no
recommendation in my book. As soon as Beta got
sacked for her reactionary hysterics, Bob Don stated
that what America was all about was freedom of the
press and he'd sure be delighted to donate his time to
the library board. The board elected him without a second (or possibly first) thought. Since then he'd been as
sweet and as fake as cotton candy to me. I guess he
knew I was a force to be reckoned with. Or he wanted
to sell me a car. Apparently for Bob Don, running a car
dealership was a lot like running for public office. He
could smell the winds of change and spit the other way
quicker than you could blink his saliva out of your eye.

I pulled my Blazer into the quiet dealership, hoping
that Bob Don hadn't dashed off to a cholesterol-filled

lunch with the good ol' boys. I parked, stepped out of the car, and made it about three feet before a fat, balding salesman arrowed toward me.

Telling him as we hustled along that I wasn't buying, but was just there to see Bob Don, I swerved and made it roughly twenty feet before a younger fellow with huge sideburns and bad teeth attempted a verbal tackle, offering to let me test-drive a Bronco. Nimbly avoiding him and his sales pitch, I made it to the air-conditioned showroom. With a plea to use the bathroom, I pushed past another sweaty salesman and got into Bob Don's inner sanctum.

A gum-chewing, beehived receptionist examined me critically before picking up her phone and announcing me to the King of the Road. Bob Don came to his office door quickly, which surprised me. He surprised me further by looking happy to see me. His broad, tanned face broke into an ear-to-ear white grin.

"Well, hey there, Jordy, it's good to see you!" He pumped my hand like I was a water well.

"Hello, Bob Don. I wonder if you have a minute to talk privately."

"Why, *sure* I do." Apparently talking to me would be the highlight of his day. I found that a little difficult to believe, what with all the unsold cars on his lot.

We went into his office, decorated in small-town prosperity. Pictures of local Little League teams that were sponsored by the Goertz dealership covered the walls, going back at least two decades. Trophies for the teams that fared well stood on a shelf. He'd backed several winners and probably sold their parents a car while the glow of victory was fresh. There were pictures of him and his wife over several years, the fashions changing somewhat but not straying far from rural Texas couture. His wife was a numbed-looking woman with heavy-lidded, blank eyes and pneumatically big hair. I'd heard gossip that she drank heavily. There were awards for excellence from the various automakers he represented; but they were cheap-looking certificates that Bob Don had mounted in expensive frames. I thought they looked rather sad.

Bob Don sat behind his desk in a thronelike leather chair and gestured for me to take a seat. Clutter covered the desk, including a huge, ceramic monstrosity of an ashtray with a few butts mashed in it. I saw it and laughed; it reminded me of the horror ashtray I used in the library. Bob Don laughed with me in the automatic, reflexive way of salesmen. I told him why I laughed and his grin grew.

"Oh, Lord, yes, Gretchen's just got too much time on her hands." He examined the ashtray as though it were an interesting part from a foreign car. "She said it represents somethin', but damned if I know what it is. Rage, I think. Insisted she had to take some damned course over at the community college in Bavary. Not pottery, but cer-a-mics. Next week it'll be photography or genealogy or some such thing." He shook his head and started to offer me a cigarette. Suddenly he withdrew the pack. "Sorry. Just remembered you're trying to quit."

"How did you know?"

"You mentioned it last board meeting." He shrugged and put the pack away.

"Actually, I'd love to have a cigarette with you, Bob Don. I decided to hold off on quitting for the moment."

He looked pleased, muttered something about not living forever, and lit for us both. I inhaled deeply and looked at him through the smoky veil. Tall guy, over six feet, probably up over two hundred pounds now. His face held strength when he wasn't trying to be a good ol' boy, and I thought he must've been handsome when he was young. He looked better when he didn't smile than when he did. His official Beta verse, according to my notebook, was Judges 5:30: *Have they not divided the prey; to every man a damsel or two?* Two women. Had Beta discovered another woman in Bob Don's life aside from the artistically challenged Gretchen? Or had some other *prey* been split? Or neither? Beta had a vivid imagination. At least I had that in common with her, I thought.

I stayed silent for a moment, watching him smoke, and wondering if he was going to set his blond-gray hair on fire with his cigarette. His hair spray was probably creating an ozone hole directly over Mirabeau. He wore it swept into a Conway Twitty–style helmet, with long matching sideburns. Bob Don could have easily been a televangelist or a Sixties country-western singer as much as a rural car dealer.

"What's up, Jordy?" he finally said, breaking my reverie.

"I wanted to talk to you about Beta Harcher."

His eyes frosted. "Oh, her. Don't pay attention to her. She's just a bit overzealous, and—"

I didn't let him continue. "Haven't you heard? She's dead."

I might as well have leaned over the table and mussed up his hair. The shock showed naked on his face. He recovered quickly, drawing on his cigarette. His eyes avoided mine. "Dead?"

I told the story in few words, omitting the list. "I thought the police might have called you by now. They're starting an investigation, of course."

"Call me? Why?" Now he looked at me. His complexion, fair to begin with, paled.

"You have a key to the library, Bob Don. There was

a key on her that Tamma Hufnagel says Beta swiped from Adam, but who knows for sure?"

"Good Lord!" He receded into his chair. He blinked his puffy blue eyes through the smoke. "Holy Christ!" he muttered. "Would you like a drink?"

"Sacrilege and booze? How un-Baptist of you, Bob Don."

He shrugged instead of arguing. "I'm a man like any other, Jordy. I believe in God, but all His rules get tiresome. I'm gonna have me a whiskey. You want one?"

"Sure." I never drink early, but I'm flexible under stress.

He produced two plastic glasses from a desk drawer, along with a bottle of Jack Daniel's. He poured solemnly and handed me a glass. He didn't make a toast and I was relieved.

"Beta dead," he muttered. "Jesus! It seems impossible." The shock faded from his face and his expression was composed and unreadable.

"Everyone dies," I observed, wondering how he'd react to such a cold comment.

"Yeah, but I always thought she'd go on her own terms." He shook his head and sipped.

"I understand you saw her yesterday, around midafternoon?"

"You ask that like you don't care, but I think you do." He fingered his red necktie, covered with little yellow horseshoes.

"You were upset when you saw her," I said.

"Who told you this?" he asked. "Tamma Hufnagel, I guess. She was leaving as I got there. Practically running. Looked as scared as a four-year-old at a haunted house."

I filed that away. "Never mind Tamma. I'm curious as to why you were there."

He frowned and I saw his fingers whiten against his

drink. "Why should I tell you?" His friendliness had not entirely evaporated, but it was drying.

I measured him. I hadn't liked Bob Don before, but in the past five minutes he'd shown glimmers of humanity that elevated him beyond the supercilious gladhander I'd known.

"Look. She threatened me yesterday in the library, then she ends up dead there from a bat I brought and left in my office. It doesn't look promising for me. The police and Billy Ray Bummel think I was involved."

He mashed out his cigarette and downed his glass of Jack Daniel's. His stare held mine. "I'll ask you a question, Jordy. I want the truth. I will help you all I can if you need it." His eyes had a frankness I hadn't expected. "Did you kill her?"

"No, I did not," I answered. "And if I did, why would you help me anyway?"

He poured more whiskey into his glass. "Because I liked your daddy, and I like your mama," he said simply. "I'd do it for them."

"Then help me. Tell me why you were there and what you know about her."

"What do I know about her?" He looked toward the window. He didn't say anything for several moments. "She grew up here. She was pretty when she was younger. She was wild, too. I remember hearing that about her, although she was several years younger than me. She didn't get religion bad until she was twenty, and then something happened to her to make her think she and Jesus together were an unbeatable team. She never married 'cause nobody could live with her. Her daddy was well-to-do and she lived off the money he left her." He shrugged. "She was obsessed with God. With judging people."

I nodded. "Do you think she ever used that judging to go a step beyond?"

"What do you mean?" he asked hoarsely.

"You can't judge someone until you know their story. She could just judge people by conduct, but that might not be enough." I watched him; our eyes never strayed from each others'. "Was she the type to dig up dirt on folks? Use it against them?" I thought of the verses she'd associated with Tamma and Bob Don; they suggested secrets best kept hidden.

"She wasn't blackmailing me," Bob Don said tonelessly. He raised the plastic glass to his lips and gulped.

Not the response I expected. I sipped my own drink, trying to act nonchalant. "So why did you go see her yesterday?"

He swallowed. "I wanted to clear the air with her about me replacing her on the board. Just make amends instead of amens." He tried to laugh but it sounded more like a sick cough. "I knew how upset she was and I thought it best to make her feel she still had a voice—through me—on the board."

That was all I needed, another Beta. "And are you her voice now? Are you going to give me as much trouble as she did?"

Bob Don looked hurt. He fumbled for his words, as though they were scraps he'd scattered on the floor. "No, not at all. Look, Jordy, please stay out of all this. Let the police do their job."

"Their job seems to be trying to find enough evidence to arrest me, according to Billy Ray Bummel."

"They won't arrest you. I promise. I—" Bob Don never got to finish. I heard the nasal sounds of the bee-hived receptionist and I recognized two other voices before the door flew open.

Junebug Moncrief and Billy Ray Bummel.

They hadn't bothered with the niceties of knocking.

Billy Ray looked at me like he'd caught me with my hands around a tender young throat.

"I told 'em you were busy talking to Mr. Poteet," the receptionist yelled from behind Mirabeau's Law and Order.

"It's okay, Bernadette," Bob Don eyed Junebug and Billy Ray critically. "Y'all come in."

Since they were already in, they stayed put. A glaring Bernadette shut the door behind her.

"Afternoon, Mr. Goertz," Junebug smiled. Billy Ray nodded and continued to scrutinize me as if I were a urine specimen.

"Gentlemen," Bob Don wheedled in his closing-the-deal voice, "usually visitors wait to be announced. Y'all trying to make ever'body here think y'all gonna arrest me?" He chuckled good-naturedly at the end.

"We just wanted to ask you some questions, Bob Don," Junebug said. "How you doing, Jordy?"

I stood, setting my drink on Bob Don's desk. "I'm fine, thank you." I didn't feel it.

"You mind telling us what you're doing here?" Billy Ray asked. "Not making a toast to Miz Harcher's memory, I hope."

Before I could answer, Bob Don leapt into the fray. "Jordy here and I were just talking about him gettin' a new truck."

"You must be a mighty cool customer, findin' a dead body then going car shoppin'," Billy Ray observed. He didn't bother to hide the vitriol in his voice.

"Billy Ray," Junebug cautioned. He looked at me, then the drinks. "Didn't know you were interested in buying a truck, Jordy."

"I'm offering him a good trade-in on that car of his, but he reckons I'm trying to rip him off," Bob Don laughed, as jovial as a host politely trying to remove unwanted guests. His verbal awkwardness was gone; the hallmark glibness that'd earned him that big car lot was back.

"Since Junebug and Billy Ray obviously want to talk to you, Bob Don, I'll be leaving." I shook his hand. "I'll consider your offer. Thanks."

"Give me a call and we'll discuss it further." His blue eyes bored into mine and there was steel in his handshake. I thought for a moment that he was reluctant to release my hand, but he did.

Junebug and Billy Ray said nothing further to me as I walked out and shut the door. I went past the still fuming Bernadette, who was muttering about the poor manners of civil servants. I emerged into the heat of the afternoon.

Bob Don Goertz, unaccountably, was acting like my ally. But even though he had been forthcoming, he hadn't seemed comfortable. Did I make him nervous? I'd half-expected him to point a finger at me and tell the officers that I was prying into Beta Harcher's death. But he hadn't. And I thought I knew why.

I'd asked if Beta was the type to dig up dirt on people; his immediate response was *She's not blackmailing me*. It seemed an odd answer for a smooth talker like Bob Don. Not a "Yeah, she was the type to do it" or "No, she was a good Christian woman who'd never commit extortion." He just said *he* wasn't being victimized. I wondered if that was a slip of the tongue, if Bob Don had been so jumpy that he'd logically leap-frogged ahead a couple of questions. Was he being blackmailed by Beta, or did he know of someone else who was? I was getting ahead of myself, I thought. But I'd definitely take him up on his offer of further discussion. He hadn't said where he was last night. I felt that honest Bob Don wasn't being entirely so.

It didn't make me want to buy a car from him.

* * *

The smell of marijuana hung faint in the air as I sat on Matt Blalock's screened back porch. I wasn't surprised that someone in Mirabeau would be toking up, but I found it disconcerting that a Vietnam vet sneaked a puff while staring out at the lush, dense growth of mossy woods that came up to his property like alien jungle. It seemed too much like a scene from an Oliver Stone picture.

Matt Blalock wheeled back onto the porch, balancing a lap tray with iced tea glasses with little mint sprigs (I hoped they were mint) topping the tea. I'd have offered to help, but I knew from experience Matt liked to do everything himself.

Stopping at the low table in front of me, he handed me a glass of tea and set one down for himself. He deftly whipped the tray around and tossed it onto another table. The tray clattered, but didn't fall.

"Good aim," I offered.

Matt shrugged. He wasn't a big guy; only five feet six or so, but his arm muscles bulged massively from years of acting for his legs. He kept his black hair cut military short. Matt's uniform these days was jeans and some cause-related T-shirt, using his big chest to advertise saving the whales, disarming the populace, or promoting world peace. Today's shirt invited us to plant a tree. His other nod to calculated Bohemianism was a perfect little trimmed triangle of beard that sprouted on his chin, pointing downward. It was like a small medal of hair pinned to his face. His eyes were dark, quick, and intelligent—without the haunted look one hears vets have. All I really knew about him was that he did occasional computer consulting for software companies in Austin and that he was involved in the Vietnam veterans movement.

"Your farm's looking good," I offered by way of conversation.

He shrugged again, an odd motion that evoked French schoolgirls more than burly veterans. "Credit my dad and my brother. They do all the work. I just live here."

I couldn't imagine my family letting me do drugs on the porch, but maybe the Blalocks figured Matt had earned special privileges.

"I hope they'll be reopening the library soon," Matt observed in his lazy, drawling voice. "I don't want to have to move our vets meeting on account of that bitch."

I loathed Beta Harcher, but even I wouldn't have said something that insensitive. "She's dead, Matt. Have some respect."

"Ding-dong, Jordy," Matt laughed. "The witch is dead. Look, I'm not one to render tears or even one moment of fake sympathy over someone I despised. She hated me and I hated her and that was fine." He turned his wheelchair to face me.

"You may not think it's fine now, Matt," I answered. "You had a key to the library. You obviously didn't get along with her. The cops have got your number."

He shrugged again. My shoulders would get tired if I only had one gesture to rely on. He kept his hands, wearing fingerless gloves, near his wheels. "They've already been out here. Chief Moncrief and that snot-nosed prosecutor of his. Those two are useless. Whoever killed Bait-Eye is going to outfox them, I've no doubt. Junebug's used to dealing with offenders who show him their monogrammed belt buckles when he asks for ID, and Billy Ray Bummel walks his kid to school 'cause they're in the same grade. Jesus!" He laughed, a dry, rustling sound deep in his throat.

"So. We've got us a clever killer?"

"Yep. Someone got her into the library, conked her, and isn't leaving a trace. Anyway"—he sipped tea—"it had to be planned. Can you imagine ol' Bait-Eye causing a crime of passion?" He slapped his leg in amusement.

"I've always thought of you as one of the smarter people in town, Matt." I smiled. "Maybe you did it."

He considered the possibility. "Maybe I did. Although I heard she got it with one blow. I'd have been slower. Lots."

I wondered if he'd seen slow killing before. The look on Matt's face made my throat tighten.

"You heard what that woman said to me at the board meetings, Jordy. When I came to talk on behalf of library patrons." I had, and I looked at the overgrowth on his property, embarrassed. As blunt and unlikable as Matt could be, Beta's cruelty toward him had been unbelievable. When he spoke against her censorship stand, she brought out her most vicious artillery. I saw the scene in my mind's eye: a red-faced Beta screeching and spitting at Matt, calling his veterans' newsletter unpatriotic and saying it was best he was crippled, since he couldn't be as seditious from a wheelchair. I do hate venom. Even Adam Hufnagel and his wife, Beta's strongest allies, had begged her to stop. I'd seen Matt's hands grip the arms of his chair, his knuckles bleached of blood, fighting for control. I think I had realized then exactly what sort of twisted person I was dealing with in Beta Harcher. The next meeting, the board removed her.

"She even called here at the house a couple of times." Matt scratched at his funky patch of beard. "Told my father he should just push me out into the countryside and leave me to die." He laughed. "Daddy told her I'd survived worse than the Mirabeau scenery and she could kiss his big white ass."

"I'm sure that mended fences."

"Screw her," he said, his voice sounding loose and a little drunk. "I'm glad she's dead."

"Were you this open with the police, Matt?"

"No. I wasn't this open," he answered—and I knew why. He'd rolled the joint I'd smelled after the visit from Junebug. Matt was a little high and a little more talkative.

I considered Matt. He appeared completely forthright, unlike Tamma and Bob Don. I decided on unmitigated honesty. "Did Junebug mention a list of Beta's that they found?"

"Yeah, he did. Allowed I was on some list of hers, didn't say who else was on it. I told him it was probably her shit list 'cause she sure wasn't doing her early Christmas shopping for me."

"Well, I'm on the list too. Along with others who have connections to the library."

"So? She was pissed at everyone at the library. Tell me something new."

"Each name had a Bible quote next to it, Matt. Would you like to know what yours is?"

That threw him. He actually moved back slightly in his wheelchair. "Not that it matters, but yeah, I would."

"It's appropriately a quote from Matthew. A famous one. *'Verily I say unto you that one of you shall betray me.'* " I paused. "What do you think she meant by that, Matt, putting that quote by your name?"

His fingers tented over his mouth, containing his laughter. "How could I betray that bitch? I sure wasn't on her side. You can't betray an enemy." Matt gestured with his tea, sloshing some of it on the porch floor. He ignored it and smiled at me, like a general at untrained troops. "And what was your quote, Jordy? Something about keeping objectionable library materials? I'm not up on my Bible. Never had much use for all that claptrap anyway."

I set my tea down and repeated my quote about good

and evil. Matt laughed again. His merriness gave me the creeps. I thought he might keep laughing and just not stop.

"Je*sus*! I wish I had so much spare time to muck around in other peoples' lives. Making lists with fucking Bible quotes—what total horseshit!"

"Where were you last night, Matt? Around ten or so?"

He quit laughing and glared at me. "I think I resent you even asking me such a question."

"I'm sure Junebug and Billy Ray asked you."

"Oh, they did. But they were more interested in you." He didn't need to put the extra stress on the last word; it hit me like a rock.

"Is that the purpose of this little social call, Jordy? To start pointing fingers of blame at everyone else to get the heat off yourself?"

"I don't need to point fingers," I retorted. "I didn't kill her, but I want to know who did. I don't care much for being implicated in a murder. You hated her and you had keys to the library."

"But I'm in a wheelchair," he said mockingly.

"Don't you hide behind it, Matt. Those arms of yours are plenty powerful. I'm sure you could hit a home run with a bat or bash in Beta's head, just as easy as pie."

"But I was here, Jordy," Matt whispered with a smile. "I was here, with my family to back me up. Is your alibi that good?"

It wasn't, and it made me feel mad. I stood. "Alibis can be broken, Matt. I'm sure when Junebug interrogates everyone else involved in the censorship fight, the hatred between you and Beta will become an issue. I may have to mention it to him myself." With that, I turned for the door. Matt didn't permit me the last word.

"Don't interrupt him, Jordy. He'll be busy reading you your Miranda rights." Then low, bitter laughter.

I slammed the porch door and headed for my car.

CHAPTER FIVE

A BRILLIANTLY SPLITTING HEADACHE HIT ME after my confrontation with Matt. As I drove back into town from the Blalock farm, I massaged my temples and reviewed my predicament.

I'd always rather liked Matt, although I didn't know him very well. He had a reputation in the town for being a smart aleck and a loudmouth, but I'd seen him face down Beta's abuse without ever sinking to her level. What surprised me was the depth of his venom; he abhorred Beta Harcher as much as she did him. I'd thought he'd be above that, with his concern for baby seals and whatnot. I wondered what the autopsy on her body would show; could the blow have come from someone seated? If so, Matt made a prime candidate.

I turned from the farm road onto Mayne, still a bit outside the city limits. I wasn't making too spectacular a debut as an investigator. I had some possibly meaningless Bible verses and a list of suspects: a Baptist minister's wife who seemed too mousy to say boo (but maybe wasn't); a used-car salesman who wanted to protect me (but maybe didn't); and a bitter, antagonistic activist (no doubt there). I didn't place any of them above suspicion. Unfortunately no one was understudying my unwanted role of prime suspect.

I hadn't eaten lunch, so I swung toward home. I took

the long way around; instead of going right onto Lee Street for the straight shot I turned early, driving down Gregg Street. Beta Harcher's house sat at the end of the road. Gregg would have gone farther, but a hundred yards beyond Beta's backyard the land tumbled down to the Colorado. I drove slowly past the house, deciding to look like any gawker. A TV van from one of the Austin stations was parked by the curb. An immaculately groomed blonde with a microphone chatted with a heavy, elderly woman who'd put on her Sunday best for the cameras. In olden days, vultures attended sudden death; today we have the media.

On impulse, I U-turned and headed to the library. There were a couple of official-looking cars there, but no cameras or lollygaggers. I steered homeward, hoping that there wouldn't be cars I didn't want to see.

I wasn't entirely lucky. Candace's Mercedes was perched in the driveway. I sighed, parked, and went in.

Mama was animated, telling a politely nodding Candace about her marriage. Nuptial bliss wasn't Candace's favorite topic of conversation, at least in public. Candace had changed clothes, wearing a stylish Banana Republic T-shirt, faded (and nicely snug) jeans, and a fancy belt studded with silver conchos. She looked gorgeous and I reminded myself again that she was a co-worker. As I walked in, she jumped to her full if diminutive height.

"And where the hell have you been? Excuse my language, Mrs. Poteet, but I'm mad at your son."

Mama assured herself I was her son with a glance and seemed satisfied.

"Uh—Out," I answered. What was I supposed to say? Sleuthing? Interrogating suspects?

"Well, I want you to know what I've had to go

through to protect your good name," Candace said archly.

I raised a hand to fend off the oncoming torrent. "Where are Sister and Mark?"

"They've run to the grocery store," she paused. "The police called Mark to confirm you were here last night. I came here 'cause I got tired of hunting you down and—I needed to see you, after this morning's shock."

I swallowed. She *needed* me? I deflected a blush by asking a question. "What happened at the station?"

"You'll be delighted to know I wasn't body-searched," Candace huffed, "although I wouldn't put it past Billy Ray. Honestly. I told them what little I knew, and that nasty Billy Ray kept trying to hint that you'd killed Miss Harcher. I repeatedly—mind you, repeatedly—told him that was utterly ridiculous, but he didn't get the hint. What a moron! Wouldn't surprise me a bit if his family tree didn't fork."

"He's still trying to implicate me?" I wanted details.

Candace threw her hands up in the air. "Tried, but I set him straight. I gave him a piece of my mind and then some."

"Thanks, Candace," I said, happy that she was on my side. She smiled then and I felt a bit awkward. I didn't want to encourage her. After all, she's my assistant and we have to keep our relationship professional, not personal.

"I don't understand any of this," Mama said, looking to Candace.

Candace heaved air, horrified at what she'd said in front of my mother. "Now, Mrs. Poteet, don't you worry about Jordy, I'm going to take care of everything. The police are just misguided. It'll all get settled." She patted Mama's hand. "Would you like some lunch?"

Mama shook her head. "No. I want a nap."

Candace volunteered to take Mama upstairs and get her settled, so I made turkey sandwiches, with lots of mayonnaise, tomato, and lettuce on wheat bread. I dumped a small bag of corn chips on each plate and popped two cold cans of Dr Pepper. I put the plates on the table and sat down with my lunch and my ruminations.

Holding true to the rule that I get little peace in my home, Candace rejoined me before I was half through. "Now, Jordy," she said, pulling up a chair, "I want the truth. Where have you been?" She dug into her sandwich and, after the first bite, smiled. I guess I'm not a bad cook for a bachelor.

I told her about my interviews with Tamma Hufnagel, Bob Don Goertz, and Matt Blalock. Candace was quite prepared to be my Watson.

"Aha! That Tamma Hufnagel. Probably a crazed killer. You always have to look out for the quiet ones," she asserted.

"She acts timid, but I think there's a toughness underneath. Maybe she's too quiet."

"My point exactly. Or there's Bob Don. I'd never buy a car from that crook."

"You'd never buy American, Candace, and he doesn't sell imports."

"Well, if I get the sudden urge for a Chrysler, I'm going to Honest Ed's in Bavary," Candace announced.

"He seemed to have a secret, but he also seemed inclined to help me." I finished my sandwich.

"Of course." Candace slapped her forehead. "He wants to find out how much you know 'cause he's the killer. Makes perfect sense. Stay away from him, Jordy."

"Bob Don didn't get nearly as upset as Matt Blalock."

"Warped by his wartime experiences," Candace intoned. "Poor guy. Beta made him snap and he saw her as a Vietcong. Probably called her Charlie right before he whacked her."

The phone rang and I reached for it, grateful for the interruption.

Candace grabbed it away. "Reporters," she hissed, as though there were lepers on the line. She spoke guardedly into the receiver: "Poteet residence."

A moment's silence, then a "May I ask who's calling?" Was it suddenly cooler in here or was it just me?

"Let me see if he's available." The cold front swept through, as swift and sure as one from Canada. "Ruth Wills for you."

I took the receiver, hoping the frostbite would be minimal. "Thanks, Candace." She made no move to give me privacy.

Ruth sounded amused. "I see you have an answering service these days, Jordy."

"Um, yes. Just for today."

"I'm not surprised you're screening calls. I hear you discovered the late Beta Harcher this morning. Are you okay?" The amusement left her voice to be replaced by husky softness, a murmur to be heard on the next-door pillow. Not a voice you'd expect to hear inquiring about your emotional well-being.

"Fine, thank you. Did you hear that from Junebug?"

"Yes, I did. He stopped by the hospital this morning to talk with me." She paused again. "I need to speak to you. In person. Could we have dinner tonight?"

I was a little taken aback. Finding Beta dead and Ruth Wills asking me out? Fortune's wheel was spinning every which way today. "I don't know—"

"Please say yes, Jordy. Look, I'm still on duty. I wanted to see you sooner, and not under these circumstances, but please, please meet me tonight." The voice had me, like a pipe enchanting a snake.

"Okay. When?" Out of the corner of my eye I saw Candace stiffen.

"Seven? Meet me at Rosita's?" That was a nice Mexican restaurant in Bavary.

"Fine," I said. "Thanks." She hung up without a goodbye, and I replaced the phone in its cradle.

"What did Ruth want?" Candace examined the last of her corn chips with profound absorption.

"She wanted to discuss some . . . library business with me. Maybe regarding Beta." I shrugged. "No big deal."

Candace measured me on some internal scale. She tented her cheek with her tongue and looked at me again. I felt awkward. Why did she always do that to me? It was damned annoying. Suddenly I wanted her gone.

"I have some other matters to attend to today," I said, but Candace didn't let me finish.

"You go and do that. I'll stay here and keep an eye on your mom."

"That's not necessary, Candace. Really. I'll wait for Sister to come home."

"I don't mind. I'll watch TV. Arlene should be back soon. Go talk with Ruth or whatever it is you have to do."

I decided not to mention that Ruth invited me to dinner. Best to beat a diplomatic retreat out of my own house. Leaving, I shook my head at my own cowardice.

A tall, bronzed teenager who was my third cousin tended the dense flower beds that made up most of Eula Mae Quiff's lawn. He was almost hidden in the wild explosions of rhododendrons, roses, daisies, and every other odd mixture of flower that Eula Mae favored. Her garden had as much order and as much color as her novels.

Hally Schneider, his tan face damp with sweat, looked up and favored me with a friendly smile. "Hey there, Jordy. You lookin' for Miz Quiff?"

"Yeah."

"She's inside getting me a drink. She oughta be right back."

Like a stage cue, Eula Mae appeared on her porch with a glass of iced tea. She came down the stairs, her baggy dress hanging about her bony, fortyish body and fluttering in the breeze. Her hair was its usual explosion of red curls, pulled into a semblance of order with a paisley scarf. She wore large earrings that looked like they were handmade in Africa. Her hands were elegantly bejeweled and her nails were long and lacquered; I wonder how she typed on her keyboard.

I'd known Eula Mae a long time; her daddy and my daddy had been friends. Since she was a little over ten years older than me, we hadn't been close when I was a kid. But when I moved back to town, she'd been my staunchest supporter in the library wars with Beta. She handed Hally the drink and favored me with a sly eye.

"Here you go, Hally, dear. Drink up."

"Thanks, Miz Quiff," Hally said, gulping down the tea. I saw Eula Mae ogling him, her avid eyes locked on where his thick neck met his broad shoulders.

I coughed. "I'm sorry to interrupt your labors, Eula Mae, but I need to speak with you."

"Of course, Jordy. Where are my manners? Come sit on the porch with me and have some tea."

I turned to Hally. "You going to be here for a while?"

He nodded. "Still got a fair amount of weeding to do."

"Okay. I'd like to talk with you when I'm done visiting with Eula Mae."

If Hally seemed surprised, he didn't show it. He just nodded and knelt back to his gardening.

Eula Mae and I walked up the long path to her gracious home. It reminded me of a shrunken antebellum mansion, one you might find on a Hollywood lot. She'd lived there alone since her terminally shy sister Patty died ten years ago. I'd always wondered if Patty simply succumbed to Eula Mae's ego.

She gestured languidly toward a porch chair and went inside. Loose pages, lying on a wicker table, caught the breeze at their corners and gently turned up. Printing and red marks covered the paper. Eula Mae's latest. I leaned forward to peek, and one of Eula Mae's multitude of cats yowled at me from a white whicker chair. I stuck my tongue out and the cat raised its head snidely.

My hostess returned with another glass of tea and handed it to me. Absently, she shoved the cat out of the chair. The cat mewled in protest at the declining social standards on the porch while Eula Mae kept an eye on her gardener.

"Jesus, Eula Mae. Why don't you just go out there and undress the poor kid?"

She looked at me with reproach. "Simply because I find your cousin aesthetically pleasing doesn't mean I want my way with him. Please. I'm doing research."

"Research?"

The displaced cat growled again, and Eula Mae scooped him into her lap. She stroked his fur contritely, and he allowed her to place her cheek on him while she spoke. "Yes, Jordy. That boy is going to be the hero of my next work. Well, someone very like him in form."

"What about in mind?" Hally was a good kid and a great athlete, but not a straight-A student.

"My hero will have a bit more on the ball than Hally, but nothing more in terms of physical endowment," Eula Mae answered. "We must always look for inspiration and never turn it away. He'd look divine painted on the cover of my next novel."

"I think you could find all sorts of inspiration round here if you were writing a murder mystery," I observed dryly.

"I was working up to that," Eula Mae answered, "but I didn't know your mental state. You over your shock, sugar pie?" She patted my knee in a friendly way. The cat glared balefully at me.

"The shock of finding her body? Yes, for the time being. The shock of being suspected of killing her? Not quite yet."

Eula Mae played dreamily with one of her errant curls. "Yes, the police have already been here asking me about you and our beloved Beta." She saw me tense and shook her head. "Junebug can't possibly think you killed her. You know he's really a sweet boy underneath all that bluster. Billy Ray's a different story, though, and Junebug gets pressure from him." She paused, giving me a speculative stare. "So what was your quote?"

I told her. She shook her head, the ringlets dancing around her face. "Makes as much sense as mine. Job 31:35: *My desire is, that the Almighty would answer me, and that mine adversary had written a book*. Well, I've written several award-winning books and I was her adversary. Big whoop. What's the damn point of it all?"

"I take it Junebug shared the list with you."

"Just my part. He wouldn't divulge who else was on it."

I did. She sat and listened thoughtfully, harrumping at

Tamma Hufnagel and Bob Don Goertz's names. At my mother and Hally Schneider's names, she frowned.

"Don't understand that at all. How could she hate or want to hurt someone with Alzheimer's and"—she gestured in the direction of her gardener—"someone as sweet as Hally?"

I shrugged. "Mama can't remember any connection with her. And I don't know about Hally. Maybe it's some sick way of striking at me or Janice Schneider."

"My Lord," Eula Mae said, but not to me. Her eyes were back in the garden. Hally had removed his shirt and his bunched muscles moved smoothly as he worked. Eula Mae sighed like a dieter in front of a candy store.

"Youth is wasted on the young, Jordy. Remember that." With Hally out of reach, she appraised me. "You and Hally do favor each other, you know. You both got those fine Schneider looks. Shame you're still just an infant compared to me. But of course Candace is a different story—"

I rolled my eyes. "Look, Eula Mae, let's concentrate. You know damn well that I didn't kill Beta and I'm willing to give you the same benefit of doubt—"

"Are you so sure?" she interrupted, her voice as sweet and fake as sno-cone syrup. I stopped dead.

"I'm kidding!" she exclaimed, but her eyes showed merriment at my discomfort. I ran a tongue over dry lips.

"So when was the last time you saw her?" I asked.

"Oh, that nastiness in the library. When she slapped the tar out of you."

"Not since?"

"No, Jordy. Lord, what do you want, an accounting of my movements? All right, Perry Mason, I'll be delighted to oblige. Murder's one of the few crimes I'm still innocent of and I want to keep my unstained reputation. After that little scene at the library, I came back here, did some work on the newest book—it features Charity Keepwell, who I am sure you'll remember from my very well-received *Lily of the Alamo* two books back. Then I had my dinner, watched some television, did a little editing, and went to bed."

"What time was that?"

"Around ten. And alone." She seemed to have spotted something interesting on her nail. The cat batted her sleeve, wanting attention.

"I see. And you don't know of anyone who had a motive to kill Beta?"

"Lord, sure I did. That crazy Matt Blalock for one. And I suppose even *you*."

I tried not to look menacing. "I hope you didn't make any such statement to the police."

Eula Mae leaned close to me and I could smell the slightly sour odor of old perfume. "No, sugar pie, I didn't. Motive, yes; but you're not stupid enough to commit murder. But someone like Matt Blalock is, or that Ruth Wills."

"Ruth?" My dinner date? That possibility didn't promote good digestion and it might make conversation just a tad strained.

"Surely you could tell there's no love lost between Ruth and Beta."

"I knew they didn't get along, but—"

"Are you keeping your ears in a jar? Beta tried to get Ruth fired." Eula Mae leaned back, delighted in the miniature drama she'd caused. A beringed hand ran through her curly mane to heighten the effect.

"What for?"

"I don't know all the details. I just heard about it from my friend Joan. She's a secretary over at the hospital and a very ardent fan of mine. Of course sheer numbers preclude my having a real relationship with most of my fans, but I've made an exception for Joan. Such a perceptive reader and an extremely reliable source. Joan said Beta claimed Ruth tried to poison her when she was in the hospital last January."

"What?" This was news to me.

"Oh, the hospital shut it up because it was groundless," Eula Mae sniffed. "Just Beta getting a visitation from Satan and blaming it on Ruth. No one filed charges or anything; I think the D.A. over in Bavary talked Beta out of it 'cause it was so blasted silly."

"So what happened between them?"

Eula Mae waved her hand, dismissing the need for details. "I don't know. Apparently Beta was in the hospital—she'd had some chest pains and they were keeping her for observation—and she said Ruth entered her room and tried to give her an injection, when she'd just been given some medication by another nurse. According to Beta, Ruth told her she was going to get *hers*—and Ruth tried to stick the needle in her. Beta screamed bloody murder—you know what a set of lungs the old witch had—and some other nurses rushed in. Of course Ruth denied the whole crazy thing and there was no evidence to support Beta's charge."

"I don't get it. Even if it were true, why would Ruth want to kill Beta?"

"Back then, who knows? Community service, perhaps? It's a lot of bullcrap if you ask me. But now"— Eula Mae slid her glance slyly over her shoulder—"who knows? I mean, Beta did try to ruin her career."

"But she failed. Ruth didn't lose her job. They didn't even file charges. Why kill Beta now?" This made little sense to me.

"I don't know what else might have transpired between them. Ruth supported you in the censorship fight. Maybe there's some other dark secret between them." Eula Mae's eyes glowed with creativity, as though she were plotting her next potboiler. "Was Ruth on that list? What was her quote?"

Ruth's was easy to remember, especially in light of this revelation. It was 2 Kings 4:40—to wit: *There is death in the pot.* When I read it earlier, I had no story such as this to relate it to. Now it sounded like Beta considered Ruth as Mirabeau's own Lucrezia Borgia.

I repeated the quote to Eula Mae and enjoyed the momentary silence. "Well, my Lord. Sounds like Beta still held a grudge."

"Great. I have a dinner date with Ruth tonight." My enthusiasm waned.

"Mind your cocktail, sweetie." Eula Mae laughed. Then her merry face darkened and grew serious. "Well, what if it's not bullcrap and Beta was right? Maybe you shouldn't go."

"For God's sake, even if it was true, she'd have no reason to poison me." I stood and watched Hally fill a trash bag with pulled weeds. "Hey, maybe Hally's pulled up a toxic plant I can take with me for defense."

"Don't joke, Jordy." I turned and looked at her. The pretend drama was out of her face. "Someone killed Beta. Maybe someone on that list, maybe not. But it's for the police to handle. Let them."

"Ruth called me. She can't think that I'm snooping into her life." I brightened. "Maybe because of Beta's earlier accusation, the police'll think of Ruth as a bigger suspect."

"Now you sound guilty," Eula Mae reproved. "No one looks more culpable than the fellow who goes around trying to prove his innocence."

I stood and rested my forehead against the porch pillar. "Thanks for the catch-22. Look, if you saw how Billy Ray guns for me—"

"You were panicked this morning, sug." Eula Mae rested her knobby hand on my arm. "You found the dead body of someone you know in your workplace. That's a profound shock. I think you've borne it quite well. But you've got to quit thinking that you're going to be arrested in the next ten seconds unless you find the killer. It's not healthy to worry so."

I hated to admit it, but she made sense. Junebug surely wouldn't arrest me—or anyone else—without hard evidence. He was a professional, after all. I kept picturing him as the boy I'd grown up with and not as the responsible police chief he was. He'd done a good job for Mirabeau. Billy Ray was another story.

"Thanks, Eula Mae. I appreciate that."

"Yeah, yeah, right." She wagged crimson fingernails at me. "Just give me first rights to be your biographer from the hoosegow."

"Deal." I nodded toward her scattered pages and then toward Hally, who was drying the sweat from his firm body with his shirt. "I'll let our beloved Jocelyn Lushe get back to work."

"Have a good dinner. Don't let Candace know. She might poison you even if Ruth doesn't."

You could always count on Eula Mae for moral support.

I headed back down the walk, watching Hally toss open another trash bag for the mound of weeds he'd pulled. I suppose Eula Mae was right. Even distantly related as third cousins (still considered kin in this part of the country), there was a family resemblance. We both stood tall with thick blondish hair and green eyes, and we had the distinctive stubborn Schneider cheekbones that could freeze into refusal and mulishness at a moment's notice. But where I was lanky from running and idle reading, Hally was thickly-built from years of football and work. I'd been a much gawkier kid. Hally was a senior at Mirabeau High and was probably years ahead sexually of where I'd been at that age. I just hoped he wasn't ahead of where I was now.

I shook his hand, ignoring the dirt on his palms.

"Hey, Jordy. How's Cousin Anne doing?" he asked.

I admit surprise; the Schneiders live no more than three houses down from us but they've only shown a passing interest in Mama's decline. Hally's annoyingly peppy mother Janice boasted a better attendance record at library board meetings than she did in checking up on her neighboring kinfolk.

"She's about the same, Hally."

He shook his head. "Damn shame. I know Mom keeps meaning to come over and see you and Arlene and Anne. I see Mark in the neighborhood, but I get the feeling that he doesn't care to discuss his grandmother."

I suspected that Hally didn't do much to curry a friendship with Mark. Hally was a senior, a popular athlete from a perfect family; Mark was a moody freshman loner stuck with a mouthy mother, a mouthier uncle, and a diminishing grandmother.

I sighed. I halfway felt like telling Hally that the Schneiders had been crappy kinfolk, but I decided it wasn't the time or place. "It's hard. Listen, Hally, I wanted to see you about something else."

He looked bemusedly at the porch. "Hope it's not about Miz Quiff. I assure you my intentions are honorable."

I laughed. "No, not about Eula Mae." Curiosity couldn't resist though. "She hasn't acted, uh, inappropriately toward you, has she?"

It was his turn to laugh. "Not at all, although I'm sure she thinks I never see her looking at me. I kind of like older women, but Eula Mae's not my type."

"No, I need to discuss a different topic with you. I guess you heard about Beta Harcher."

Hally's smile faded. "Yeah, I heard. Mom told me about it. You found her in the library?"

"Yeah." And why didn't you ask me about that straightaway? I wondered. Not every day someone you encounter has stumbled across a corpse, and you'd think the topic would debut damn early in the conversation. "Did you know her?"

Hally blinked. "Why are you asking?"

I figured a football player like Hally appreciated bluntness. I told him about the list. Shock spilled across his face.

"Honest to God, Jordy, I don't know why that woman would have my name there." Hally wiped a sweaty lip with the back of his garden-gloved hand.

"There was a Bible quote by each name. Yours was Proverbs 14:9. *Fools make a mock at sin.*"

Hally's tongue darted out to his lips and back again, nervously. "Why would she write something like that about me?"

"I thought you'd know. You been doing any sinnin' lately?" I said it as nicely as I could, but I've never believed in treating errant family members with kid gloves. Or garden gloves, in this case.

Hally looked spooked. He took a step backward and fell over the bag of weeds. Dirt and twigs stuck to his sweaty back and he jumped up quickly, brushing them off his jeans and mumbling about being clumsy in the off-season.

I'd seen that boy play football with the grace of a

dancer, so I crossed my arms and frowned at him. "What's got the chigger in your pants?"

"It's a little unnerving, you know, to hear some dead person was writing shit—I mean stuff—about you." Good thing sweet cousin Janice wasn't there to hear her little boy cuss. Janice would smile big as day while she scrubbed your mouth with lye soap.

"So how did Beta know you, Hally? She must've, to write what she did."

The words came quickly. "She knew Mom from the library and the church. I knew her from Sunday school; I'm president of the youth group there. And she baby-sat for us sometimes, when I had a date or something for school and Mom and Dad went out." Hally had been an only, extra-adored child until his little brother Josh arrived five years ago, much to Janice's embarrassment. She was the kind of woman who'd prefer no one know she was still getting sex at forty.

"So you knew her socially."

"I saw her at church. She had some definite opinions about how the youth group should be run." I remembered what Tamma Hufnagel said in the same vein. Beta's need for control was an equal-opportunity annoyance. Hally continued: "And I saw her about a week ago when she baby-sat Josh. After going to the movies in Bavary, I got home before Mom and Dad did, so I relieved her. Put Josh in the car and took her home."

I sighed. Hally seemed shook by all this, and I couldn't blame him. I was shook, too. But I didn't like that he wasn't able to meet my eyes for more than a second or two. What was he hiding?

"How did she act when you saw her?" I asked.

Hally shrugged and pulled his T-shirt back on. "Same mean old bat as always, I suppose. She was still mad at Mom for siding with you about banning books. Mom told her that didn't mean they couldn't still get along, even if they disagreed. So I think that's why Mom asked her to baby-sit Josh, maybe to patch up. Miz Harcher really seemed to like Josh; she'd play games with him, read him Mother Goose and Pooh Bear stories. I kind of thought she'd wished for a grandkid of her own."

Beta Harcher? Being nice to a child? I imagined Beta's baby-sitting activities to include recanting of cartoons, a delicious serving of cold gruel (with a side order of guilt), a spirited game of Name That Heretic, and basics of book incineration. Kindness and stories that didn't involve retribution for sins hadn't occurred to me. Maybe there'd been a heart under that stony skin.

"And nothing unusual happened when you took her home?" I pressed.

Hally looked nervous again, running his tongue tip over his chapped lips. His jaw worked. "Well, yeah. But I'm sure it doesn't mean anything. It was probably library business or something." He glanced nervously toward the house. "I don't want to get in trouble and I don't want her in trouble."

I followed his eyes to the empty porch. Eula Mae had vanished into her inner sanctum to be Jocelyn Lushe and chronicle the escapades of her latest pair of starcrossed lovers.

"Eula Mae?" I asked. "What do you mean?"

"She was sitting on Beta's porch when we pulled up. Waiting for her. Miz Harcher had left her porch light on and I could see Miz Quiff sitting up there. Miz Quiff looked madder'n hell. She was sitting in a porch chair, and she got up real slow from it when Miz Harcher got out of my car." Hally paused. "Real slow. You know, like someone who's so mad that they've got to move like molasses to keep from knocking the tar out of someone?"

"I know what you mean. So what happened then?"

Hally scooped weeds from the ground and stuffed them in a bag. "Nothing. Miz Harcher said something like 'Finally,' kissed Josh goodnight, and told me to get on home. So I did." Hally tied off the lawn bag with a green piece of wire. "But I'm sure it doesn't mean anything." He still didn't look at me. If he'd been making a mock at sin, as Beta suggested, he wasn't going to look me in the eye and fess up.

"You don't mind me asking, do you, Hally, where you were last night?"

He did meet my eyes. "No, I don't mind. I was out with a girl. Chelsea Hart. Didn't get home until after midnight." He smiled, and added, "Even with a later curfew for spring break, I missed it. Mom was mad."

"I see. Well, listen, I got to go. Tell your mother I'll stop by soon."

Relief moved across his face like a shadow. "Okay, Jordy. You take care."

I walked away from my cousin, and away from my friend's house, feeling as if even the people I knew and trusted weren't being up front with me. Eula Mae hadn't mentioned her little late night excursion to see Beta last week. Hally behaved as if he'd done worse than miss curfew. Knowing he was on that list shook him up. And I wondered why Hally, rather than his library-board mother, had made Beta's mysterious catalog.

CHAPTER SIX

"EXCUSE ME, BUT A DINNER WITH RUTH Wills?" Sister demanded. The bathroom door didn't do a lot to mute her. "You can't go out on some date. Who's gonna stay here with Mama?"

"Mark can stay. He's old enough to take care of her." I made a face at the door. The shaving cream made me look rabid. I already felt it.

"I think an adult should be here. God have mercy, you just found a body this morning and the police think you might've killed her. Decent folks'd stay home."

"Then I guess I'm indecent." I ignored her reply and finished shaving. "I'll call Dorcas Witherspoon and see if she can come over." I splashed water on my face and turned to the shower.

"Maybe I can just call Candace," Sister offered. I couldn't immediately tell if she was teasing but I had my suspicions. "I'm sure she'd be delighted to baby-sit Mama while you've got a hot date. Bet she wouldn't mind at all."

"Give it a rest." I turned the taps and drowned out her babble. I stepped into the shower and let the water sluice over me. I had found when I returned to Mirabeau that the bathroom was a simple haven from Mama, Sister, and Mark. No wonder many middle-aged men spend so much time there.

Worry nagged at me more than Sister did. In a small town, gossip runs rife. Beta's charges against Ruth had certainly been effectively muffled. And it seemed doubly interesting that Beta, who was never stingy with accusations, never mentioned her feud with Ruth at the library board meetings. The hospital, Ruth, or someone else had managed to keep Beta from hellfire-'n'-brimstoning against Ruth as Mirabeau's resident poisoner. That bothered me no end.

Sister had returned downstairs when I snuck from the steamy bathroom down the hall to my old bedroom. There's nothing quite like growing up in a house, leaving it for years, then coming back and living in your own room again. I'd expected to hate the arrangement, but with the stress of Mama's disease it comforted me. It's like putting on a very old and comfortable pair of jeans and finding they've stretched a little to match your longer legs. The bed I'd slept in as a teenager—the one I'd lost my virginity in one thunderous spring afternoon when Mama, Daddy, and Sister had gone to visit friends in Bastrop—was still there. My legs still stuck out a tad over the edge during sleep. I'd taken down the dusty academic awards and the track trophies from Mirabeau High and replaced them with art that'd hung in my condo in Boston. The Mark Rothko prints and the Ansel Adams photographs looked out of place with the antique furniture, but I didn't care. I needed some link to my middle life, the one I'd sandwiched between childhood and unexpected adulthood in Mirabeau. I slipped a CD into my portable stereo I'd put on my old study desk and got dressed while Miles Davis made his trumpet sing a sketch of Spain. I picked khakis, brown loafers, and a nicely tailored chambray shirt. Rosita's wasn't fancy by Boston standards, but I wanted to look presentable for Ruth. I thought about a tie, decided I'd look like a doofus wearing a tie if I wasn't going to church, and tossed it back on the bed.

I didn't get away scot-free. The phone rang and I scooped it up.

"Get your business wrapped up with Ruth Wills?" Candace asked archly.

"No, Candace." I didn't feel like fibbing. Maybe Sister really had called her? "Just about to, though."

"So where are you meeting her?" She must've smelled my cologne through the receiver. Some women can do that.

There was no getting past this, and I got a little hot. Candace was my friend and co-worker, but nothing more. No matter how cute and caring she could be, she could also be damned aggravating. I didn't owe her an explanation.

"Look, Candace, she asked me out to dinner. She wants to discuss Beta. And I've found out some other information that makes me want to talk to Ruth even more."

"Well, I want to discuss Beta, too."

"Candace—" I began but didn't finish. Didn't have a prayer.

"I'll tell you this, but if my mother finds out I'm in deep mud. Beta banked at Mother's bank here in town. And she deposited $35,000 cash into her savings account a week ago."

"Good Lord! Where—"

"—did she get that kind of money?" Candace finished my sentence with a vexatious amount of smugness. "Damn good question."

"God, Candace, how'd you find that out? That's supposed to be confidential."

"Mother better not find out. I got one of the tellers to help me. She told me the police were already looking into Beta's accounts."

"Well, that's interesting, Candace. I assume that Miz Harcher didn't generally deposit that kind of money in her account."

Candace snorted. "Nope. Hardly ever had a balance over five thousand, and most of that from the trust her daddy left her. She wasn't poor, but she wasn't wealthy either."

I recalled the conversations I'd had today, and how that money might fit in. I glanced at my watch; I was going to be late getting over to Bavary.

"I got to go, Candace. I'll phone you later tonight."

That placated her. "Okay. Don't have any fun with that witch."

I hung up and my male pride roared at me. Why on earth did I promise to call Candace after seeing Ruth? I didn't owe Candace an up-to-the-minute activity report.

As I descended the stairs, Sister lectured a sullen Mark about taking care of Mama. Mark turned hostile eyes on me. "I had plans tonight, you know. You ain't the only one with a social life."

"Sorry, Mark. I'll make it up to you." Maybe if I bought him a *Playboy*, he'd warm up to me. Only problem was if Sister found out, she'd warm up even faster. As in nuclear meltdown.

"Well, just make sure you come home tonight," Mark said.

"Don't worry, I'm not out to score."

"I don't mean that, Uncle Jordy. Just don't get arrested."

Rosita's screamed with color. The walls were a riotous lime green (to accompany the riotous behavior the margaritas could cause), adorned with oversized and vibrant paintings of red parrots, rainbow-beaked toucans, and black sombreros. Tinny Latino music chirped from mounted speakers. There was a patio that faced a side street in Bavary, but it overflowed with customers who were slurping down drinks, stuffing nachos in their faces, and all talking simultaneously. I wanted quiet for my tête-à-tête with Ruth.

I went in and was heartened that most patrons were taking advantage of the nice, clear night outdoors. The dining room wasn't too crowded. A beautiful young woman with ebony eyes and luxurious black hair approached me with a smile.

"I'm meeting someone—" I began but she didn't let me finish.

"You Mr. Poteet?"

"Yes."

"This way, please."

I followed her to a dim corner booth, where Ruth Wills sat as comfortable as a cat curled up on a pillow. Her brown hair swept up in a flattering way, and her eyes were dark in the pale light. She looked a little more urbane than the typical customer, in a black mock turtleneck and tailored gray slacks. A simple diamond pendant hung about her neck. I tried not to stare at the diamond, since it reposed on her shapely breasts. I didn't want her to mistake why I was here. Her physical attractiveness hadn't lured me here, I reminded myself—I wanted answers. But suddenly I found myself swallowing when a simple *hello* would have done nicely.

"Jordy," she said, offering me her hand. I took it, wondering for a moment if kissing it was out of the question. Her customary attire was a baggy sweatshirt and jeans; she looked lovely that way, but now she was positively gorgeous. And had she changed her voice? She spoke as smoothly as the curve of her hip.

"Ruth. Nice to see you." You could tell I was making my small talk extra-suave and elegant. I coughed for refuge and sat.

"I've taken the liberty of ordering a pitcher of margaritas," she murmured. "I hope you don't mind."

"That's fine." I tried to get seated comfortably without making the vinyl squeak.

"I wanted us to get together socially. I'm sorry that I waited until such sad circumstances." She placed a hand near her pendant, as though taking a pledge. "Granted that Miss Harcher was not the most beloved person in town, but as a nurse I find it hard to wish anyone ill."

This girl couldn't have poisoned a rabid rat, I thought, then pulled on the mental reins. Keep actions related to mind, I told myself. I'm a weak man in some regards and Ruth sapped my strength.

"Let's not talk about that right now." I made my voice purr as best I could. "How about an appetizer?"

We made it through the meal without mentioning any bodies I'd recently discovered. The conversation stayed safely within limits: the hopes for next season's Mirabeau Bees high-school football team, Ruth's life in the coastal city of Corpus Christi before she'd come to Mirabeau, my life in Boston amidst all those Yankees. It was a nice dinner: quesadillas stuffed with jalapenos and cheese, chicken flautas for her, beef enchiladas smothered in cheese and chili con carne for me, Spanish rice and refried beans for both, and margaritas served in blue-rimmed glasses that could have doubled as goldfish bowls. I finished one, feeling tip top, and hardly noticed when Ruth poured me another. Beta didn't rear up from the grave until we were filling our powdered, sugary sopapillas with honey.

"It must have been"—Ruth finished loading the hollow pastry with honey—"horrendous, finding her body. Terrible shock for you and poor, dear Candace."

"More for me, I guess. Candace was a rock."

"Yes, I would think so," Ruth bit into the bottom of

her sopapilla, pulled it away from her mouth, and let the honey drip onto her tongue. And yes, I watched. It was downright fascinating. She swallowed the honey, then sipped at her margarita. "Candace seems to be quite strong where you're concerned."

I felt a need to explain. "Candace is my friend and my assistant. We have a professional relationship."

"Really? I think if you were a library book she'd have you checked out constantly."

I smiled thinly. "Let's not talk about Candace."

She gave a quick cut of her hand over her glass. "Fine. It's a dull subject anyway."

I didn't let that pass. "You brought her up. Why do you care if she's interested in me?" I normally wasn't so forward, but I didn't like her picking on Candace. And the margarita felt like liquid bravery.

"What makes you think I care?" she asked.

"You invited me to dinner, Ruth. Not the other way around." I shrugged. "I figured that Beta Harcher was the proposed topic."

She laid her fork down, as though in surrender. Her eyes, dark with smoke, met mine and for the first time I felt a little afraid of her. She'd poured the margarita for me and now I wondered if it didn't have the slightest lethally chemical taste.

"*Touché.* And I'm sorry I picked on your"—her mind searched for an appropriate term for Candace—"little friend."

"So what about Beta?" I asked.

"Who killed her?"

"I don't know. Who do you think did it?"

Ruth leaned forward. "Not you. I'm not saying that out of any sort of fear toward you."

"Gee, thanks. That'll keep me from cutting your throat later."

Unexpectedly, she broke into raucous laughter. Other tables glanced our way, saw the empty pitcher, and lost interest. I couldn't keep from smiling at her despite feeling that the joke just wasn't funny.

She poked my arm with short painted fingernails. "I like you, Jordy. You're on the edge."

"Thanks. I think."

"I mean it, Jordy. You're so different from most people in Mirabeau. God, the entire town's a bore."

I stiffened, the margarita glass halfway to my lips. "You don't like Mirabeau?"

She made a dismissive noise. "I suppose there are worst places. But don't you find it unbearable after the big city?"

I finished the sip of margarita I'd started. Did I hate it here? Perhaps I had when I'd first come home; the shock of Mama's illness, the tension between Sister and me, and the stress of taking over at the library hadn't made Mirabeau seem congenial. But when I thought about it, Mirabeau was still home. You can take the boy out of the country, but not the country out of the boy. Coming home had been a rediscovery of sorts; that people waved and spoke to you on the street, even if they didn't know you (and they weren't begging or raving), that neighbors all knew each other, that you could sleep with a window open on a lovely spring night without fear. So what if we didn't have a sushi bar? I'd just as soon use raw fish for bait down on the Colorado.

I smiled thinly. "No, I like it here."

She flicked her tongue across her smile. "Maybe I am in trouble. Didn't mean to bash sweet ol' Mirabeau."

"Let's get back to Beta. I didn't mean to debate Mirabeau's merits."

She lowered her eyes, staring at her empty glass. "Beta. Y'know, I've seen plenty of people die in my line of work. You avoid sympathy because you just can't spend the energy. I've cried more over an unknown child that died in the emergency room than I ever will over Beta Harcher." She shrugged, a slow uncoiling movement.

"You didn't have a cordial past with her," I said.

She sipped at her margarita, rolling the crushed ice and salt in her mouth, and studied me over the glass. "No, I didn't. We didn't agree about the library."

"And even less about the hospital."

Ruth's nerves didn't move, much less jump. She smiled. "So you know about that little stink she made."

"I have a distinct feeling that if she'd been poisoned last night, you'd be spending quality time with Junebug Moncrief right now."

"That whole incident was utterly ridiculous. Crazy woman that she was, I almost felt sorry for her. Until she died."

"One item confuses me no end," I said. "Why she didn't raise this issue at some point in the censorship fight at the library? With you on my side and her against us, she would have vented full steam. She sure in hell didn't spare me, Eula Mae, or Matt Blalock."

I wasn't certain that breath was still escaping from her lips. Her dark eyes traveled my face, as though looking for a crack. I blinked. I waited. Finally she shrugged as if the question were unimportant.

"It didn't happen. I never, ever tried to poison her or harm her in any way. She made it up because she hated my guts."

"How did the hospital keep her from making—uh—unfounded accusations?"

She straightened. "They know me there, and they knew her story was bullshit. The hospital told her they'd sue her for slander, libel, whatever if she claimed that I tried to hurt her. They meant it and she saw that. So she shut up."

"I should have tried that approach with her at the library. Got me an attorney." Considering that the only attorney I knew was my uncle Bid, that was a wholly unappetizing prospect.

Ruth laughed again. "We could have kept a whole firm litigating against her."

"So why did she make that charge against you, Ruth, if it was foundless? I'm curious as to her motive."

"What possessed that woman—no pun intended—anyhow, Jordy? You know how judgmental and demanding she was. She'd get into her head that you were a sinner and that she was going to get you good—before God had a chance." Ruth's eyes held mine for a long moment. "Crazy people don't need motives."

"So she just made up that story about you trying to kill her? For no good reason?"

"That's right. Like I said, she was nuts."

"Odd. I always thought she knew exactly what she was doing."

"If she did it, it was because she didn't like me. Maybe she was planning her censorship campaign then and knowing I'd side against her, she decided to smear me off the board. Look, Jordy,"—her voice imparted frustration—"she redefined pathetic, okay?"

"I won't argue with you on that point."

"You might want to save your arguments for the police." Ruth frowned. "You said you didn't know who killed her. The police and that bumpkin D.A. asked me about you and Miss Harcher. Like how bad did it get between the two of you at the board meetings. They wanted to know if you threatened her at the meetings. Someone told Billy Ray that you said you could've killed Beta."

I kept from groaning. Who had been standing there after Ruth hustled Beta out? Eula Mae, Tamma, and almost six other library regulars. I wished I'd bitten off my intemperate tongue.

"Billy Ray asked me to confirm that when I told him I saw the fight between you and Beta, but I told him I hadn't heard you say any such thing."

"Thanks. Billy Ray's hot on my trail."

Ruth shook her head. "I already told you I don't think you did it. Whoever killed that woman had to hate her from the get-go. It couldn't have been a crime of passion; no one loved her."

"Passion can mean hate, too. And Matt sure seems to have hated her."

Ruth Wills drew back from the table, resting against the booth. She shook her head. "No. I don't believe Matt could murder anyone."

It was an unexpected defense. "You should have seen him today. He hated her guts. I didn't like her; neither did you or Eula Mae. I think she irritated Bob Don and the Hufnagels more than they'd admit. But Matt despised her."

She shook her head again. "I don't know Matt very well, but he served his country and I don't think he'd kill Beta."

"Then who?"

She leaned forward. "It obviously had to be someone she knew. She wouldn't have been in the library with a stranger. She didn't have a key."

"Tamma Hufnagel says Beta swiped Adam's key," I interjected.

Ruth snorted. "Whatever. Regardless of who had the key, she wouldn't have been there, late at night, with someone she didn't know. So why was she at the library?"

"I don't know."

"She was meeting someone there. Someone she couldn't meet elsewhere because they needed privacy. If she had to meet with someone on the library board, why not at the deserted library?" She tapped fingertips on the table. "She could have met me at my place—I live alone. Same with Eula Mae. But not so with Matt, Bob Don, Janice Schneider, Reverend Hufnagel, or you. You all have keys and you all have families in your homes. Now I don't think that you or Matt did it. Adam Hufnagel's the biggest stuffed shirt I can imagine, but he is a preacher and I don't think he's a killer. Janice Schneider—pardon me, I know she's kin to you—is a wimp. That just leaves Bob Don."

I opened my mouth and shut it again. I hadn't given much thought to why Beta was at the library; I'd assumed she'd wanted to get rid of books she'd objected to.

"So why would Bob Don want to kill her?" I asked.

Ruth smirked. "I would pick him, when you start narrowing down the options."

"Why Bob Don?" I thought of Bob Don's heartiness toward me, his seeming willingness to help me. And Tamma's story of his arrival at Beta's as she left, looking angry.

"Something that happened last Saturday. I've been looking at buying a pickup truck and Bob Don'd told me he'd give me a good price. I stopped by the dealership late Saturday after I got off my shift at the hospital. He'd told me he'd deal with me direct. So I went back to his office." Ruth fidgeted for a minute. "Beta was there. I heard her voice even before I was at the door. She was screaming at him, telling him he was nothing but a lousy lying sinner. I opened the door—I actually thought something violent was going on. Beta and Bob Don were in there, all right. And Bob Don looked like I'd just kept him from committing murder. His face was all bloated and red, he was so mad. Beta had spit on her chin and she was waving that damned old Bible of hers in his face. The tension, the hatred in that room." She shivered.

All news to me. "My God! What happened?" I asked.

She drained the last of her margarita. "I muttered something about how they were yelling loud enough to raise the dead. I thought Bob Don was going to have a stroke. He's got one of those pulsy veins in his forehead that jitter when he's mad. Beta gave me one of those triumphant little sneers. She told Bob Don to remember what she said, 'or you know who'll pay. You don't want 'em hurt, do you?' I can't forget the words, because she said them with such contempt. She threatened him, with me right there. I was speechless. She called me a name—I believe *hussy* was her new vocabulary word—then she pushed past me and left."

"I saw Bob Don today. Junebug and Billy Ray paid him a visit."

Ruth nodded. "They saw me at the hospital this morning. I told them where I'd been last night. That was their first question, and then I told them about Bob Don and Beta."

"So where were you last night?"

She didn't seem to mind the question. "On duty at the hospital. I worked a double shift 'cause I'm taking off some time later this month."

"So did Bob Don say anything to you after Beta left?"

"Like I said, I was ready to call the cops. I thought his aorta was about to conk out. He just sank into his chair and looked up at me like he'd never seen me before." Ruth fell silent as a smiling, talkative waiter cleared the table of the empty pitcher and plates. After he hustled away, she continued:

"I asked him if he was okay, and he didn't even answer me the first time. He finally said he'd be fine, so

I left. It was weird. I've seen a look like that in my work. When somebody hears a loved one has died, or that they're terminally ill."

Bob Don. He'd been hearty, not shaken, when I was in his office. From Ruth's account you might have thought he'd weep in relief when I told him Beta was dead. He'd acted like he was hardly affected. What had she done to him? Who were the *they* she threatened to hurt?

I was still thinking when she propositioned me. I almost didn't hear her. "What?" I said, thinking she'd misspoken.

"I said, let's go back to my place. We've both had rotten days, Jordy. Maybe we can help each other relax." Her voice already felt like hands gently massaging my shoulders. A red fingernail idly traced the hair on my wrist.

Now I grew up a hick, but that awkwardness was long past me. I'd been a big boy for a while and could handle a sexually aggressive and confident woman. God knows I was attracted to her. The *yes* half-formed on my tongue till I thought of Beta's allegations against her and Eula Mae's warning to be careful. I liked Ruth, but I wasn't sure I trusted her. *And* I was suddenly far too tired. Not that Candace did not influence my decision in any way. Remotely.

"No, thanks, Ruth. I appreciate the offer, but it's been a long and stressful day. I need to get on home."

She smiled a smile she didn't mean. I saw her eyes crinkle in anger for a bare moment; she wasn't accustomed to refusal and she didn't like it. The crinkle faded. "I understand. Why don't you call me when you're feeling more up to par?"

I nodded, wondering if she was challenging my potency with that last remark.

I walked her out to her car. It was a red Miata. "Cool wheels," I said.

She patted it. "My vice," she said. "I know it's an indulgence, but nurses don't get many chances to spoil themselves. I got an inheritance from my aunt in Corpus and decided to splurge." She opened the door and slid inside. Elegantly. I fought back a sudden fantasy of checking myself into the hospital and letting Ruth give me a sponge bath.

"How's your mom?" she asked unexpectedly.

"Best as could be expected."

"Must be hard on you," she said, thoughtfully. "Emotionally and financially."

"Yes, it is. On both counts."

She gave me a speculative smile and cranked her engine. I promised to call her later and watched her drive off. I walked to my Blazer, thinking what an idiot I was. Here was a gorgeous woman who was practically throwing herself at me and here I was, too tired, antsy, and distrusting for even a roll in the hay. Lord knows my sex life had evaporated since I'd moved back to Mirabeau. Maybe I'd entirely lost my drive. My pants felt tight and I decided that wasn't my problem. I liked Ruth, but I didn't particularly relish bedding anyone on Beta's list. There were too many unanswered questions, and I wasn't entirely sure I believed Ruth's disclaimers about Beta's lies.

I pushed in the Blazer's cigarette lighter and fished a pack out of my glove compartment. I'd stuck them there last week, vowing to quit. If Ruth could have her Miata, I could have my vice, too.

As a smoking spot, the Blazer was a damn poor substitute for Ruth Wills's bed.

CHAPTER SEVEN

I GOT HOME, RELIEVED TO SEE THAT I WASN'T going to be policed, either by Junebug or Candace. The carport was empty.

Inside, Mark sat close to the TV as Arnold Schwarzenegger shot his way through a group of extras in one of the *Terminator* films. The gunfire whispered with the sound turned low. Mama watched the movie, a sure sign of her illness. She'd never have countenanced one of those bloodfests before she got sick.

"Hey. How are y'all?" I asked. Mark glared up at me from the couch.

"Well, despite that I didn't get to go to Randy's house tonight, I'm trying to have just a little fun—" Mark started unidoly, but I held up a hand.

"Listen, Mark. Listen real good. Since you're about to hit puberty, you'll soon realize life isn't fair. And you'll realize that life is too short to listen to whiners. You've got about one-twentieth of the problems of everyone else in this house, so having to forfeit one evening isn't going to kill you. Your grandmother's sick, your mom's busting her ass at that crappy truck stop to clothe and feed you, and I'm trying to figure out who really killed Beta Harcher so I don't end up in jail. So, my dear nephew, just shut up."

His jaw fell as if the hinge had vanished. Mama certainly wouldn't have cottoned to me chastising her adored grandbaby, but she wasn't sure who Mark was. His eyes flashed again and then went back to the TV.

I went into the kitchen and brewed some decaf. Leaning over the sink, I rinsed out my mouth with tap water, trying to clean out the sting of lime and tequila. I was buzzed from the drinks, yet I was too hyper to go to bed and plop down.

Too many fingers pointing blame. Tamma pointing at Bob Don. Bob Don pointing at Tamma. Matt pointing at me. Eula Mae pointing at Ruth. Hally pointing at Eula Mae. Ruth pointing at Bob Don, giving him the early lead. And worst of all, Billy Ray pointing at me with the finger he'd chiseled off the statue of blind justice over at the county courthouse.

I poured my coffee, then stirred in milk and some Sweet'N Low. None of that he-man black coffee for me; I'd rather chew barbed wire. I went past the on-screen carnage in the living room, wished Mama and a blissfully silent Mark goodnight, and took my coffee upstairs.

In my room, I slid a Mary-Chapin Carpenter CD into the player and let her wistful lyrics croon in my ear. Country music has sure improved in the last couple of years, even bringing back fans like me who didn't know there were other kinds of music until we were teenagers (when we jumped over to other parts of the jukebox). Most of my CD collection remains jazz and classical (I'd fallen for both in college), but the country stack kept growing with folks like Mary-Chapin, Lyle Lovett, Jimmie Dale Gilmore, Tish Hinojosa, and Rosanne Cash putting out beautiful, intelligent albums.

I needed to put my thoughts in order. I wrote down the names of everyone on Beta's list. It was the key to the mystery, I was sure. I also wrote down what questions remained, as far as I could see. I wrote steadily, trying not to lapse into the bad habit of chewing on my pen. I fought back the craving for a cigarette while I sat and thought over the day's events. Mary-Chapin finished her songs and I replaced her with Lyle Lovett's dryly witty mix of jazz, blues, and country. I made three trips downstairs for coffee. The last time I helped Mama up to bed and got her settled for the night. Her medicine had relaxed her and she didn't argue as I got her into her nightdress. She lay back on her pillows. Her eyes looked dull and listless compared with the highly intelligent eyes that I'd stared into during dinner.

"You were gone. Did you have a nice time?" Mama asked.

It was unusual for her to notice that someone was around or not. Maybe this was a sharper moment for her.

"Yes, Mama, I did have a nice time. Thank you for asking."

"That's good." She patted my hand.

Might as well try. "Mama, do you remember Beta Harcher? She was a lady at the Baptist church. And she did work for the library." Worked *against* the library, but that was too many details for Mama.

Mama didn't like questions; they frustrated her. "I don't know. I don't know."

"It's okay. I just thought you might remember her."

"Ask your father," she said sleepily. That advice wasn't particularly helpful. I counted my blessings anyway; many Alzheimer's patients spend their nights keeping their caretakers awake. Mama embraced sleep tonight. I kissed her cheek, turned out the lights, and went down to retrieve the cup of decaf I'd left when Mama asked me to take her upstairs.

The television fell silent as I came down the stairs.

Mark crouched on the couch, staring at his beloved high-top sneakers instead of me. I ignored him and picked up my cooling mug of coffee.

"Sorry about before," he muttered. I'm sure it's the same kind of apology his daddy never bothered to give my sister.

"Apology accepted." I sat down next to him and lifted his chin so his eyes met mine. God, he was growing up quick. It'd only seemed like yesterday he'd been a baby that gurgled and cooed happily at his uncle Jordy. "Look, Mark. I'm not mad at you. It's just that you have to understand the situation we're all in. As you pointed out to me yesterday, your Mamaw is not getting better. She is never going to get better. I shouldn't have kidded you that she's ever going to improve. And we all have to do what we can to hold together as a family. We're all making sacrifices. Your mother's working ungodly hours. I gave up a good job and moved back here, where I have practically no career opportunities. So you have to help do your share, too. And sitting with your Mamaw when we need you to is not too much to ask."

"And how long till you get tired of it, Uncle Jordy?" Mark asked acidly. "I'm sorry I snapped at you before. But this noble act isn't flying with me. Everyone's saying how great you are for coming back here and helping with Mamaw. Well, big fucking deal." He waited to see if the language shocked me. I stayed as still as stone. He continued, his words spilling out:

"You'll get tired of it sooner or later and you'll haul butt back to Boston or wherever you damn well please. You're not going to find any job in Mirabeau to make you happy. Living here's going to wear thin and you'll take your nobleness, say thanks to me and Mom, and you'll be gone." His thin face paled and those young, dark eyes dampened with angry tears.

"Is that what you think, Mark?"

"That's what happens. It always happens." He got up and started up the stairs.

"I'm not your daddy, you know. I'm not going anywhere." I would've called louder but I didn't want to wake Mama. Mark's steps paused for one brief moment on the stairs, then resumed their pounding. I heard his door shut.

Maybe that explained the anger and the snotty comments. He was thirteen, starting that terribly awkward age, and he'd never known a man who stuck around. His father cut out when he realized Mark and Sister meant responsibility. My and Sister's dad had inconsiderately died. Sister's subsequent few boyfriends didn't seem much taken with the idea of an ill mother-in-law and another man's child. Why should this faraway uncle suddenly appear as the silvered knight of trust?

I leaned back on the couch. I understood his worry. God knows I'd been tempted to leave. Sister still tended to treat me like a pesky little brother who foiled her plans. Mama could drive you crazy with her repetitive behavior, her restless nights, her lack of being the woman who raised me. Mark's mouth outdid mine at his age. And Mirabeau didn't offer much in the way of employment in my field. I'd gotten calls from friends at Brooks-Jellicoe, the publisher I'd worked for in Boston. Seeing if I'd changed my mind. Seeing how Mama was doing and inquiring if I was considering coming back. They wouldn't keep calling forever. And what would I do after Mama passed away? That could be next week or in twenty years. I wouldn't have a career left. That's what being a caretaker did to you; stripped you of yourself and replaced it with a distorted mirror image of the sick person you sacrificed your life for. I'd look in the mirror someday and see Mama instead of myself. I groaned; I was turning into Norman Bates from *Psycho*.

I warmed my coffee and went back upstairs. I'd nearly finished my notes. I turned off the stereo then read over what I'd written:

QUESTIONS ABOUT BETA

1. Why did she make that list of names connected to the library, and why was she carrying it around with her?
2. Why was she dressed all in black? Not her usual attire.
3. Why was mud caked on her shoes? Had not rained in the past couple of days.
4. Why was she at the library at night?
5. How did she get a key? Tamma Hufnagel says Beta swiped Adam's key.
6. Why did the killer use the bat in my office? Because it was handy or to implicate me? Handiness indicates that the killer came into my office; bat was behind my desk.
7. Where did that $35,000 in her account come from? Who benefits under her will? (Maybe this has nothing to do with the library after all.)

BETA'S LIST

1. Tamma Hufnagel—minister's wife. Her quote is Numbers 32:23. "Be sure your sin will find you out." What sin had Tamma committed that Beta knew about? Something that could ruin her, or just something that Beta used to irritate her?
2. Hally Schneider—my third cousin, 17, son of li-

brary board member Janice Schneider, works part-time for Eula Mae. Claims he was on a date with a girl named Chelsea Hart last night at time of murder. Mirabeau native. His quote is Proverbs 14:9. "Fools make a mock at sin." Another quote related to sin. Did Beta think that Hally had done something sinful then hadn't worried about it? Or joked about it? Hard to see how quote pertains to him.

3. Jordan Poteet—I can say categorically that I did not kill Beta Harcher! My quote is Isaiah 5:20. "Woe unto them that call evil good, and good evil." Beta's death has brought me woe all right. Have no interpretation for her quote for me, unless it's that I considered books she called evil to be good and worth keeping on the shelves.

4. Eula Mae Quiff—successful romance writer, known professionally as Jocelyn Lushe. Her quote is Job 31:35. "My desire is, that the Almighty would answer me, and that mine adversary had written a book." Beta objected to Eula Mae's passionate little paperbacks, called them smut. Did she bruise Eula Mae's considerable ego one time too many? Why was Eula Mae meeting Beta late at night and why didn't she mention it to me?

5. Matt Blalock—Vietnam vets activist, contract computer programmer for software companies in Austin. His quote is Matthew 26:21. "Verily I say unto you, that one of you shall betray me." What betrayal had Matt committed in Beta's eyes? Of God, Mother, or Country? Beta called Matt seditious for his vets activities that challenge the rightness of the war (she was so old-fashioned). This is the best interpretation I know so far.

6. Ruth Wills—nurse at Mirabeau Hospital. Claims to have witnessed a violent argument between Beta

and Bob Don last Saturday. Her quote is 2 Kings 4:40. "There is death in the pot." Guess is that it refers to Ruth's alleged attempt to poison Beta.

7. Bob Don Goertz—local car and pickup truck czar. His quote is Judges 5:30. "Have they not divided the prey; to every man a damsel or two?" Sounds like Bob Don had either reaped a windfall of women; or that he possibly had a mistress on the side? Could it have been Beta herself, if not now then in the past? Knew her since she was young and claimed she was *wild* then.

8. Anne Schneider Poteet—my mother. For whatever reason, her quote is Genesis 3:16. "In sorrow thou shalt bring forth children." I have no idea what this means in connection with my mother. Probably the sorrow was to be that I (someone Beta loathed) was her child.

I closed my eyes as I finished reading my notes. Mama. This of all made the least sense. My mother hadn't hurt a fly in her whole life. She was caring, forgiving, loving. Yet she'd made it onto this list of Beta Harcher's sinners. Perhaps Ruth was right; crazy people didn't need motives. Putting my mother on that list was proof enough.

I paused, then realized I'd left something out. I scribbled again:

BOARD MEMBERS NOT ON LIST

9. Reverend Adam Hufnagel—preacher at First Baptist Church of Mirabeau (for past five years). I haven't spoken with him regarding Beta's death—must do soon. Why is his wife on Beta's list? Why isn't he?

10. Janice Schneider—homemaker, my cousin-by-

marriage (married to my second cousin Harold
Schneider). Mother of Hally and Josh. Perky,
Stepford-wife, greeting card type. Had Beta baby-sit
her son Josh on occasion—apparently tried to make
up with Beta after library incidents. Why is her son
Hally on Beta's list? Why isn't she?

I drummed my pen against the paper. Those ending
questions were both damned good ones. Perhaps there
was no reason to it; after all, Mama was on the list.
Maybe Tamma and Hally were there as well to strike
against imagined betrayers Adam and Janice. Janice had
voted against Beta and Adam hadn't argued hard when
the board voted to remove her. That assumed this list
was some sort of weapon Beta could've used against
those she hated. Or maybe Hally and Tamma had been
doing their own wrongs against Beta. I decided talking
to Brother Adam and cousin Janice was a priority.

There was one more addition to the notebook:

BETA HARCHER

Mid 40s. Never married, as far as I know. Mirabeau native. Did not work; lived off trust left to her by family.
No close relatives in town; has a niece in Houston, according to Tamma Hufnagel. Do not know of anyone
that she considered a close friend or confidante. Extremely religious; a zealot. According to Bob Don, got
religion in her early 20s; previously had a reputation for
being wild (whatever that means). Had served on library board less than six months when she began at-
tempts to ban books she considered unwholesome.
Ejected from library board by other members. Acted as
though she operated by divine guidance; even stated as
much when she assaulted me in the library. Deposited

large, unexplained amount of cash recently in her savings account. Apparently argued with Bob Don Goertz (if Ruth is to be believed) and was having a late night meeting with longtime enemy Eula Mae Quiff in the week before she died.

Eula Mae and Bob Don. A well-to-do writer and a prosperous car dealer. And $35,000 in Beta's savings account. I wondered if for all her moralizing, Beta Harcher considered blackmail a sin.

I switched out the light and considering the length and stress of the day I'd had, collapsed quickly into a deep sleep. Beta Harcher kindly stayed out of my dreams.

CHAPTER EIGHT

THE NEXT MORNING STARTED OFF AS MOST mornings did, except I kept wondering whether or not I could open the library and whether Junebug still considered me a prime suspect. I fixed breakfast for Mama and Mark and checked on Sister; she snored in her room, worn from an evening of cooking up homestyle food for wayfarers.

I'm not nearly as good a cook as Sister, but Mama and Mark didn't complain. Course it's hard to mess up toaster waffles and Rice Krispies, but I do pride myself on my ability to coordinate every part of the meal so it reaches the table simultaneously.

Junebug didn't disappoint. He showed up about eight-thirty and I was glad to see that Dilly Ray wasn't in tow.

"Hey, Jordy. Good morning," Junebug held his Stetson in his hands, as if sparking Sister rather than grilling me.

"Good morning, Chief Moncrief." I kept my tone formal. He frowned.

"I'd like to speak with you for a minute, Jordy."

"Don't you need a backup, Chief? After all, I'm a dangerous suspect."

"Come on, Jordy," he sounded like the Junebug of old, asking for his baseball back when we'd disagreed about a hit being foul. "Quit being pissy about this. I got a job to do. I'm not here to arrest you."

113

I relented. "I just made some coffee. Come on in."

He came awkwardly into the kitchen, watching Mama. "Good morning, Miz Poteet, Mark. How y'all doing?"

Mama stared at Junebug, as if she feared he might be here to escort her to a nursing home. She smiled cautiously in his direction.

Mark once again put himself first. "I already told you what I know, Chief," he said, sounding like a prepubescent version of a Bogart-movie thug.

Junebug regarded Mark critically. "Yes, son, I know. Thanks again for your cooperation. I'm here to see your uncle, though. Would y'all mind giving us some privacy?"

"Mark, please take Mama upstairs. Then go outside and play," I said. Do thirteen-year-olds still play?

Mark's eyes widened like drops of ink in water. "Are you going to arrest him?"

"No, son. Good to see you again, Miz Poteet." Junebug nodded politely at Mama as Mark escorted her out of the kitchen.

I poured Junebug black coffee and set it before him. I decided to act like what I was, just a bystander to all these nasty little events. "So when can I reopen the library?"

"Not today," he said in his slow voice, sipping the brew. His blue eyes flicked at me. "You make good coffee."

I sipped my own in response. "Is that what you came by to tell me, that the library has to stay closed? You could have phoned."

He set the mug down. "Jordy, I think Beta might've been in the library to burn it down."

I felt the heat of the mug in my hands, but it paled next to the heat in my face. Burn the library? Burn *my* library?

Junebug read my expression. "I didn't get into this with you before, because we didn't know. Her fingers smelled of gasoline, and the coroner found traces of gasoline on her clothes. And there was a pack of matches in her skirt pocket."

"Did you find gas cans?" My voice sounded stunned.

"In her car. It was parked down the street from the library. Found it there yesterday."

"Not enough that she tried to ban books. Not enough that she threatened to shut the library down. No, if she couldn't have her way, she'd just torch it. Even the many books she didn't object to, just to get rid of the few." I jumped up from my chair and paced the kitchen madly.

"She didn't threaten to burn the place down to you?" Junebug asked in his relaxed drawl.

"Never." I stopped. "You know I would have reported any such threat to you. I'd have had you and the volunteer fire department on twenty-four-hour alert. And I'd have had Billy Ray throw a book she couldn't burn at her skinny butt."

"Unless you decided to stop her yourself." He said it as casually as if he were reading a high-school football score from the paper.

I felt my lips tighten. "You know I wouldn't kill her. There'd be no reason for me to. You're the law. I would have come to you."

"I think you would have, too," Junebug said. "But that's not how Billy Ray sees it. He figures—"

"Billy Ray couldn't figure if you gave him both sides of the flash card," I interrupted.

"—that if you knew she might try something like that; but you didn't have solid proof, you might just take it into your head to guard the library. Maybe keep a bat handy. A bat that has only your prints on it."

Only my prints. I gulped, but pressed on. "Does that sound as stupid to you as it does to me? Tell Billy Ray to unknot his lariat from around his ankles and try throwing again. Instead of dreaming up little scenarios between me and Beta, why doesn't he get busy finding out about that money in her account? Or why Bob Don had such a fight with her last week? Or why she accused Ruth Wills of trying to poison her? Or why Eula Mae was meeting her late at night last week? Or why she bothered to make that list in the first place?" I stopped. "Or why only my prints are on that bat? If some kid just left it in the lot, it'd have to have his prints on it, too. Right?"

Junebug's jaw wavered. "How the hell—"

Open mouth, do not insert foot because of torrent of words that pour out in temper. I sat down quickly. A model schoolboy.

"I guess you've been checking up on folks," he said sternly. A model principal. "That's my job, Jordy. Mine and Billy Ray's."

"Well, do your job, Hewett." He's not real crazy about being called by that name. How inconsiderate of me. "You know in your heart that I didn't murder anybody. You know I couldn't. Get that schnauzer of a lawyer off of me."

The front door creaked and it wasn't a schnauzer of a lawyer that came in. It was a chihuahua of a lawyer, little and hairless. Bidwell J. Poteet, attorney-at-law. My beloved uncle Bid. He stood in the doorway of the kitchen, resplendent in his small-town lawyer's light gray suit, smoking an obnoxious cigarillo. It fit him. He was short, like my father had been, and he'd lost most of his hair. What little remained was scraggly and white. A soul less charitable than myself would've said it looked like cat mange. His eyes were a deep lake blue, but icy and cool. The stub of that cigarillo popped out of his thin lips and his raspy drawl pervaded the room like the nauseating smell of the smoke.

"I hope you're not trying to intimidate my client,

Chief," Uncle Bid wheedled. "He ought to have my representation if you're trying to coax a confession out of him."

Junebug frowned. "This isn't an interrogation, Mr. Poteet. Jordy and I are just talking."

"I'll be the judge of that, sir." Uncle Bid sat in the chair. He blinked at me, like a troll at a billy goat gruff. "Aren't you going to be hospitable and offer your poor old uncle some coffee?"

Soon as I find the rat poison for it, I thought, getting up and slopping coffee into a cup. "Your sister-in-law is doing fine, thank you for asking," I announced.

Bid made a hoarse reply that lacked concern. He'd done nothing to try to help Mama, the wife of his older brother. He'd dropped by only once before since I'd moved home, just to explain what an idiot I was to return to Mirabeau—and grieve that Daddy was spinning from his grave all the way to China on account of my giving up my career. Feel the love?

"Mr. Poteet, let me assure you that I wasn't questioning Jordy. We were simply discussing when he could reopen the library. It is a crime scene, you know, and we can't run the risk of tampering there," Junebug said.

Bid sucked down boiling-hot coffee as if it was ice water. Those cigarillos must build up the scar tissue fast. "Well, then, if you two have concluded your business, I'd like to speak privately with my nephew."

Junebug arched an eyebrow, but didn't argue. "Yes, we are finished, I believe. Jordy, I'll let you know when you can reopen." I nodded mutely and escorted Junebug to the door.

He paused on the porch as he adjusted his hat and blinked into the morning sunshine. "It's a nice day. Why don't you spend it with your mother? Take her out to the park or out to lunch?"

"I have other plans, Junebug."

"Remember, Jordy, I'm the law. I'll handle the investigating around here. And one thing I might have to investigate is how you knew about that money in Beta Harcher's account."

I didn't want to get Candace in trouble for sneaking around bank-record confidentiality. But I didn't want to lie to a police officer either. Best to take the blunderbuss approach. "Have you found where all that money came from?"

"No, we haven't," he confessed. "You know anything about it?"

"No," I admitted.

"Will wonders never cease? I'll see you later, Jordy." Junebug smiled at me, set his hat to his liking, and headed for his cruiser.

I went back into the kitchen. Uncle Bid leaned against the open refrigerator, his bald head surveying the shelves up close.

"Breakfast service is closed," I quipped. "If you want the special thrill of having a relative cook for you, wait till Sister wakes up. I'm sure she'll whip up your favorite. And get that smelly cigar out of the fridge. And out of the house. But there's no need to spit it out. Just let your lips follow."

He slammed the door shut and rubbed an apple on his lapel. "You'd shame my brother, talking to me that way." He could invoke a father's ghost faster than Hamlet.

"No, he'd be ashamed of how you've ignored Mama. You never call. You never come by unless it's to offer less-than-constructive criticism. Your absence is a blessing to me, though, so I guess I shouldn't complain."

"I'm concerned about you, Jordy, and I'm here to help. You need my representation. I've just had me a fascinating conversation with Billy Ray Bummel." He bit into the apple and chomped noisily. That didn't keep him from talking. "Let's look at the facts, boy. Beta Harcher popped you one and threatened you in front of a library full of witnesses. You were in the library, by y'own admission, in the range of time the murder took place. If she was going to burn down the library, that was an immediate threat not only to you but to the only employment that you are remotely suited for in this town—aside from village idiot. And only your prints are on the murder weapon. Now do you still think you don't need my help?"

"I'll get my own legal representation, thank you."

The phone rang. I scooped it up, willing to chitchat with an obscene caller rather than Bid. It was Candace.

"Glad to see you're home. I waited last night for your call."

Oops. I'd been so wrapped up in pulling my thoughts together and writing out my notes I'd forgotten my promise to phone Candace.

"Sorry," I said. "Look, this isn't a good time. Can I call you back?"

"As long as you're not fixing breakfast for Ruth Wills." It might've sounded mean if she hadn't laughed.

"I'm not. Talk to you in a minute." I hung up and turned back to Bid. He munched the apple down to the core. I kept hoping there was a seed or two he might choke on.

"I'm offering you free legal representation, just as soon as you're arrested," he said, wiping his mouth with a dainty, monogrammed handkerchief.

"I'm not going to be arrested. If they had anything on me, they'd have arrested me by now." I said it with more conviction than I felt. "And even if they do, I'll get me a good attorney, someone over in Bavary who actually hasn't been investigated by the state bar."

Bid shrugged away the history of his luminous career.

"And how will you afford it, Jordy? With your stellar librarian's salary?" He got up and thumbed his cigarillo stub into the trash. "You don't have the money to spend on legal defense. And trust me, you don't want a public defender. Bonaparte County's recruiting from the very dregs of the dreggiest of law schools."

"I'll take my chances, thank you. I'm sure any public defender would do a more conscientious job for me than you would. You've never given a crap about me or my family. You always acted superior because you had all the education and Daddy didn't. Well, I've got an education now, Uncle Bid. But I didn't need that to see that you're just an uncaring, selfish bastard."

His bony, ugly face (thank God I didn't favor the Poteet side) screwed up in anger. He turned red. "You listen to me, boy. I will represent you. You are kin and I will not have the Poteet name disgraced. I will not entrust your defense to some wet-eared kid straight out of school. There's too much at stake—"

"Too much what?" I crossed my arms and smiled. "You've never offered to do anything that you didn't get a ton of benefit from."

He fished another cigarillo from his pocket and lit it in a fluid motion. He took his time, making the end of the nasty thing glow with each suck of whispered breath. When he finally spoke, his voice was sulky but reasonable.

"Jordy. I know we've had our differences. I know I haven't been"—his face screwed up as he breathed in smoke, making him look like a little dragon—"the best uncle to you and Arlene. I've been remiss in my duties to your poor mother. I'm asking for a chance to help you." He laid his palms up in mock surrender. "Please, let me help you if the worst happens and you get charged with Beta's murder."

I watched him. He acted sincere. Acted. I'd had

enough experience with him to avoid embracing him and sobbing that all was forgiven. But maybe the old coot was genuine this time.

"Please," he said once more.

I loved hearing him beg, but I wanted him gone more. "Tell you what, Uncle Bid. If I do get arrested, I'll retain your free services. Until then, we won't have any sort of formal agreement. Deal?"

He didn't look entirely pleased, but he'd honed his ways of hiding disappointment through his many failures in the courtroom. He came forward and shook my hand. His was sticky with apple juice. "Deal, then, Jordy." He relinquished my hand and tried a new buddying-up tactic. "Although I remain staunchly convinced of your innocence, it wouldn't surprise me that you could've killed that woman. Crazy old bitch. Waste of what was once fine womanhood."

"You knew Beta?" I asked, wishing I could wipe my palm.

"I wasn't on speaking terms with her," Bid offered congenially, "but I knew her when she was younger. An eye-popper, that girl was. And knew how to have a good time." Uncle Bid thoughtfully gyrated his pelvis so I wouldn't miss his point. Beta? Bob Don had said she didn't get religion until she was in her twenties. What kind of woman was she before then? Bob Don's description of *wild* had been vague.

"You and Beta?" I asked, incredulous. Imagining oddities from the Kama Sutra was easier than conjuring up an image of my uncle and Beta Harcher coupling.

"Oh, Lord, no, Jordy. I never dated her. I wouldn't have soiled my reputation by doing so. Funny how people turn out, though. Such a wild thing in her youth, then such a dried-up old church hag." He shook his head.

"Bob Don said she was pretty when she was younger."

Bid frowned. "You stay away from Bob Don Goertz. He's nothing but a dirty liar." God only knew what brought that on. I didn't know Bid and Bob Don knew each other.

"I'll be going. Remember what I said, and you call me if you run into trouble. Give my best to Arlene, Mark, and your mother."

I nodded, not wanting to argue again. Beta Harcher, party girl turned keeper of morality. I wondered if Uncle Bid was trying to make his own metamorphosis.

Candace had nothing new to report. I told her about Ruth witnessing the fight between Bob Don and Beta, didn't mention Ruth's offer of sexual solace, and concluded by telling her that apparently my prints were the only ones on the baseball bat. At the last tidbit, she gasped.

"My God! Maybe they will arrest you."

"I don't know. It seems odd that I would have the only prints on it. Say the killer wore gloves. If a kid left it in the field, it should also have his or her prints. Why doesn't it?"

"The killer wiped it clean," Candace prompted.

"And missed my prints? I don't think so. I was the only person to handle that bat when it came into the library." I closed my eyes, remembering. "I brought the bat into the library. I put it in my office. No one else went near it, until the killer used it to bash Beta."

"The only explanation," Candace said slowly, "is that it was wiped before you handled it. A kid wouldn't do that; there's no reason to. Unless—" she stopped.

"What?"

"Oh, God. Unless the killer planted it there, already wiped clean of prints, and waited for you to pick it up."

"That's crazy, Candace," I coughed. "Doesn't that seem

like putting a lot up to chance? That I'm the first person to walk by the bat, that I notice it, that I pick it up, that I even take that path at any given time of the day?"

"Jordy," Candace's tone was flat. "You're far more a creature of habit than you realize. You always cut through the field on your way to the pharmacy."

"Yeah, but I don't go to the pharmacy on a regular basis. Whenever Mama needs her medicine."

"Maybe the killer knew when that would be. When you'd be going next."

"My God!" I exclaimed. Pictures unraveled in my mind, like a grainy, old-time newsreel. "You're onto something, Candace. Imagine you're the killer. You want to frame me for this murder. You want to get my prints on the murder weapon. You want to put me at the scene of the crime near the time of the murder, or you want to kill Beta Harcher at a place where only I—and possibly a few others, including you—have access. You can't use a conventional weapon like a gun or a knife, because how could you explain getting me to touch it? 'Please leave your prints on that registered weapon, Jordy, and I'll be on my way.' So you decide to use as your weapon something I might handle. But there's nothing in the library that's lethal enough. I don't have a heavy paperweight on my desk. I don't have an antique sword hanging over the card catalog. But there is a softball field right by the library. So you decide to use a baseball bat. You know—or learn—that I cut through the softball field when I head toward the pharmacy or downtown in general. So you find out when I'm planning on going to the pharmacy, watch me leave, then leave the bat there on the path for me to find when I return. If I pick it up, you're set. If I don't, maybe you have an alternate plan."

Candace sighed on the other end of the line. "A lot of ifs there."

I clutched the phone in excitement. "But say it's true. That could narrow the field down even further. Who would know that Mama needed her prescription refilled and that I would go down the path that day?"

"Maybe that's not the key," Candace suggested. "Maybe they just were in the library when you left to go to the pharmacy and then put the bat out for you to find when you got back. Maybe your mother's medicine had nothing to do with it."

Leave it to Candace to make simplifying conclusions. Simple seemed better. "Okay, let's take that tack. So who was around that morning?"

Candace hummed slightly on the other line. "Let's see. You. Me. Old Man Renfro, of course—he's always there. Eula Mae and her lot were just starting to arrive when you left." She harrumphed. "Ruth Wills was there, looking up something. Probably home cures for venereal disease." She paused. "Tamma Hufnagel—no, she came in after you got back, right when the fight started with you and Beta."

"Maybe she was outside the library and saw me go."

"Maybe so. And maybe anyone else could've been too," Candace agreed. "Bob Don came in to return a book that his wife'd checked out. There was a whiskey spill on one page and he offered to buy the book. That was about ten minutes before you left. I took care of it."

"Bob Don again," I said. "His name pops up more than a jack-in-the-box."

"There were a few others at the library. Older folks. That nerdy Gaston Leach. I can't imagine any of them as Beta's killer."

I rubbed my eyes. "I've got to go, Candace. I've got some folks to see. I'm afraid that Junebug knows that we know about Beta's deposit. It kind of slipped out this morning."

She sighed, disappointed in me. "Oh, well. Mother will just have to forgive me. After all, it's for a worthy cause. Saving your butt."

As soon as Sister was awake, I told her about Junebug's visit, Uncle Bid's offer, and my theory about the murder weapon.

"Uncle Bid? Being nice?" She wiped sleep from her eyes as I sat on the corner of her bed. "I'm fast asleep, right?"

"Nope. And I'm not working today. The library's still closed."

She blinked green eyes at me, rimmed with dark. Those eyes said she'd been working too much. "Why do I get the feeling that you're not going to volunteer to stay home with Mama?"

"There's some people I've got to see."

"Look, Jordy. You're trying to clear yourself before they've even arrested you—"

"How would I clear my name from a jail cell? I wouldn't count on Uncle Bid to hire a decent private investigator. I've got to do this now, prove I'm innocent." I leaned back on the bed. "I called Dorcas Witherspoon. She said she'd stay with Mama if you needed to run errands."

"Okay." Sister knotted the sheets around her. She was wearing an oversized T-shirt that said RICE UNIVERSITY. God, I'd given that to her my senior year in college and she still slept in it. "I can't believe this is happening. I can't believe anyone thinks you're a killer."

"I have you on my side, though. And Candace."

Sister squeezed my hand. It was the first legitimate sign of affection she'd shown me in weeks. I think we were both just too tired to bother most of the time, too caught up in feeling sorry for ourselves, too worn down from dealing with Mama, too frustrated at our own powerlessness in the face of her disease. We'd been close once. I wanted to be close to her again.

I offered to bring her some coffee in bed and she giggled. "You?" she asked.

I drew myself up to my full height. "I too can be sensitive and caring. We just got a book about it at the library."

I brought her milky coffee, the way she liked it. She sipped it as daintily as an English lady being gently roused in the morning by a roomful of servants. I told her about my dinner with Ruth and what I'd found out yesterday. She listened for once, and did not interrupt me. A rarity for my big sister.

When I was done, Sister finished her coffee before she spoke. "Well, I can fill in one gap. Bob Don did used to be friends with Mama and Daddy."

"When?"

"Oh, when I was real little. Before you were born. He came over quite a bit. I remember he loved to toss me up in the air and catch me. I'd squeal everybody deaf. And he and Mama and Daddy played cards some evenings, I remember that. But he and Mama and Daddy had some big falling out. I think it was over him marrying that nasty Gretchen. I don't think Mama and Daddy liked being around her. She's a real bitch."

"Candace says that Bob Don returned a library book that'd had booze spilled on it."

Sister huffed. "Then she's also a real *drunk* bitch. Wouldn't surprise me a bit. Have you ever seen that woman, Jordy? Course she doesn't get out like she used to. But I know a drunk when I see one. She must just be getting worse and worse. Poor Bob Don. Maybe he really does want to help, make up for the rift between him and Daddy and Mama."

"Maybe so," I said thoughtfully.

I offered to make Sister some breakfast, but she said she'd get her own. (She wasn't willing to take a chance on my cooking.) So I got on with my work. There were people to see and stories to be checked out. I decided to strike close to home first.

The Bavary/Mirabeau phone book listed three families named Hart. I got lucky the second time around. The lady who answered had a daughter named Chelsea.

"May I ask why you want to speak with her?" the woman asked. Her voice was nasal but polite.

I fidgeted. "Actually, she's dating my cousin, Hally Schneider. I thought she might assist me in planning a surprise party for him." I couldn't think of anything else and hoped that I wouldn't actually have to plan a social function for a teenager to cover my tracks.

The woman warmed. "Oh, yes, Hally and Chelsea did go out the other night. Such a handsome young man." Her voice faltered. "I—I didn't know that he was really interested in Chelsea."

"Oh, talks about her constantly," I chirped. Well, he'd mentioned her once. That counted for something. Mrs. Hart directed me to LuAnne's Bäckerei, a little German bakery in downtown Mirabeau. I thanked her and hung up. I could stop off and chat with Chelsea on my way to see Reverend Hufnagel, Bob Don Goertz, and Eula Mae. And when I got back, down-the-street neighbor Janice Schneider and I were going to have a little heart-to-heart as well.

CHAPTER NINE

THE WARM AROMA OF FRESHLY BAKED KOlaches enveloped me as I stepped into LuAnne's Bäckerei. Kolaches are a Czech pastry, a warm, square roll with a fruit or sausage middle and topping. Every small town in east-central Texas boasts a kolache bakery, even some left over from the earliest Czech immigrants. Kolache and coffee together are the ultimate in comfort foods; the smell alone brought back memories of my grandmother Schneider's kitchen, a tray of hot kolaches being set before Sister and me—with a gentle warning to let them cool so we wouldn't burn our mouths. Today's batch smelled of apple, peach, and heaven.

I didn't know LuAnne or any of the staff; there was one stout, matronly woman in the back on the phone and a trio of young girls brewing coffee, pulling fresh kolaches out of glass-fronted ovens, and ringing the cash register. If LuAnne's had a morning rush I'd missed it. Two plump ladies in stretch polyester pantsuits sat by the door, laughing merrily over steaming cups of coffee. A circle of older men slumped by a table, watching the women chat. One man, a Dallas Cowboys cap perched on his head, held court, talking and smoking his cigarette. The other men munched on their kolaches, and it was hard to tell if they paid the slightest attention to him. They had probably heard whatever story he was telling a hundred times already.

I approached the counter, bought two apple kolaches and a coffee, laced with milk and sugar. The girl who rang up my purchase smiled prettily. I thought she was just Hally's type.

"Excuse me. Are you Chelsea Hart?"

"No, she is." The girl jerked her head toward the ovens.

A girl I never would have pictured with Hally Schneider extracted a tray of steaming peach kolaches from the oven. She wasn't pretty and I'm not being unkind. She just wasn't. Her face was bony to an extreme, gaunt and sallow. Her nose and chin were small, but sharply pointed, like a cartoon witch's. Her hair was pulled back into a ponytail of dirty-blonde hair, with a front tuft moussed to defy gravity. A short-sleeved blouse showed arms like rails. I moved down the counter and spoke to her, aware of the cashier's eyes on me.

"Excuse me? Chelsea?" I said.

Chelsea Hart gave me an apathetic glance and moved her chewing gum to the other side of her mouth.

"Yeah? Can I help you?" she asked in a nasally drawl.

"I'm Jordy Poteet. Hally Schneider's cousin. Could I talk to you for a second?" I motioned toward a table.

Chelsea blinked brown eyes at me. She glanced back at the heavy woman, who chirped into her phone, waving a lit cigarette for emphasis. She turned to me. "Sure."

I went to a corner table with my kolaches and coffee and Chelsea followed, dragging her feet along the ground. She sat across from me, propping up her bony face with bony fingers.

"Kolache?" I offered her one of my apple pastries.

She made a sour face, which didn't help her cause any. "God, no. I get enough of them, believe me. What did you want?"

I still hadn't come up with a better excuse than planning some party for Hally. "Well, I understand you're dating my cousin."

She laughed, and it was too hollow and empty to come from a teenage girl. "I don't think one miserable evening counts as dating."

"Oh." I was at a loss. "Sorry. I'm planning a party for Hally, and I hoped you could help me. I thought—"

"That I was Hally's girlfriend?" She laughed, shaking her head. "Wrong. You must not know your cousin very well. I wouldn't be the person to help you plan a party for Hally."

I took immediate refuge in the kolache, chewing it slowly to gather my thoughts. Chelsea looked bored. I swallowed and said, "But you were out with him night before last, right?"

"Yeah, I was. My evening with Prince Charming. Right." She leaned forward and I could smell, mixing with the fragrance of coffee and fruit, a cheap, sticky perfume. "You tell your cousin something for me, okay? I don't get asked out that often, and it don't bother me. My own company suits me fine. But when a guy wants to spend time with me, I expect him to be with me, not off in his own world. He didn't give a rat's ass about being with me; it was just like he was killing time." She leaned back. "I was surprised when Hally asked me out. He ain't exactly the kind of boy that goes out with me. But I figured it out. I'm not stupid. He ain't been dating anyone in school, so I figure here's a chance for me, even though he asked me at the last minute. When we were together, he didn't even know I was around. Just kept checking his watch all through our hamburgers. Told me the same football story three times and didn't realize it. Even parked down by the river and he just wanted to talk. If I want to talk I can stay home and listen to my sister." Chelsea Hart smacked her gum emphatically. "He probably thought he was doing me some damn big favor, just breathing the same air as me. Well, I don't need that. If he was out with me just to make some other girl jealous, he can kiss my ass."

"Can I ask you one question?" I interjected. Enough pretense. She shrugged bony shoulders.

"When did he bring you home?"

"Midnight. I got a curfew. I was ready to go home hours earlier, though, but he insisted on sitting and talking. Christ, what a bore he was. And if you're having some stupid party for him, cross my name off the invite list. I don't need him." With that, she stormed back to the counter, leaving me with a kolache halfway to my mouth. Hell hath no fury and all that.

I finished my coffee. Chelsea Hart might be as ugly as the day was long but damned if she wasn't her own person. That would help her in life far better than comeliness ever would. Why was Hally spending time with a girl he had no apparent interest in? Where was his mind when he was on the date from hell?

I had a sinking feeling that Hally was more concerned with providing himself with an alibi for Beta's murder than with winning Chelsea's heart. Why had my cousin gone to the trouble? What did he have to hide? I hurried out of the warm smell of the bakery, the dull throb of suspicion beginning in my heart.

Matt Blalock was the last person I expected to see at the First Baptist Church, but there he was. Adam

Hufnagel was helping him into his Taurus, storing the folding wheelchair and putting it in the back seat. I pulled up next to Matt. The good reverend and Matt ignored me. By the time I was out of the car, Matt's exhaust churned in the air and he tore out of the parking lot.

I blinked at Reverend Adam Hufnagel. He smiled thinly at me. I don't think he was pleased to see me.

Adam Hufnagel was a tall, rangy man, thinner from his bout with cancer last year. He was a tough old bird and he'd beaten the disease. His hair was iron gray, the color that gives a man the look of resolve. Strong-featured, he looked more distinguished than handsome, the ideal father figure. I wondered if his wife Tamma thought of him that way.

Brother Adam slipped on his smiling parson's face for me. "Jordan!" He came forward, shaking my hand in the warm, intimate way that all clergy use. "Good to see you, son. How are you doing?" His voice, a rich-timbred instrument, oozed just the amount of concern a Southern gentleman would permit himself.

"Fine, Reverend, considering what all's happened in the past couple of days. Do you have a minute to talk?"

He inspected his watch. "Just for a few minutes. I have to meet with the ladies who are planning Vacation Bible School."

Ah. "Weren't your wife, my cousin Janice, and Beta doing that?"

He steered me toward a church side door. "Why, yes, they were. Horrible about Beta's murder. Horrible."

"No one should die that way," I agreed. "That's why I'm trying to find out who killed her." I felt his fingers on my arm stiffen for a moment, then relax.

We went down a short, tiled hallway, the walls covered with a rainbow of felt cutouts done by the Sunday school children. Crosses, trees of life, doves, hands grasping. The nursery school interpretation of religion. It seemed better than Beta's version.

Adam Hufnagel's office was immaculate. Files were stacked neatly on his desk. Pencils and pens stood in holders, with not a single stray on the desk. An assortment of silver-framed photos ranged the credenza behind his comfortable leather chair. So much for vows of poverty. The pictures were nearly always of Hufnagels: Adam and Tamma vacationing in a sunny place, Adam and Tamma wearing T-shirts of the church's soccer team, Adam and Tamma getting married, he looking more like her father than her husband.

Adam gestured toward a seat. "When will the library reopen?"

"Hopefully soon. Junebug makes that decision." I paused. Adam Hufnagel was a little intimidating, but I hadn't backed down over the book banning and I wasn't about to back down now. I swallowed and said, "Is that what Matt was here to see you about? The library?"

"Sort of." Adam smiled at me like he might at a child who'd asked if God really existed. "He wanted to know if he could use the church hall for his veterans' meeting, since the library is temporarily closed. Of course I gave him permission, and he was very happy."

"Oh." If I hadn't kept eye contact with the good Reverend I might have believed it. Eyes betray us. Adam Hufnagel's eyes darted down to my lap and back again as he spoke. He didn't want to look at me. And when I thought of Matt Blalock and Adam Hufnagel, who'd been on opposite sides of the censorship battle, I couldn't see Matt asking Adam for help.

"Matt can be difficult, but these are veterans." Adam shrugged, keeping his eyes steadily on me. "I thought perhaps letting Matt use the church would mend fences

broken during our recent"—he fumbled for a word—
"disagreements."

"Matt doesn't strike me as a fence mender. He wasn't
exactly broken up over Beta Harcher's death."

Adam raised palms in supplication, and it was a dis-
tinctly annoying gesture. It said: don't ask me—I just
work here. "Matt has many burdens to carry, Jordan. I
hope I can minister to his needs. Now what did you
want to see me about? Surely not to ask questions about
Matt Blalock?"

I licked my lips. I felt as nervous as the proverbial
whore in church. Grilling regular folks was one thing,
but trying to worm information out of a man who was
supposed to be above reproach made me uneasy. I swallowed down my unease and forged ahead. "I understand
that Beta took your key to the library to get in."

"Apparently so." Adam nodded. "Tamma noticed it
missing when the police called. Beta was here the afternoon before she died for a brief time. I don't keep the
office locked during church hours. It would have been
easy for her to take."

"Thou shalt not steal," I intoned. "Seems she only
observed commandments that were convenient to her."

"Jordan, let me be frank." He leaned forward over his
spotless desk. "Beta Harcher was a committed member
of this congregation."

Should've been committed, I thought, but held my
tongue.

"She didn't have much of a life outside of church.
Old maid, with no family left here in town. She practically ran this church for me." He smiled but there was
no feeling behind it.

"And that didn't bother you? Tamma suggested to me
that she tried to tell you what to do."

"I'm an ordained minister of the Southern Baptist

Church, Jordan. I'm the one responsible for my flock, not Beta Harcher. She knew and understood that."

"She appointed herself custodian of other people's morality quick enough, Adam." Hell, he was on the board, wasn't he? First names were a leveling field. I leaned forward, rudely putting my elbows on his desk. I meant to be rude. "She was going to burn down the library. That's the latest theory. They found traces of gasoline on her hands. If she couldn't ban some books, she'd burn all of them. Are you still so proud of her now, Adam?"

He didn't rattle. "No, of course not. That would have been wrong of her." He narrowed his eyes at me. "Seems to me that points the finger of blame more at you, Jordan. Quite possible you'd do anything to protect that library."

I shrugged. "Someone who doesn't know me very well might think so." I curled one leg up under myself and he glanced at his watch. I didn't hurry. "Did the police tell you about the list she made?"

They hadn't. I told him about it and watched the color seep from his face. His blood traveled pretty fast for an older man.

"Interesting, isn't it, Reverend? You didn't make the list. She must not have been mad at you."

"You don't know that the list is of people she had a bone with," Adam answered. "I didn't have any problems with Beta."

"Did your wife? She made the list. She's not on the library board." Neither were Hally or my mother or Matt, but I didn't mention that.

"You're making a mountain out of a molehill. Tamma and Beta got along fine. Tamma felt she ought to be in charge of certain church events as my wife. Beta disagreed. There was some conflict between them for a while, usually with Beta winning. Tamma does not usually have a confrontational personality."

"No, she doesn't. Beta had the monopoly on that."

Adam Hufnagel raised an eyebrow at me. "They worked on their differences. I asked Tamma and Beta to serve together as chaperons at a youth group retreat over at Lake Travis at the beginning of March. They returned with their disagreements resolved, as friends." He looked sternly at me. "I'm sure their shared love of Jesus brought them together."

"Must've," I concurred politely.

"And I have no idea why Beta would put Tamma's name on this list. You're judging Beta too harshly. Perhaps it was a prayer list. We should pray for our enemies."

I shook my head. "Maybe with me and some of the others who are on the list. But not your wife, right? You just said they were pals."

"I can't help you. I don't know the answer to why Beta did that." He stood, trying to end the interview. "I must meet with my wife and Janice. We have a lot of planning to do for the Vacation Bible School."

"Just another minute, please," I said, keeping my seat. His comment reminded me of something Tamma mentioned yesterday. "She said she'd also worked with Beta on the church rummage sale."

Adam smiled briefly as he sat back down. "That was the first sign that their little battles were over. Beta volunteered for it, then just took it over entirely from Tamma. Tamma realized that it was important to Beta to feel busy, so she let her."

"When was that sale?" I asked.

Adam glanced at his calendar. "About two weeks ago. Beta, I'm afraid, didn't do a very good job. She left many things undone that Tamma and I had to do at the last minute."

"Like what?"

He shrugged, impatient. "Sorting through contributions. Pricing them. She'd made a start on some, but then it was as if she forgot to finish the rest."

That didn't sound like Beta. If she was anything, she was thorough. She'd shown that in her war against the library. I thought hard. I hadn't considered one important part of the formula that equalled death for Beta Harcher. Why had she died now, at that particular time? What had happened in her life that led to her death? I had only concentrated on her war against the library and me, but she might have had other mischief up her pilgrim's sleeve. The church was her other main means of contact with her fellow human beings. Perhaps I needed to start looking for an answer there. Aside from her general involvement in the church, there was her involvement in the Vacation Bible School, the rummage sale, and the youth groups.

"Do you have a list of everyone who contributed to the rummage sale?"

Adam Hufnagel looked suspiciously at me. What was I—Herod hunting down innocents? "Why would you want that?"

"I'm curious as to who donated to the church. Surely you keep a list of contributors."

"I do, but I don't see that it's any of your business."

"Look, Adam. You can play this the easy way or the rough way. Beta Harcher had an unusual amount of money in her banking account, enough to overflow most coffers. She hadn't had that money long. It hasn't been traced yet, so I don't think she got it from stock options or winning the lottery. She was getting it from someone."

It took a moment for it to register with Adam. "Blackmail? Beta? That's absurd." The music of his voice was slightly off-key.

"No more ridiculous than her trying to burn the library. I'm just curious about who she dealt with in the past two weeks. It wasn't just the folks on the library board. It was people in this church."

Adam looked uncertain. I stood. "That's okay. I can just take my story to Junebug. He doesn't think I killed her. He's just itching to have someone else to hand over to Billy Ray Bummel. He can get a warrant to search every record in this church."

Tamma interrupted us. She stepped inside her husband's office, not seeing me at first, but deciphering the look on her husband's face. Her eyes, so downcast yesterday, found me and weren't happy.

"Jordy. What are you doing here?" Her voice showed anger.

"Talking to your husband," I answered. I'm a stickler for politeness.

"Bothering him, you mean. I wish you'd leave him alone." The mouse was now roaring.

I ignored her. Adam held the power in that relationship, so it was him I dealt with. "That list, Reverend?"

He weighed it in his mind. A tongue, used to spouting Scripture and metaphor, fell silent. He walked out of the office. Tamma glared at me.

"Why are you doing this? Why are you bothering us?" she demanded. Her hands balled into fists, unsuitable for prayer.

"I didn't realize looking for truth was a bother to you. Isn't that why we have churches?"

"I used to think nicely of you, Jordy. But you're a thoroughly unlikable person. Leave us alone."

Adam returned with a file. He sorted through the papers, found one, set the file down, and walked back out. I heard his footsteps stop, the hum of a copying machine, and the crisp sound of paper sliding into a tray. His footsteps resumed and he entered, brandishing a paper at me.

"Here. I hope you don't bother these people too much." He glanced at his wife, who wouldn't look at me. "I can't see how this has anything to do with Beta's death."

"Thanks. Good day, Reverend. Mrs. Hufnagel." I nodded to the unfriendly Tamma, and left. Walking out into the morning sunshine of the parking lot, I scanned the list quickly. It was interesting that two of the names matched two of the names on Beta's list.

I changed my plans. I went home. Sister sat in the living room, watching Mama sweep the back porch. Mama loved to do that; repetitive actions hold a fascination for Alzheimer's patients. It's almost as if their repertoire of tasks is so limited, they get a sensual pleasure out of repeating endlessly the few actions they can still do well. Mama swept even the microbes off that porch, weaving back and forth for hours if uninterrupted. We didn't want her to do it at first, but her doctor said it was decent exercise. It was better than the walking in circles that she also favored.

I decided to try out a theory. No more taking folks at face value. I picked up the kitchen phone, cleared my throat, and dialed Matt Blalock's number.

"Hello, Blalock residence."

"May I speak to Matthew Blalock, please?" I sounded just like my friend and co-worker Gil Camden back in Boston, just watering down the Yankee accent a tad. Making fun of Yankees when you live up there tends to make you into a good mimic. At least it did me.

"This is Matt Blalock."

"Hello, my name is Gil Camden. I'm a Vietnam vet who just recently moved to Bavary. I understand you hold a weekly meeting over there in Mirabeau for vets. I'm interested in attending."

"Yes, we do. But not this week." Matt coughed. "We don't have our usual meeting place available. We should have it back next week, and we'll meet then. If I can get your address and phone number, Mr. Camden, I'll—"

I set the receiver gently back into its cradle. The good Reverend Hufnagel had lied right to my face. So why were he and Matt together at the church? The two of them were a pair that just didn't match.

I went up to my room and laid out my notes. Since I didn't have enough answers about the suspects, I decided to concentrate on the victim. Beta brought death on herself; this was no random act of violence, no crime of passion. Her presence in the library at night, her attempt to torch the building, her careful list of names and Biblical verses, the unexplained money in her account pointed to some system she'd imposed on her life. Beta, in other words, was up to something and it got her killed. I was the person most attached to the library; I'm the only one who would have arguably killed for it (and I wouldn't have gone that far). That list had kept me focused on Beta's relationships at the library, but Mirabeau was a small town and lives overlap in other areas. I needed to cast my net further, and I'd decided to start with the church.

I wrote out another list on paper:

TIMETABLE OF EVENTS IN BETA'S LIFE

January—Beta in hospital, accuses Ruth Wills of trying to poison her. Incident dropped.

February—Beta forced off library board after censorship battle. Rough fight with bad feelings between Beta and library board and vice versa. Particular animosity between Beta and Matt Blalock. Bob Don Goertz appointed to replace Beta.

Beginning of March—Beta chaperones with Tamma Hufnagel on youth group trip to Lake Travis. Beta and Tamma mend fences.

Late March—church rummage sale. Beta drops the ball on it.

Beginning of April—Beta begins planning work on Vacation Bible School with Tamma and Janice Schneider.

Monday, April 7, evening—Hally Schneider takes Beta home after baby-sitting job. Sees Eula Mae Quiff meeting Beta at her house.

Tuesday, April 8—Beta deposits $35,000 in her savings account.

Saturday, April 11, evening—Ruth witnesses violent argument between Beta and Bob Don at his dealership. Beta makes some threat toward someone Bob Don cares about. (Perhaps his mistress—remember his assigned quote about a damsel or two!)

Monday, April 13, morning—fights with me at library. Also present: Tamma, Eula Mae, Ruth.

Monday, April 13, afternoon—at her home apparently meets with Bob Don, then Tamma. Goes to church and takes library key from Adam's office.

Monday, April 13, late night—goes to library with intention of burning it down—alone or with killer? Killed with baseball bat.

I read again where Beta deposited all that money. The day after she met Eula Mae. And Eula Mae was one of the few folks in town who could cough up that much cash. Beta must've been dangling something over Eula Mae's head—

The palm of my hand slapped up against my mouth and I felt as stupid as a Bummel at birth. Beta did have something over Eula Mae, but it had to be something Beta didn't know about when she made her censorship stand at the library. If Beta had dirt on Eula Mae, she'd have used it to get Eula Mae to switch her vote. The same for the others on the board: Janice and Ruth. But Beta hadn't. No embarrassing revelations came to light when Beta got tossed. Whatever she'd had on Eula Mae, she hadn't had it in February.

But at some point, Beta got smarter. She'd gotten $35,000 worth in smarts. Meeting late with Eula Mae. Threatening Bob Don. Who else?

I tore through my notebook, back to the list of names. Maybe this was a list of people Beta could blackmail. But then why were my name and Mama's on it? I'd been as virtuous as a monk since coming home, and Mama could only get into a limited amount of mischief in her condition. It didn't wash.

Sister rapped gently on my door. She'd never done that as a teenager but she'd broken her filthy habits.

"You have a visitor, Jordy. Beta Harcher's niece is downstairs."

CHAPTER TEN

THE YOUNG MISS HARCHER WASN'T WHAT I
expected. Although I hadn't given it much thought,
when I'd heard Beta had a niece it wasn't hard to imagine some tight-lipped, proper young clone of Beta. Apparently self-righteousness and primness aren't in the
genetic code.

The girl was around five feet eight, with shoulder-
length reddish brown hair and a finely featured face.
Her eyes were blue as a jay, and they darted around
with the same cunning and speed. Her figure was firm
and shapely under the black T-shirt and faded, acid-
washed jeans she wore. She also wore large, funky tur-
quoise earrings and black cowboy boots. I guessed she
was young, around twenty-three.

Mark had come in from the backyard. As Sister and
I came down the stairs, the girl laughed at something he
said, a high, musical bell of a giggle. He blushed madly
and kept gawking at her. I obviously needed to have a
talk with that boy when all this calmed down. Had Sister explained the facts of life to him? Lord, all my re-
sponsibilities.

I kept those facts of life firmly out of my head as I
introduced myself. I'm not sure she did.

"Well, Mr. Poteet, you sure don't look like any librarian I ever met. I'm Shannon Harcher." Her hand was cool and firm in my grasp.

"Please, sit down," I indicated the sofa.

She did, neatly, and I sat next to her. I glanced at Sister, asking with my eyes for some privacy. Sister made herself comfortable in the easy chair. Mark leaned against the wall, trying to look older and nonchalant. It didn't work.

"My sympathies on your aunt's death," I said, not knowing what else to say.

To my surprise, a hint of a smile tugged at her mouth. "You're very kind, Mr. Poteet. But I know you and Aunt Beta weren't exactly friends. She gave me updates over the phone about her book-banning efforts."

I opened my hands, then closed them back together. No use in denying that little fact. "No, we weren't friends. I—" She raised a well-manicured hand to interrupt me.

"Look, Mr. Poteet, there's no need to explain. I know what kind of person my aunt was." Shannon Harcher shrugged. "You don't have to pretend with me that you liked her. I won't hold you to all those small-town niceties."

"Okay, Miss Harcher—"

"Shannon."

"Then call me Jordy. Okay, Shannon, your aunt and I weren't friends." I paused. "You've probably already heard that from the D.A.'s office and the chief of police."

Her lovely eyes narrowed. "I haven't talked with the D.A.'s office. The chief told me you'd found the body."

So Junebug hadn't told this girl I was a suspect. Maybe he didn't consider me one anymore. I felt relief that she hadn't talked with Billy Ray Bummel. She wouldn't have come around me if he'd been allowed to paint my picture.

"I did find the body." I told her the story, quickly. I left out the part about Billy Ray wanting to nail my butt to the wall. While I spoke, Sister got up and fixed us iced tea with sliced limes. Shannon nodded her appreciation and sipped. She didn't interrupt my story and sat thoughtfully for a moment when I finished.

"A baseball bat, of all things," Shannon finally said. "I still can't believe it. I always thought that she'd go down frothing at the mouth, waving her trusty Bible."

"Not to be indelicate," I said, "but I take it you didn't share your aunt's religious views."

One of her fine, high, arched eyebrows (which probably already needed a building permit) went up a little farther. "No, I'm afraid I didn't. I know you didn't get along with her, Jordy. Sometimes, I didn't either. My folks died when I was seventeen in a car wreck in Houston. They didn't leave me enough for college, and I didn't have the grades for a scholarship. Aunt Beta gave me the money for college." She smiled. "With provisions. As long as I went to Baylor. As long as I went to church regularly. As long as I majored in religion."

"Sounds like Beta," Sister put in.

Shannon smiled her gorgeous smile. I might have majored in religion myself to see that more often. "It turned out to be negotiable. I ended up majoring in music instead. I just told Aunt Beta I specialized in church music, and that made her happy."

"I'm glad someone could negotiate with her; I never mastered that particular talent." I shifted on the couch. "Don't take this the wrong way, Shannon, but why are you here to see me? Surely not just to meet the man who found your aunt's body?"

Shannon lowered her eyes, staring down into her iced tea. She looked soulful and lost. It was a pose that she seemed comfortable in, carefully made to tug at a man's heart. I could hear Mark's sigh across the room.

"In going through some of Aunt Beta's things, I found these library books. I was going to drop them off at the library, but it was closed. And I was curious to meet you anyway, after Chief Moncrief told me you'd found my aunt." She dug into a book bag at her feet which I hadn't noticed before. Pulling out four hardbacks, she offered them to me.

I took them from her, scanning the titles. *A Writer's Guide to Getting Published. Drug Abuse: Traitor to Humanity. Videotaping for Fun. Living with Alzheimer's Disease.* It made for a curious reading list.

Shannon watched my face. "That book on Alzheimer's made me wonder if she was coming down with it."

"Hardly. My mother has Alzheimer's, though, and she made that list of Beta's." I set the books down. "I have no idea why Beta was interested in these other topics."

"My aunt never had a wide range of hobbies," Shannon said dryly. I liked her even more.

I ran a thumb along the book bindings. Alzheimer's and my mother, and now Beta with a book on the painful subject. I wondered if some similar connection existed between Eula Mae and this book on writing. And what about the others? I couldn't imagine Beta doing drugs—but I did know that Matt Blalock smoked dope. Maybe Beta knew, too (although I couldn't imagine Matt caring). If she did know, she hadn't turned him in. And I couldn't picture Beta submitting an entry to *America's Funniest Home Videos.* So why the videotape book?

Shannon cleared her throat and stood. "Well, I appreciate your hospitality, Jordy." She nodded to Sister. "Thanks for the tea, Mrs. Slocum. Nice to have met you, Mark. Now you stay handsome, hear?" Before Mark could burst a blood vessel, I put my hand on Shannon's arm.

"Stay for just a moment, please. I want to ask you something." She shrugged and sat back down.

"Your aunt had just deposited $35,000 in her savings account before she died. I understand that was an unusual amount for her to have."

Shannon examined one of her fingernails. "I'm not sure I should discuss my aunt's financial situation with you. That was, after all, her business." *And now it's mine* was the unspoken ending to that sentence. I waited patiently for her to look at me. She did when I didn't speak.

"Those of us who are involuntarily involved in this case have thought that Beta might have been getting money. By extortion."

Shannon looked at me with wry amusement. "My aunt? A blackmailer? Get real, Jordy." She sighed. "I guess I have to tell her secret, not that it matters now. She was hoarding that money for a long while. She was going to open up her own church in Houston."

Her own church? I was glad my jaw was hinged, otherwise my chin'd be scraping the ground. "Beta wasn't an ordained minister." I managed to say.

Shannon laughed. "Oh, that didn't matter. It was going to be a nondenominational, fundamentalist church. She didn't need to be ordained for that; she just needed money, time, and some real estate." Shannon shook her head. "She'd told me all about it. She'd saved up a bunch of money, and she was going to go to Houston and find her some office space she could convert. No pun intended." She laughed, any grief over her aunt forgotten. "She was supposed to come out to Houston next month and sign a lease. She was going to drag me into this whole mess. I work as a music promoter for several bands in Houston. She kept going on about how I could be the music director for her church. God, I wanted to avoid that, if possible."

Enough to kill her? I wondered. "If she'd saved all this money, how come she made it in one big deposit? Why not let it grow in the account and accrue some interest?"

"I don't know. She was goofy."

"But she wasn't stupid. If she was saving up to start a church, she'd want as much money as possible." I shook my head. "I'm not calling you a liar, Shannon, but I don't believe she had that money stuffed into a mattress all these years and just decided to put it in her account."

Shannon's eyes steeled. "Then it must have been donations from supporters. You know, like the TV evangelists get. It doesn't matter anyhow; that money is mine now."

"Not if it came from illegal means," I said simply. "You already know she had a list of people on her when we found her. I've been talking with all those folks and they're each as skittish as a waterbug during a drought. Maybe there's a connection between her list, these books, and that money."

"Maybe she was researching her first sermons," Sister volunteered and I shot her a black look. She shrugged.

"She was religious," Shannon argued. "Religious people don't break the law."

"She was in a library after hours, ready to torch it,"

I retorted. "I bet you if we look in the Texas Penal Code we'll find arson mentioned."

"So what do you want from me?" Shannon demanded. Her eyes flashed, and I guess the thought of losing that money was the spark.

"I want you to save yourself a lot of grief later on," I answered. "If the money is genuinely your aunt's, then it's yours and the matter's settled. But if she got it through blackmail, we need to know now. That way you won't have to worry about the police coming and asking you for it down the line."

Shannon weighed her choices. The lovely skin tightened across her high cheekbones as she thought. She was a smart woman.

"Fine," she finally said. "I'll cooperate. What do you want?"

"I want us—meaning you, me, and Chief Moncrief—to search your aunt's house for any evidence that she was blackmailing someone."

She shook her head, but not in disagreement. "The police already went through the house when she was killed. They didn't find anything."

"Then we go through it again. Junebug's fellas probably wait for something to announce itself before they notice it. If we don't find anything there, your aunt is probably innocent of extortion and I'll apologize to her at her grave. But if she was, we might find who killed her."

"I want that," Shannon said bluntly. "I want to know who killed her and I want them to pay for it. I won't pretend that she was my favorite person in the world, but she helped me when I needed it. It's not right that she died that way."

"I want that, too," I said, but for an entirely different reason. It wasn't right that Beta was murdered, but in my humble opinion it was less right that I be arrested for it.

She glanced at her watch. "I have an appointment with Reverend Hufnagel. He's conducting the funeral service. How about around three this afternoon?"

"I'll call the chief," I said, sure that he would not be pleased about me inviting myself along for the ride.

She stood, eager to be gone. She said her goodbyes again to Mark and Sister. I walked Shannon to her car, noticing that two doors down Janice Schneider was pulling into her driveway. Time to pay my kinfolk a visit.

I went back into the house. Mark was still moon-eyed over our visitor, but that wasn't keeping him from toying around with expensive hardware. He pulled wires and cords from the TV and the VCR.

"Wow, she's real pretty, huh, Uncle Jordy?" he said, yanking on a cord that looked costly to replace.

"Yes, she's very attractive. And too old for you and too young for me." I watched as he broke the bonds that hooked together TV and recorder. "What exactly are you doing, Mark?"

He began lugging the VCR up the stairs. "You said we all had to make our adjustments with Mamaw's illness. Well, my adjustment for today is watching a Schwarzenegger tape on the TV in your room, so I can blare the volume and not freak out Mamaw." He vanished up the stairs and into my private sanctuary. Great, I thought. That room always had been a magnet for teenage male mischief.

Ever go into someone's house and feel more like you've stepped into a catalog than a place where people actually live? I felt that way everytime I went into Janice Schneider's house. Note that I said house, not home. I swear to God there was no way this woman had three males actually living in this house. It was as pristine as new crystal and as tasteful as money could make it. There had been enough money, all right.

Janice's living room wasn't much bigger than ours, but it was as white as a snowy field. The carpet, the upholstery, the throw pillows were all various shades of ivory. The furniture that wasn't white seemed to be all glass and chrome, so you could see through it to the white or have the white reflected back at you. I thought the TV might only pick up static, just to fit in. If I'd been a speck of dirt in that room, I would have died of loneliness.

Janice bravely served me coffee in that expanse of snowy home furnishings. I say bravely because if I were her, I wouldn't allow anything that could make a stain in that room. Janice seemed to have total confidence in my ability to not spill, however.

She was still as pretty as she'd been in school, with brown hair and pert features. She looked strained, though, around her eyes and mouth. I think it was all that perkiness. She was always the happiest, smilingest person you ever saw. God, she was annoying. Civilization could be falling around your head and Janice'd just giggle and say we could have a bake sale to help the survivors. Where Beta had been dour about folks' relationships to their Maker, Janice was sure that God really did love everybody and that he'd give those extra bad sinners a pat on the head and forgive them right away, so they wouldn't even get their toes warm before they strapped on their angel's wings. She sided with me against Beta in the censorship fight, to my surprise. But I felt that Janice had stuck by me because her God liked Mark Twain and Maya Angelou and Jay McInerney and all those other folks Beta objected to. Her God liked everyone, even me.

"I just can't tell you how devastated we all are," Janice sniffed as she dumped a chunk of sugar in her coffee. I didn't think she could get any sweeter, but I refrained from comment.

"I saw Hally the other day. He said that Beta baby-sat for y'all sometimes."

Janice nodded, looking desolate. She caught herself, though, and perked right up. "Yes, Miz Harcher was real sweet to our Josh. I know that might be hard for you to believe, Jordy, but she truly was fond of Josh. I think she sometimes wished she had children of her own."

"I must've missed her maternal streak."

"Oh, it was there," Janice assured me. "But, you know, living alone in that old house, with no real involvement in her life but church—" Janice faded off, shaking her head.

"We all make our choices," I answered.

"Yes," Janice agreed. "But I tried to help her. Before all that to-do over the library, I even tried to set her up on a date."

"Date?" My throat caught. A date. With Beta Harcher. One could only imagine the possibilities, since none of them would ever take place.

"Yes," Janice smiled, remembering, "but her reputation preceded her. I couldn't find a willing widower in all of Bonaparte County."

That seemed to me the saddest part of all. I felt bad for Beta all of a sudden, despite everything. No matter how much trouble she'd caused folks, each day she had to wake up and live the hell of a life she'd created for herself. Alone and unloved, and now cold in the morgue with hardly a person to mourn her.

I got up from the couch and walked into the warming sunlight streaming through the sliding-glass window that led to the Schneiders' porch. I felt Janice's eyes follow me.

"You were working with her on the Vacation Bible School plans, weren't you?" I could almost hear her relax behind me.

"Yes, I was. I have to admit, I think both Tamma and I were dreading it after her getting kicked off the library board. But she was easy to work with, undemanding and even calm."

"Did you know that she was planning on moving to Houston and opening a fundamentalist church there?" I asked, turning back to her.

Janice obviously didn't. Her perky face tightened in surprise. "Beta? Her own church? I find that hard to believe."

"Believe it. She told her niece all about it and stashed away a little money as her start-up funds."

"How . . . surprising. I'm sure folks at church didn't know anything about this." She paused. "If it's true, maybe that's why she'd gotten even more involved in the administrative side of the church lately. The youth trips, the rummage sale, the school. Maybe she wanted to learn how to run such things."

I nodded my agreement.

Janice cleared her throat and tried to change the subject. "How is Anne doing? Are you and Arlene holding up?"

"Fine, thank you for asking," I answered, keeping the sarcasm out of my voice. I wanted to say: come down and see her for yourself—it's not catching; but I refrained. I walked back to Janice, sitting perfectly on her perfect little couch in her perfect little house. I pressed onward.

"You know that when I found Beta, there was a list of names in her pocket. With Bible quotes next to them."

Janice set her coffee cup back in its saucer with a rattle. "Yes, I know. Junebug Moncrief told us when he came to ask Hally some questions."

"Then you know that Hally's name was on that list."

She nodded. "The whole thing's silly. Hally had nothing to do with Beta."

"Except that she went to his church, he headed up a youth group that she chaperoned, and she baby-sat for his brother."

Janice took refuge in silence. She sipped at her empty coffee cup.

"Most of the other names of people on that list are library board members. There are a few, though, that aren't. Hally made it onto Beta's list, and you didn't. I'm curious as to why."

"To know that, I'd have to know why she made that list," Janice countered. "I don't. Do you?"

"I have my suspicions," I answered airily. Suspicions and no proof. "The quote next to Hally's name was 'Fools make a mock of sin.' Do you have any idea what that means?"

"None whatsoever. Hally is beyond reproach," she snapped. I must've hit a nerve; she'd stopped smiling.

"Please, Janice," I smiled. "He's a teenager. Teenagers do dumb things sometimes. It doesn't mean he's not a good kid." I glanced around at the ideally pristine room and wondered if anything less than perfection was acceptable in Janice's eyes.

"I don't know of anything that Hally has done that Beta could find fault with," Janice asserted.

"Beta found fault with things most people would consider faultless. Like D. H. Lawrence and Nathaniel

Hawthorne," I reminded her. "I had a talk with Hally yesterday. At the very mention of Beta Harcher and her death he was as nervous as a long-tailed cat in a room full of rocking chairs. I'm just wondering why."

"How dare you!" she sputtered, jumping to her feet. "How dare you come into my home and suggest that my son had anything remotely to do with a murder."

I crossed my arms. "Spare me the histrionics, Janice. I'd never have suggested it if Beta hadn't had his name on that list and if he hadn't acted so skittish."

"Of course he was skittish. He knew her. She was murdered. That's upsetting to people!" It certainly seemed to upset her.

"Remorseful, maybe. Saddened, maybe. But not skittish. Hally acts like he has something to hide, Janice."

The very suggestion enraged her. Her arms, hanging at her side, cocked into L's, and her fingers jerked with anger. If I'd been within reach, she would have slapped me.

"Get out. Get out of my house," she whispered.

I obviously hadn't handled this well. My approach of forthrightness with Hally hadn't worked on his mother. I set my coffee cup down on her table and I raised palms in supplication. "Okay, Janice, okay. Don't bust an artery or anything, I'm going."

She stood there, trembling, watching me leave. I felt like I'd smeared something nasty across her spotless white interiors.

Hally was pulling up in his little Mustang when I walked out onto the yard. He smiled uncertainly when he saw me.

"Hey, Jordy," he called as he unfolded himself from the car.

"Hi, Hally," I said, deciding to take the offensive

again. "Look, I've upset your mother. We were discussing Beta Harcher."

Hally's blue eyes flashed. "What is it with you, Jordy? Why don't you just let the police do their job and leave everyone else alone?" He was mad at me, but he was more scared. I could see the fear in his face, lurking behind the braggadocio he wore like a mask.

"I'm sorry. I didn't mean to rattle your mother."

Hally ignored me and stormed toward the house. I couldn't resist.

"Oh, Hally, I did see Chelsea Hart this morning. Charming girl. She sends you her best." He tottered, torn between the idea of coming back across the yard and dealing with me and going in the house to either see Janice or possibly hide under his bed. Mom won. The door slammed hard behind him, rattling the bay windows Janice had added to give her house extra class.

I exhaled slowly, not feeling proud of myself. Well, I'd stirred up the hornet's nest at the Schneiders. I retraced my conversation with Janice in my head. I could have been a lot more diplomatic, I supposed. I turned and headed down the street, walking along the line where grass met road and balancing on it like a highwire walker.

Josh Schneider nearly ran me down before I saw him. He came pedaling down the road, carefully perched on his little shiny blue bicycle. He stopped about three feet dead from me, the tires pealing pleasantly as he halted.

"Josh. Hi, how are you?" Even as I asked, I glanced back at the Schneiders'. We were in front of my house, so I didn't think Hally or Janice could see. I'm sure if they could have, Josh would've been snapped up quick. "Got a second to talk?"

"Sure," he sniffed. Where Hally was a younger version of his father (my cousin Harold), Josh was a petite

Janice. He resembled her, with his fine looks and brownish hair, but more than that, he acted like her. I'd never smiled so much as a child. I don't think I'd seen Josh without a grin before, cheering up the other kids. He wasn't smiling now, looking a sad figure in dusty jeans, a cartooned T-shirt, and neon-lined tennis shoes.

"Hey, buddy, you doing okay?" I squatted down next to him.

He shrugged. "I guess so."

"You sad about something?"

Josh nodded. "I miss Miz Harcher. I loved her."

My throat tightened. Someone did actually care about the old battle-ax. I chastened myself for thinking that. Beta's parents must have loved her, surely. Perhaps some young man once considered her pretty and smart and fascinating. But that was all long ago. Maybe Josh's love was the only love Beta knew. My jaw felt tight as I looked into Josh's dark, unhappy eyes.

"I know you did, buddy. She loved you, too." I said it with no knowledge of its truth, but it sounded fair. If she could have loved anyone, maybe it was this little boy who was so unsullied by the sin she saw in everyone else.

"Then why'd she have to die, Jordy?" Josh asked, his face frowning into tears he was repressing.

God, how do you explain death to a five-year-old? I couldn't do it. I didn't have a clue. I took one of Josh's hands in mine. "Someone took her away, Josh." I fumbled for an explanation to help, but Josh didn't need my words. He had his own.

"One of the bad people did it," he said, folding thin arms over his stomach. The little Martian man from the Looney Tunes cartoons peered at me from Josh's T-shirt, his head peeking above Josh's crossed arms and daring me to contradict the boy.

I didn't know what defined a *bad person*, but Josh was correct to a degree. "Yes, a bad person killed her."

"She said they were here," Josh added mournfully, and wiped his nose with the back of his hand.

"Bad people were here?" I asked, trying not to sound too stupid in front of this bright little boy. This was no news to me, though. I was stupid much of the time, it seemed, and Beta thought just about everyone was pretty bad.

"Yeah, she said they were." Josh blinked at me, then glanced around, as though bad people might creep up right behind us.

I tented my cheek with my tongue, thinking. "What did she say about the bad people, Josh? Who were they? You can tell me." I just hoped I wasn't on the dishonor roll.

Josh shrugged with the same I-don't-know attitude I'd experienced far too much lately. He must be learning it from all the adults around him. "She just said all the bad people were going to pay."

"Pay? For what?"

"They were going to pay her. So she could build this place to talk to God," he said, glancing toward his house. My eyes followed his, relieved to see his front yard empty.

The church. They were going to pay her for the church. I took Josh's shoulders and made him look into my eyes. "Josh, listen to me. What you just said to me is very important. Could you tell someone else about it? Would you tell Chief Moncrief?"

Josh considered his civic duty. "Would he give me a ride in the patrol car and lemme run the siren?" he asked seriously.

"Yes, he will. And I'll call you every time we get a new children's book at the library," I offered. This literary bribe didn't have the glamour of the patrol car, but it was enough. Josh took my hand and followed me into the house.

A glass of milk, two slightly stale cookies, and a phone conversation with Junebug later, I dispatched Josh home. Junebug was still on the line when I came back in.

"So now do you believe my blackmail theory?" I demanded.

"It gives us something to work on, which is only a shade better than nothing. We need some solid proof, Jordy," Junebug opined.

"So let's go over to Beta's and get it," I insisted. "Look, it's coming up on three. I told Shannon we'd meet her there around then and she'd help us look around."

"Shannon, eh?" Junebug asked. "She's still Miz Harcher to me. I must not have your charm."

"We all have our small burdens to bear. You going to be there or not?"

"I'll be there," he huffed. "See you shortly."

I replaced the phone in the hook. The bad people indeed, Josh, I thought. From the mouths of babes.

CHAPTER ELEVEN

I KNEW SOMETHING WAS WRONG THE MOMENT I saw the door of Beta's house. It stood ajar. Shannon might be visiting a small town but she was a big-city girl and didn't strike me as the type to leave front doors open. I jogged up the path to the porch. It creaked when I stepped on it.

"Shannon?" I called.

No answer. The second step creaked louder than the first and I paused again. "Shannon? It's Jordy Poteet."

The wind answered me, brushing across my face and bringing me the scent of honeysuckle from a neighbor's bush. I pushed the door open, calling Shannon's name again into the dimness of the entry hall.

I walked into the living room. The curtains were still drawn as Beta probably left them, but in the light of the doorway I could see the whole room had been trashed. Chairs were knocked over, books spilled down from the high-standing bookshelf, drawers from a desk lay yanked free of their snug home. I had taken four steps into the room when I heard and saw Shannon.

She lay crumpled by the sofa, and the cushions were stained with the blood from her face. Her arms were flung outward, as though ready to give a hug, but not a kiss. Her lovely face was a wet mass, stained with blood and hair and what looked like bone. Her citified black T-shirt was ripped at the collar and I could see her bra strap and a white expanse of shoulder. The acrid smell of bullet fire pervaded the air, in contrast to the sweet honeysuckle on the porch.

I crouched by her, hearing her wet intake of breath before I tried to find a pulse. I couldn't bring myself to touch her neck; I found a pulse in her wrist. The beat had almost faded, but it was still there, like a last echo on a stage.

I stumbled through the mess to the phone, hearing the porch boards creak under weight. Junebug's shadow fell into the hallway.

"Call an ambulance!" I hollered. "She's been shot!"

The next few minutes were a daze. Junebug bolted back to his car and radioed for help. I held Shannon's cooling hand, telling her that help was on its way, for her to hold on. I don't know if she heard me; there was no replying grasp on my fingers, and the only noise she made was her breathing. I held each breath of mine until she drew another one.

The ambulance came, along with two of Junebug's officers. Someone pulled Shannon's fingers from mine and I watched them take her off in the ambulance. Wordlessly I turned back and walked into the house that still smelled of gunfire. I stood by the gore-stained couch and suddenly needed to sit down, but not there. I sagged and a strong arm, one that felt familiar, caught me.

"Here, Jordy," Junebug said gently. "Sit here." He steered me to an easy chair in the corner under a lamp. I trod right over the books and smashed bric-a-brac that littered the floor. I sank into the chair.

Junebug squatted by me, and over his shoulder I saw a wall of crosses. They were of every size and shape, some of metal and some of wood, and right away I saw they formed a larger cross that stood well over seven feet tall.

Home decor à la Harcher, I thought crazily. It made the scene even more unreal. I sunk my face into my hands.

"Listen, Jordy," Junebug said. "Tell me what happened."

I told him, remembering that it was only two mornings ago I'd had to relate a somewhat similar story. If I kept finding bodies, I wasn't going to get invited anywhere. Shannon wasn't a body, I reminded myself. She was alive. For now. I felt cold, despite the spring warmth outside.

Junebug squeezed my shoulder when I was done. "You okay?"

For the first time in all this he sounded like my old friend and rival. I looked up at him with gratitude (not a common occurrence with me) and he smiled grimly.

"I just can't believe this, Junebug. What the hell is going on here?"

One of Junebug's officers, the nervous one with the cropped hair that'd been at the library, stuck his head around the corner. "Busted window in the back bedroom, Chief," he reported crisply. "Looks like the pane was smashed and the window forced up from outside."

"Thanks. Keep checking around; let me know what you find." Junebug shook his head, surveying the wrecked room. He walked through the mess, and I followed him. The destruction wasn't quite complete. One shelf of cheap glass over a secretary-style bureau glittered intact, and another row of Bibles stood on the topmost shelf, probably out of the attacker's reach. Pictures on one wall, of a younger Beta, a far primmer-looking Shannon in her Baylor graduation gown, and of a nearsighted-looking couple from the Forties peered back at us, still hanging straight from the wall. Shards from a china collection that had seen far better days crunched under my feet. Junebug glanced back at me.

"Maybe you were right, Jordy. Beta must've been

hidin' somethin' in here. This ain't from any struggle Shannon had with her attacker. Somebody was either looking for something or being a vandal."

"If someone broke in, Shannon must've walked in on them," I guessed. "She told me she had an appointment with Reverend Hufnagel before she was meeting us back here. She must've surprised the intruder."

"Is that the story you're peddling now, Poteet?" a nasal voice behind me demanded. Billy Ray Bummel sauntered in like he owned the place. He sniffed the air, like a wine connoisseur inhaling tenderly over a glass of vintage red. "There's been a crime here, I do believe."

I was ready to tell him the only crime was his continued employment by Bonaparte County, but Junebug had his own ax to grind. "Lay off Jordy, Billy Ray. He didn't have anything to do with this."

Billy Ray whirled on the law like it was a misbehaving dog. "And how are you so sure about that, Chief? Let me remind you that Mr. Poteet here has found both members of the Harcher family dead in the past two days."

"Shannon's not dead," I argued.

He waved off that technicality and tried to get as close to my face as his stunted height would allow. "Not yet. And why not? Because you're a lousy shot, probably. Because Chief Moncrief here caught you before you could snuff out that poor young thing's life. What is it that spawns your violence against womenfolk, Poteet?"

He was about to see what spawned my violence toward balding, onion-breathed lawyers. Junebug intervened.

"Stop it, Billy Ray. Jordy, you take two steps back and don't pay him heed." There was a snapping noise and I saw Junebug pulling on plastic gloves. "Billy Ray, Jordy was on the phone with me immediately before all this happened. He wouldn't have had time to get over here, trash this room, and shoot Shannon."

"We are not talking about running across Houston here, Junebug. We are talking about being three streets over. He would have had plenty of time." Billy Ray fumed, the struggle of doing such calculations draining his energy.

Junebug began picking through the debris of Beta Harcher's den carefully, not looking at Billy Ray. "Nonsense." He told Billy Ray about me finding out what Beta had told Josh, bolstering the theory that Beta was using blackmail to build funds for her proposed church. Billy Ray didn't care for that theory. He turned back on me.

"You've spun a might tricky web here, Poteet," he sneered. "I guess you think havin' lived in the big city, you're going to outfox us reg'lar folk. Let me just divest you of that notion, mister. You're going to have a lethal injection pumped into you if Shannon Harcher dies, and even if you don't, you're gonna have one for killing Beta."

"I bet my uncle Bid could sue you for saying something like that to me," I said hopefully. My temper was in full force now. I'd seen a lovely young woman lying near death and now this little minnow of a barracuda had the audacity to accuse me, with no proof. "Of course I wouldn't sue you as an officer of the court. The people of Bonaparte County suffer enough every time you open your mouth as their representative of law and order. I'd see about suing you just as you. Of course, what could I ask for as restitution? I have no burning need for cheap suits, and I just don't think that I want a cardboard diploma from a mail-order law school with a post-office address."

Billy Ray showed he had some hot blood by having it all rush right to his face. One big vein popped up on his forehead and I wished for a shrimp deveiner. The little lunk might have actually tried to hit me. Our arguing had brought the pale-faced young deputy back into the room, but Junebug kept shuffling through the dross of Beta's den. The young deputy stepped between Billy Ray and me, but it was hardly necessary. I wasn't going to stoop to hitting the worm and he wasn't about to strike me and get a rep for slapping around taxpayers and fellow civil servants.

"Jordy," Junebug said in his regular, polite, slow drawl, "what was the name of Eula Mae's first book?"

The question was so unexpected Billy Ray and I quit glaring at each other and turned to him. Junebug stood, setting an open Bible on a table. A yellowed piece of stationery was in his hand, and he peered at it like it held the wisdom of the ages.

I had to think over Eula Mae's impressive publishing credentials. *"The Rose of San Jacinto,"* I finally said.

"And she published it, right?" Junebug said.

"Not a vanity press if that's what you mean," I answered, misunderstanding. "It was published by one of the big New York houses."

Junebug chewed his lip. "Y'all better look at this."

I nudged in front of Billy Ray and scanned the aged letter Junebug held in his hand. My breath caught at the end:

411 Blossom Street
Mirabeau, Texas 78957
January 12, 1975

Ms. Eleanora Parkinson
Parkinson Literary Agency
200 East 52nd Street
New York, New York 10022

Dear Ms. Parkinson:

I've written a romance novel, set during the Texas Revolution. The working title is *The Rose of San Jacinto*. It's the story of a young woman who is torn between her arranged marriage to a Mexican officer and the gallant rebel that she loves. The book is in finished form and is around 100,000 words. I haven't been published before, but my sister thinks it's good. Please let me know if you would be interested in representing this novel to publishers.

Sincerely,
Patty Quiff

"Patty? Who the hell's Patty?" Billy Ray muttered.

I found my voice. "Eula Mae's sister. Her older sister. She died in, oh, about 1976. Cancer."

Billy Ray drew in a long breath, like a bloodhound scenting a deer. "Well, well, well. Isn't this interesting?"

Junebug pulled a plastic bag from his back pocket and eased the document inside. "Doesn't prove anything yet, Billy Ray."

Billy Ray coughed. "Kind of indicates to me ol' Eula Mae's been pulling the wool over the literary eyes of not just Mirabeau, but New Yawk as well."

She was working on her latest book when we got there. Billy Ray had tried to send me home, but Junebug said I could stay. He told Billy Ray that Eula Mae was a friend of mine and I could talk to her perhaps a bit easier than either of them.

Eula Mae greeted us with her usual civility and charm. Today she wore some long dashiki-type of robe, speckled with bright purples, oranges, and blacks like the plumage of a tropical bird. Her eyes darted from face to face, as though we were predators of the rainforest.

She bade us sit down in her living room, for which the operative word was *wicker*. I hadn't seen so many

swirls since my teenage job in an ice cream shop.
Junebug and I settled on a couch with a back of dizzy-
ing arabesques, and Billy Ray perched next to us on a
straight-back chair.

"Y'all wait just one second and I'll get us some tea,"
she trilled, heading into the kitchen.

"You ought to have someone watching the back
door," Billy Ray hissed at Junebug. "She might try and
go over that rose hedge in the back."

"I don't think that'll be necessary, Billy Ray,"
Junebug said mildly.

The cat I hadn't befriended the other day wandered in
and eyed our merry band. He regarded me with disdain,
Junebug with curiosity, and—perceptively—Billy Ray
with contempt. He hissed at the assistant D.A., arching
his back (probably the only time Billy Ray has seen a
back arch in his presence), and scurried from the room.
I liked cats better all of a sudden.

Eula Mae returned with a tray of iced-tea glasses,
each topped with a sprig of mint from her garden. We
made momentary small talk as she served us. Nervous-
ness hit me like a rock and I sipped at my tea, for once
not wanting to say anything. Finding Shannon wounded
had dulled me; reading the letter by Eula Mae's sister
had stunned me; and now I sat in my friend's parlor,
with Law and Order on each side, to debate fraud and
murder. God, I wanted a cigarette.

Eula Mae sat in a comfortable chair next to the
wicker sofa, across the coffee table from Billy Ray. "To
what do I owe the pleasure of this visit?"

Junebug raised a warning hand to Billy Ray, and for
once Billy Ray leashed his tongue.

"I don't suppose you've heard that Miz Harcher's
niece was shot today at her house," Junebug said.

Eula Mae's face crumpled. "Oh, my Lord! No, I

hadn't heard." She paused. "I didn't even know Beta had kinfolks still around here."

"Girl's from Houston," Junebug replied. "Someone shot her in the face. Don't know yet if she'll live or not. Young girl, too, early twenties."

"How horrible." Eula Mae shook her head, then looked uncertainly at me.

"Jordy found Shannon Harcher," Junebug said, as if that explained my presence. "He also found another witness that said, basically, that Beta was extorting money from folks to finance a church she planned to start over in Houston."

I saw the fight for control on her face. The wrinkled corners of her lipsticked mouth jerked, just once. Her silver bracelets, choking with charms, tinkled as she smoothed out her skirt.

"And why are y'all telling me this? Trying to give me the plot for my next potboiler?" She laughed, and it sounded jagged.

"We think Shannon Harcher walked in on someone ransacking the house. Looking for something, maybe something Beta was holding over their head and using to get money," Junebug explained.

"So answer me, Junebug," Eula Mae's voice rose. "I don't know anything about Beta getting killed or this Shannon girl getting shot. Why are you here to see me?"

Junebug set his mouth in a thin line. "We found a letter there, Eula Mae. A letter apparently from your sister to a literary agent, asking about representing a book she'd written called *The Rose of San Jacinto*."

Eula Mae did not withstand adversity as well as her heroines. Her face blanched, the lines in it seeming to darken as she frowned. One hand flew up to her forehead, like a startled bird returning to roost. "I—I—," she stuttered.

I saw Billy Ray starting to uncoil like a striking rattler. "Perhaps, Junebug," I suggested, "Eula Mae should have some legal representation present if you're going to accuse her or—"

"No!" Eula Mae thundered, and I fell silent. "No lawyers," she whispered, and her eyes flicked across each of our faces. "No one else. Who else knows about this, Junebug?"

"Just the three of us," he answered softly.

"I—I want your help. Each of you, please," she whispered. This woman seemed crushed; not like the Eula Mae who always tried to run the library board meetings, who played her local fans like a string quartet, who had beaten the odds to make a living as a writer. Even her curly, uncontrollable hair was listless. Her eyes, usually sparkling with gossip and merriment, stared at the floor.

"What kind of help?" I asked.

"I want you to help my sister," she said, which left us all silent. Eula Mae waved a tired hand and began an explanation. "A few weeks back the Baptist church committee came by looking for items for their rummage sale. I gave them a box of old books that had been my sister Patty's. I didn't think to look through them—they were just old books of hers, writers she'd admired as a teacher. Welty, Balzac, Thoreau, Turgenev, Robert Penn Warren. I gave them those books and never gave it a second thought."

"Till Beta paid you a visit," I said, finishing her sentence for her.

Eula Mae stared at me and through me. It didn't matter what I'd said.

"She'd gone through the box I donated, and found a letter Patty wrote to an agent—about her book." Eula Mae's tongue flickered across her lips. "I never knew Patty even wrote a draft of such a letter. She never sent one. She was a wonderful writer, but she was just too afraid of rejection. I kept urging her to send it, but she didn't want to hear anyone say no to it. Then she thought people around here would tease her for writing a romance novel. I suggested she publish it under a pseudonym, but she just laughed. She said if she ever did, it'd be under a joke name like Jocelyn Lushe. She just made up that name out of the blue." Tears formed in Eula Mae's eyes. Junebug offered her a handkerchief and she took it, wiping her eyes.

"After Patty died, I just hated the thought of that manuscript sitting there. I started submitting it, but I was afraid no one would touch it if they knew a dead woman had written it. Those romance houses, they want to know they can buy a book and expect others to follow from the same author, build a series and an audience. So I said the book was mine, and I used the Jocelyn Lushe name. It didn't seem like I was taking credit for her, or stealing from her, because it wasn't my name. It was her pseudonym. I didn't plan on continuing it—I just wanted to get Patty's book published. So I did. And it did really well; it made a lot of money. The publisher started asking me for my next manuscript." She paused and wiped her eyes again. "I didn't want to stop. Writing those books was like having Patty back around. She'd had gobs of notes for ideas, so I went through those and wrote another book. Then I got a three-book contract, and I just had to keep writing them."

"Stealing from a dead woman—your own sister—to make yourself famous," Billy Ray snorted, shaking his head at Eula Mae with contempt.

He got as good as he gave. "Think what you want, Billy Ray," she snapped. "There have been eleven Jocelyn Lushe books. I wrote ten of them, and they've done damned well. I didn't steal from Patty; I kept her dream alive. I did all the hard work."

"But Beta found out," Junebug prompted.

She nodded, miserably. "Beta found out. She came to me with the letter. I'd never known Patty had written it; it would have been just like her to write it, then not mail it. Just slipped into that book to mail when she got her courage up. I guess her cancer took all her courage." She dabbed at her eyes, and when she looked up again they blazed, free of tears. "Beta told me, as payback for helping to remove her from the library board, that she'd expose the first book as being Patty's, not mine. She'd call my publisher, the Romance Writers of America, the news stations in Austin. It could have been very ... professionally devastating."

"So why didn't she just do that?" Billy Ray demanded.

"She wanted money. Money for her silence," Eula Mae replied.

"So you gave her $35,000," I finished, eager to hear and have my theory entirely justified.

Eula Mae blinked at me. "No. I gave her $10,000."

"So who gave her the other—" I started, but Junebug shushed me.

"When'd you give her this money, Eula Mae?" Junebug asked.

She sniffed, wiping her nose with the handkerchief. "The week before she died. I met her at her house. She'd been babysitting little Josh Schneider. The Schneiders dropped her off at her place and I gave her cash. She wanted more, but I said no. I decided I wasn't going to keep paying blackmail to that horrible woman, and—"

"And so you killed her," Billy Ray interrupted. "I'm gonna guess you didn't tell her no more payments; you agreed to make one final payment. At the library, two nights ago. You killed her to shut her up and stop the extortion. But you still needed to find that letter. So you broke into Beta's house, tore up her den looking for it, and when Shannon Harcher walked in on you, you shot her in cold blood." The assistant district attorney leaned as far forward as he could, spewing his accusation like he usually spewed bad breath.

Eula Mae trembled. "That, sir, is what's known as a damnable lie," she retorted, and one of her characters couldn't have said it better. I leaned over and took Eula Mae's hand.

"I don't know who killed Beta," Eula Mae said, "but it wasn't me. I had nothing to do with that."

"Had you told her you weren't going to pay her any more money?" Junebug asked quietly.

She shook her head. "She told me she'd want more later, but not when. I decided the day after I'd paid I wasn't going to give in to that holier-than-thou witch."

"You didn't need too, Miz Quiff," Billy Ray asserted. "You'd already decided to take action, and you did. Well, this little scandal should help your book sales."

Her eyes blazed, like an irate devil's. "You little shyster," she barked. "I might've expected that from you. I told you this 'cause I said I wanted you to help my sister. Help me keep her dream alive. Don't tell anyone what Beta knew. Do what you like to Eula Mae Quiff, but don't ruin Jocelyn Lushe."

Billy Ray shook his head. "No way, Miz Quiff. There's no way to keep that quiet when your trial starts."

"Miz Quiff," Junebug said, not using her Christian names. I didn't take that as a good sign. "Where were you between two and three this afternoon?"

Her hand trembled in mine. "Here. Editing a manuscript." She paused. "Alone."

"Did you see or talk to anyone?" he pressed.

She shook her head. "No, I did not."

Billy Ray stood. "I think we've heard enough, Chief."

Junebug looked up at him, not wanting to get up from the wicker sofa. The air in the room had taken on a dense, thick quality. I felt choked.

Junebug finally rose to his feet. "I'm sorry, Miz Quiff. I'm going to have to take you down to the station for further questioning—"

"Junebug, please!" she gasped. "I didn't do it. I didn't kill Beta, I didn't shoot that girl. You know me, you know I couldn't."

He stared into her face. His mouth worked for a moment, then he found his words. "You're under arrest for the shooting of Shannon Harcher. You have the right to remain silent. Do you understand?"

Eula Mae sagged against me and I held her up. She only needed a moment. She found the strength in herself and stood straight. I stood next to her, listening to her Miranda rights. She said she understood everything he said to her. I felt like I didn't understand a damned thing. Eula Mae had lied, and taking credit for her sister's work wasn't too acceptable, but I didn't think she was a killer.

"The handcuffs, Chief," Billy Ray said when her rights were read.

"That's not necessary, I assure you." Eula Mae looked shocked at the very suggestion.

Billy Ray began a whiny protest, but Junebug shook his head. The police chief took her by the elbow and led her toward the door. I finally found my voice.

"Eula Mae! Do you want me to call my uncle Bid?"

"God, no," she retorted. "You better get me a real lawyer."

CHAPTER TWELVE

"SHANNON SHOT AND EULA MAE ARRESTED? You're kidding, right?" Sister was incredulous.

"No, I'm not. He arrested her." I poured Dr Pepper over ice cubes and listened to them pop. I forced a grilled cheese sandwich into my mouth. It was tasteless.

"What does Junebug think Eula Mae did, read one of her books to Beta and bore her to death?" Sister snorted. "He and Billy Ray must be out of their minds. What proof do they have?"

I chewed. I'd come straight home to find Mark watching gory films in my room while Mama napped and Sister ran midafternoon errands. I'd called a respectable-sounding lawyer in the Bavary yellow pages—having the biggest ad does make a difference in dire straits—and hired him for Eula Mae. I'd made some food I didn't have an appetite for and tried to eat. Sister's demands for information kept my mouth busy. "It's a case of sorts. Eula Mae doesn't have any alibis, she's got a key to the library, and she sure as hell had a motive."

Sister pressed me for what motive in particular, but I'd decided to keep Eula Mae's reasons to myself. I wasn't going to be the one to wreck her career. Hell, maybe this wouldn't wreck it. But obviously Eula Mae thought her literary reputation was worth at least $10,000.

The phone jangled. Sister scooped it up with a quick hello. "You listen here, Junebug," she said after a moment. "If you work late tonight, you come over to the truck stop and I'll fix you up with some of my peach cobbler. I want to have a word with you." Silence while Sister listened. "Don't you jaw that old line at me, Hewett Moncrief. You sound like one of those ventriloquist's dummies, sitting on Billy Ray's knee." Eyes rolling, she handed the phone to me.

"Jordy here."

"Hey," Junebug said, subdued. "I guess y'all can open the library. My officers are busy doing scene-of-crime work over at Miz Harcher's house. They're all finished up with the back room at the library."

"Thanks. I might even reopen this afternoon. I'm going nuts just sitting around here."

"Well, I would like for you to come over right now and give a statement about finding Shannon Harcher."

"Okay," I said. "Let me make a couple of phone calls and I'll be down."

We both hung up. I called the hospital. They wouldn't provide information about Shannon's condition. I asked for Ruth, but they said she was on duty in the emergency room. I had a feeling she was working on Shannon.

I called Adam Hufnagel. His wife Tamma answered, sounding like she'd caught a bad cold and had just woken up.

"What did you say?" she asked after I'd asked for Adam.

I sighed, trying not to sound impatient. "I need to speak with Adam."

"He's trying to take a nap, Jordy. He's had a hard day."

"Well, maybe you can help me, Tamma. Do you know, did he keep his appointment with Shannon Harcher today?"

There was a moment's silence. "Yes, he mentioned he saw her. Why do you ask?" Her voice held the edge of suspicion she'd shown when she confronted me in her husband's office.

"If you have an extension, please put him on it," I said. "I have news he needs to hear—you both need to hear."

There must've been something in my tone, because she didn't argue. I held while she roused him. When he came on the line, I waited until I heard Tamma pick the phone back up.

"Shannon Harcher was shot today at Beta's house. Junebug and I found her. She's in critical condition at the hospital. They've arrested Eula Mae," I said.

Adam wheezed and Tamma was silent. "Why Eula Mae?"

"I don't want to get into that, but apparently I was right. Beta was profiting from her involvement in your church's activities, like your rummage sale. Just thought you'd like to know. You might want to be a little more choosy with your volunteers." I hung up, not wanting to further my conversation with those two.

I called Candace, told her what all had happened during the course of the afternoon (including Eula Mae's confession—I trusted Candace to keep a secret to the grave), and asked her to open up the library. I asked her if she'd mind working late so folks could use the library a bit longer than usual, since it'd been closed for two days. She didn't mind a whit and kept inquiring as to my well-being. I told her I'd see her shortly.

I finished eating and told Sister I'd be home later than usual. We went upstairs and checked with Mark. He'd laid in a big supply of borrowed videos and wasn't averse to taking care of Mama. I put the VCR on pause and told him about Shannon.

Mark's dark eyes grew wide. "Can we go down to the hospital to see her?"

I shook my head. "Not now. She's in intensive care, I'm sure. Maybe later."

"Is she going to die? Was it gross? Do you think she's in a lot of pain?"

"I don't know, Mark, and yes, it was gross." I glanced at the videotapes he'd borrowed from friends, every one a bloodbath. "I don't think I'll ever want to see one of those movies again myself."

Mark looked at the collected Arnolds and Dirty Harrys with new eyes. He pushed the off button and the VCR fell quiet. "Maybe not these, tonight. Maybe I'll just read a book for a change."

I went to the police station and made my statement. It was fairly short and simple. Billy Ray wasn't around to taunt me this time; he was too busy arguing with Eula Mae and the lawyer from Bavary I'd hired. Apparently she and her lawyer were getting along just fine; they could both yell you deaf. I nearly felt sorry for Junebug.

I picked up my notes on the case and shuffled through them. I thought a lot of questions were still unanswered by Eula Mae's arrest. I stuck my notebook under my arm and headed out.

I parked in front of the library. It was nearly four and we usually closed at six on Thursdays. I suppose it was hardly worth opening for two remaining hours, but I figured Candace and I could wrap up any loose ends from having been closed for a while. Plus, we might stay open a bit later, let the curiosity seekers get it out of their systems.

Going in was a little harder than I thought it would be. My hand froze as I reached for the door. Beta's bludgeoned face, eyes wide open in death, wasn't waiting in there for me this time. But I couldn't erase her easily from my thoughts. I made a concerted effort and instead of Beta's battered head, I saw Shannon's bloodied face. My fingertips massaged my eyes. Too much death, too much suffering for one little town.

I heard the door open and Candace was there, wrapping her arms around me. "You okay?" she breathed against my chest.

"Yeah. God, what a week," I said, then chortled nervously. My own laughter sounded tinny in my ears. We put arms around each other and walked into the library together.

The air had the same dense quality about it that Beta Harcher's house had. I told myself that it was just from the library being shut up for two days, not death lingering in the air like some foul fog. The old air-conditioning system sputtered and cranked away, but it hadn't yet dispelled the foreboding, pressing atmosphere.

She'd brewed coffee, in the only brewer we had—back in the room where Beta's body had lain. I set my notebook on the counter and I went back there. The tape outline was still down, etching where she fell. I didn't know if I was yet allowed to pull the tape up, but I did, yanking it up violently. I wasn't about to velvet-rope this section of the library and charge a quarter a peek. I felt mad—mad that Beta had hurt people, mad at what I'd been through, mad that Shannon was lying near death, even mad that little Josh Schneider got an awful early introduction to what death meant. Candace watched me, waiting for me to talk.

"If Eula Mae killed her," I finally said, "that means Beta died for $10,000. I never thought of a life in monetary terms." I realized I was lying as soon as I said it. I'd thought of how much money Mama would need to live her limbo existence over the next twenty years. I closed my eyes, feeling more anger and shame. I got up, poured coffee, and went back to my tiny office. I sat down and Candace sat across from me. She was watching me with a concern that made me uneasy. I wondered—not for the first time—what it would be like to kiss her. Instead I coughed.

"I suppose we should reshelve and check in books in the drop slip," I said, attempting to sound professional. "Doesn't look like we're going to get any takers today."

Candace shook her head. " 'Fraid so. I felt creepy when I got here, and I didn't know how long you'd be at the station. So I called some of the regulars. Old Man Renfro and Gaston Leach both said they'd be over shortly."

"Followed, undoubtedly, by the town curious who'll want to tour the death scene. Shall you be the docent or shall I?" I said. I sipped at my coffee. I kept thinking about Eula Mae, in jail and accused of murder and attempted murder. Something niggled at my mind, something in all this that didn't fit. I thought of Matt Blalock and simmering hatred. I thought of Ruth Wills, an accusation of poisoning that didn't stand up. I thought of Hally Schneider, who had been right about a secret connection between Beta and Eula Mae, yet still seemed awfully nervous for an innocent bystander. I thought of Bob Don, who seemed to want to help me and fought violently with Beta less than a week before her death. I thought of the Hufnagels, and how their church wasn't good enough for Beta's ambitions. And I thought of my mother, her presence on Beta's list still unexplained. Billy Ray thought he had his woman now, but I wasn't convinced.

I went over to the local-authors shelf. Eula Mae was currently the only Mirabeau resident with fulfilled literary aspirations, and her collected works sat in a row. I plucked her first novel from the shelf; the copyright was in Eula Mae's name. I'd thought for a moment that if it was copyrighted under the Jocelyn Lushe pseudonym that Eula Mae would have had an easy out; no one could have necessarily accused her of lying. But it wasn't so. She'd claimed each book as her own. I replaced *The Rose of San Jacinto* on the shelf and went back to Candace.

"There's still $25,000 that was in Beta's savings account that didn't come from Eula Mae," I told Candace. "So where the hell did that come from? She embezzle from the Girl Scout cookie fund?"

The bells above the front door jangled, and from my office I saw Old Man Renfro and Gaston Leach come into view. I couldn't have conjured up a more unlikely pair. Old Man Renfro always wore a threadbare suit; he must've had a whole armoire of them. Snowy white hair topped his dark, wise face. He was retired from the post office and when he had tired of reading people's addresses, he'd ended up spending his days at the library. It would not be unreasonable to guess he'd read everything in the library at least once. Even the children's section, reading them to his several grandchildren. According to what I'd heard, he'd attacked the shelves methodically, moving through the Dewey decimal system as if it were a grocery list and devouring every book. His real name was Willie, but every one called him Old Man Renfro.

Gaston Leach was what every kid in high school aspired not to be. He was a gawky youth that might one day, the charitable among us said, turn from ugly duckling to swan. We could only pray he'd develop some social skills to go along with any external improvements. He had a mind I'd have killed for and a face I'd have committed suicide over. His parents apparently had little concern for Gaston's ability to interact with others, because they sent him out in tacky clothing the dead wouldn't wear and bought him eyeglasses with lenses that could double as drink coasters. Not to mention the pairing of his first name with his last. His thick mop of black hair fell in a bad cut across his forehead. Today he was resplendent in too-long gray trousers that hung low on his bony hips and a shirt with a nauseating orange plaid. Never failing to accessorize incorrectly, he held up his pants with a western-style brown belt and wore black shoes. He'd missed being cool by several feet today.

"Glad to see y'all are back open," Old Man Renfro proclaimed. "Well, Miss Harcher did manage to close the library for a while, but not in the way she thought she would."

Gaston was less philosophical. "The new McCaffrey come in while y'all were closed?" he demanded, turning those powerful lenses on the new-arrivals bin.

"No, Gaston," I said, having no idea. I hadn't checked our mail drop, but I didn't want to get into another long discussion with Gaston about the relative merits of the science-fiction selection at the Mirabeau Public Library.

"Oh," Gaston muttered, high-beaming reproachfully at Candace. She must've bribed him to come over. Apparently the idea of being supportive of folks he saw every day was an alien concept. That couldn't be right,

I thought. Gaston explored alien concepts every day, what with his reading list. Old Man Renfro took Gaston by the elbow and steered him to a chair in the periodicals section. Candace and I followed.

"Candace says that there's been a shooting, and that Eula Mae has been arrested for that crime and for Miss Harcher's murder," Old Man Renfro said. His voice was a carefully modulated tenor. He was one of those gentlemen who is very careful about how he speaks, because he'd grown up in a house where it hadn't mattered and he'd made a conscious decision to be correct. If his voice was any deeper he could've subbed for James Earl Jones.

I nodded. "So I guess I'm not under suspicion any more. But I can't believe that Eula Mae is some calculating plotter."

"Having read her books, neither can I," Old Man Renfro agreed with a tad of asperity.

"Yes, Eula Mae's strong suit has always been characters," I retorted. I didn't feel picking on Eula Mae's writing skills was helpful at this critical time.

"Her character hasn't always been above reproach," Old Man Renfro said, turning his own wordplay, "but I find it hard to believe Eula Mae would willingly hurt another person, much less a young woman she didn't know."

"What'll happen to Eula Mae's cats when she's in jail?" Gaston wondered. "Maybe she'll donate them to science."

"Gaston, dear, I'll take care of her cats, don't you worry." Candace patted his arm, looking a mite green.

"I only know what I read from Sayers, Christie, and Hammett." Old Man Renfro tented his fingers across his face. "But if Eula Mae was going to kill someone, I don't see her swinging a baseball bat or firing a gun.

I think a nice, quick poison would be her choice. Not to sound morbid, but I don't think Eula Mae would want to see someone die at her feet. She would much rather spike their iced tea with something that would not act immediately, get out, and leave their final sufferings to her overactive imagination."

I opened my mouth and shut it again before flies made it a home. He was absolutely right.

"What I don't get is why Miz Harcher was even in the library when she got killed," Gaston interjected, wiping his nose without benefit of facial tissue. "She didn't even like this place."

I quickly explained Junebug's theory that Beta had intended to incinerate this den of evil. Old Man Renfro's eyes hardened, and Gaston wheezed with dismay at the thought of all his unread Anne McCaffreys, Piers Anthonys, and André Nortons that would have gone up in smoke.

"I don't understand that," Candace put in. She ran a hand through her lovely, tawny hair and frowned. "Does that mean the killer was here to help her burn down the library?"

"Maybe that's how the killer lured her here," I said. "Offering to help her burn down the place she hadn't been able to censor or close. That would've appealed to Beta."

"And the person must've been someone she wasn't afraid of," Old Man Renfro added. "Someone it wouldn't bother her to be alone with."

"I don't think she was afraid of anybody," Candace said.

I thought of that list of names. "I think more folks were afraid of her than the other way around." I pulled out my notes and flipped to the questions. "I wrote this up after she was killed." My eyes flicked to Old Man

Renfro and Gaston. "There are things mentioned here that aren't mentioned in the paper. Can I count on y'all's discretion?"

Old Man Renfro nodded, and him I didn't worry about. Gaston was another problem, though. Anything he knew about the case, he'd brag about to his classmates in a futile attempt to move up the high school food chain.

"Now, Gaston, don't go blabbing about what we talk about here. If you do—and rest assured I will hear if your lips start flapping—I'm going to cut back on the science-fiction orders. No new David Brins or Greg Bears. Do you understand me?"

He nodded like a scared addict, afraid that his supply would be terminated. I could almost imagine Gaston stealing TVs so he could hit the used bookstores in Austin to keep the narcotics of his favorite literary pastime available.

I opened the notebook and went down the list of questions. I still don't know why Beta had made that list of names and Bible verses, but I suspected it had to do with blackmail. She knew Eula Mae had faked her first book, and Eula Mae's quote talked about an enemy writing a book. Some of the other quotes—such as Tamma's and Bob Don's—also hinted at secrets preferably kept. I realized though, I still didn't have answers to most of my questions. I still didn't know why Beta was dressed in black (unless it was supposed to be in vogue for nighttime book burnings), why her shoes were caked with mud, and why the killer used the bat in my office. I did know why she was at the library now, but her having a key still bothered me. If Eula Mae had met her at the library to kill her, Beta wouldn't have needed a key; Eula Mae had one. So why swipe Adam Hufnagel's key, the one found on her person? I only had the Hufnagels' word that Beta had taken the key; could they have given it to her, knowing she might burn down the library? Did they still hold a grudge for having lost the censorship fight?

Old Man Renfro looked through my notes, humming. Gaston leaned over his shoulder and I fished out a tissue for him, just to protect Old Man Renfro's jacket. Allergies are tough here in the spring.

"I hope at the end of our lives, there are no questions," Old Man Renfro said softly. "I used to think I knew who Beta Harcher was, but I didn't."

"Who did you think she was?" Candace asked.

"I'd heard she wasn't always the paragon of religious virtue she pretended to be," I added.

Old Man Renfro leaned back. "She was a very pretty young woman. I remember she used to come into the post office when she was young, back in the Fifties; she had a pen pal in Europe. I remember that because those were the only letters I ever remember mailing to Norway. She always seemed to be in a sweet, good mood."

"Sourness crept in somewhere," I interrupted. "That Norwegian pen pal send her some pickled herring that stuck in her mouth?"

Old Man Renfro shook his head. "I don't like to repeat old gossip, especially if there's no way to prove it. But I guess when you die by violence, you lose all privacy. Your life's not the only thing your murderer steals from you." His dark eyes met mine. "There was a rumor, long ago, that she got her religion on a trip to Mexico."

"Mexico?" Candace said. "She wasn't Catholic."

"No, she didn't get any particular faith," Old Man Renfro agreed. "But back then, young ladies could get . . . problems taken care of over the border they couldn't always get taken care of here."

Gaston appeared utterly lost, but I swallowed. "You mean she'd gotten in trouble? An abortion?"

Old Man Renfro nodded. "That was just the rumor that swept through town, but I don't think anyone really believed it. My sister told me she'd heard it from a lady who cooked for one of the Harchers' neighbors. Of course, Beta started going to church on pretty much a twenty-four-hour basis and I guess that rumor died, like most do."

I shook my head. "I'm not going to go chasing thirty-year-old shadows on rumor."

Gaston scanned the list again. "Her shoes were real muddy?"

"Caked with it," Candace answered.

"Maybe her car broke down again," Gaston offered helpfully.

"What d'you mean?" I asked. "You working for Triple A now?"

Gaston sniffed. "Naw, I just saw her car last week, out on the dirt road that goes out to the east side of Bavary. Late last Wednesday night I was coming back from my D and D game—"

"D and D?" Old Man Renfro asked, sounding as though he thought Gaston was engaging in kinky hobbies with Bavary housewives.

"Dungeons and Dragons," Gaston explained with a sigh. "It's this really cool game where you pretend to be a fantasy character and you have adventures—"

"Thank you, Gaston, but you said you saw her car?" I wasn't in the mood to hear about Gaston's latest escapades as a slayer of dragons and saver of virgins.

"Oh, well, yeah. See, I wasn't really concentrating on the road because I was mad I hadn't killed the Black Druid with my enchanted broadsword when I could've and I was wondering if I'd have a second chance next week—"

"Gaston," I interrupted again. "I'm sure Tolkien fans will be in a mad dash to buy your adventure when you get it all written down, but where did you see Beta's car late at night?"

He looked hurt behind those thick lenses and I felt bad. I squeezed his bony shoulder. "Sorry," I said, "I'm just a little jumpy."

"As I was saying," Gaston began with great dignity, "I was concentrating on my poor strategy in the game. I nearly ran her car down. She was barely parked on the shoulder. I knew it was her car 'cause it had all those Jesus bumper stickers on it."

I nodded. Beta had driven an old Ford Tempo with enough religious bumper stickers on it to look like a scout car for a Billy Graham revival.

"Anyhow, I stopped, because I thought her car must've broken down and it was awful late—around eleven. I got out, but she wasn't in the car. I called out her name, but there wasn't any answer. I figured someone else had picked her up and she hadn't come back for the car yet."

"Where on the road was this?" I asked.

"Not too far out of town," he shrugged. "Maybe a couple of miles, no more. Near the Blalock farm."

"Isn't that interesting?" I said to Candace.

"I was sort of glad she'd gotten picked up," Gaston continued. "She didn't like me."

"Well, Gaston, you did speak out very eloquently against censorship when she tried to—" I started, but Gaston shook his head. Fortunately no grease flew off.

"No, that's not it. I go to the Baptist church. She heard about the kind of books I like to read and the role-playing games I like to play. I tried to get some of the other youth-group kids interested in playing one that doesn't even involve swords and sorcery on a retreat, and she chewed me out good!" Gaston said, the picture of wounded innocence. "She said they were Satanic and evil. Of course she didn't know that Bobby Jay Tumpfer and Lila Duke were sneaking into each other's rooms during that whole trip. And all I wanted to do was play a game!"

"Hey, Gaston, was this the trip to Lake Travis that Beta chaperoned?" I asked.

"Yeah, she and Mrs. Hufnagel went with us. It rained, so there wasn't much to do 'cept listen to Miz Harcher preach at us."

"Sounds like she was warming up for her church with y'all," I muttered. "Anything else happen on that trip?"

Gaston thought. "No, we were all just trying to figure out when Bobby Jay and Lila were going to get caught and what old Beta would do if she caught 'em. And nobody really picked on me too much during that trip." It seemed a fond memory for him, and he paused. "Oh, well, that was the trip that Hally's daddy's camcorder got stolen."

"A camcorder?" I asked.

"Yeah, one his dad loaned him for the trip. He left his room unlocked or something and somebody took off with it. There were a couple of other youth groups there, too, so I suppose someone from one of them took it. It never did turn up and Hally was awful upset."

A missing camcorder. Beta had checked out a book on using camcorders. Had she swiped it and not gotten the instruction manual at the same time?

The phone jangled, interrupting my thoughts. Candace scooped it up. "Mirabeau library, Candace speaking," she said. Her eyes frosted lightly. "Why, yes, Ruth, he is. One moment." She handed me the phone.

"Your little friend in white. Although why she's allowed to wear that color I don't know."

Old Man Renfro and Gaston stared at this unusual ferocity from Candace. She smiled sweetly at them.

"Hello, Ruth?" I said.

"Jordy, hi. Listen, I only have a minute. I understand from Junebug that you found Shannon Harcher today."

"Yeah."

"I thought you might want to know her condition."

"I tried earlier, but they wouldn't tell me anything."

"She's in a coma," Ruth said, her voice lowering. "She's got a depressed skull fracture. There's been a lot of bleeding around the brain. She's going to need surgery."

"My God! Do you think she has a chance?" I thought of telling Mark that she didn't and dreaded it.

"Yes, I do," Ruth said. "The bullet didn't actually penetrate Shannon's brain. It hit and deflected at a fairly thick part of her skull. Her face is going to need some fixing later, but if they can relieve the pressure around the brain, I'd say her chances are good. She's young and strong. They're getting in a specialist from Austin tonight."

"Oh, God, I hope she makes it," I breathed. "Thanks for calling and letting me know."

"I knew you'd be worried about her," Ruth said, her voice sweetening. "And I have a selfish reason for calling, too. I hoped you might be able to come by the hospital now. I have a matter I'd like to discuss with you."

"I don't know, Ruth. We just reopened the library and I'm pretty backlogged."

"I'm sure Candace can handle that. She seems extraordinarily capable of taking care of all those mundane, boring details," Ruth said. "Please, Jordy, it's important. I'll expect you here in about fifteen minutes. Meet me in the front lobby."

I hesitated, then decided to take her up on her offer. "Okay, fine. I'll be there. Goodbye." I replaced the phone receiver in its cradle. I looked at the trio before me. "Shannon Harcher's in a coma right now, but they think she has a chance. She's undergoing brain surgery." That last part seemed a good segue, so I added: "They need me to come down to the hospital."

Candace's eyebrows arched. "They do, do they? Are they looking for a brain donor?"

"Yes, I mean, no," I muttered. "Look, Candace, can you keep this place open just another hour or so? I really do need to go down to the hospital and see how Shannon's doing."

"Sure, why not?" she said. "It's not like I had any other pressing engagements this evening."

I thanked her, and thanked Gaston and Old Man Renfro for their help. Picking up my notebook on Beta, I dashed into the late afternoon sunlight.

I hate the smell of hospitals. I tried to ignore the heady mix of antiseptic, bland food, and general illness that pervades that mecca of modern medicine, Mirabeau Memorial. Ruth met me in the front lobby, holding a Baby Ruth candy bar that she said was her snack for a quick break. She munched on it as we walked through the hallways.

"Junebug has Shannon Harcher under police guard," she told me. "Whoever hurt her isn't going to get another try."

"You know they've made an arrest?" I asked.

She shook her head. I told her about Eula Mae.

For a moment, there was complete shock on Ruth's finely featured face. She blinked and the surprise dropped away like flaky makeup. "I suppose they must have had good reason for that. Yes, I can see Eula Mae killing someone."

I stopped and waited for an overweight aging candy-striper to lumber past us, out of earshot. "Really? I thought you looked surprised there for a second. Were you expecting someone else to be arrested? Bob Don? Matt? Me?"

"I'm sorry Eula Mae was arrested. I know she's your friend. You don't have to take your anger out on me." Ruth pouted, her pretty little lip trembling.

I frowned. I don't like pouters and I especially don't like fake pouters. "Sorry. Didn't mean to blame you. Now what was this business that was so darned important, Ruth?"

The lip slid back in like it was automated. Ruth took my hand, looked both ways down the empty hospital hallway like she was crossing a street, and led me into a room. It was an empty private patient's room, the only light burning a dim one from the bathroom. She leaned against the heavy door and it slowly closed.

"Ruth—" I began, but her mouth didn't let me finish. She pulled my head down to hers, kissing me hard, tangling her fingers in my hair. It's no excuse, but I hadn't been kissed like that in ages. Her mouth tasted of warm chocolate and caramel. My body responded while my mind continued to mull over the implications.

Her hands ran across my body, feeling, lightly exploring. Fingernails nipped playfully at sensitive areas and I gasped, pulling her closer. She broke the kiss but kept her mouth scantly off mine.

"See there? We make a good team. I knew we would," she breathed softly into my face. "See? I can help you and you"—she squeezed my buttocks—"can help me."

"Okay, Ruth," I said, restraining the urge to kiss her again. This sounded more like negotiations of commerce than declarations of affection or even lust. "What do you mean by all this?"

She kissed me hard again. I pulled back.

"How would you like," she said, pressing her breasts against me, "to be sure your mother's never in a home?"

It wasn't the question that I was expecting. My mouth opened in surprise and she covered it with her own. She pulled away and flicked her tongue across my bottom lip. I closed my mouth and pulled away from her.

"What do you mean? What are you talking about?"

"Be at my house around ten tonight, and I'll tell you," she said.

"No, Ruth, tell me now. I came all the way over here—"

"So I could let you know how I felt. And see how you felt." She laughed, sliding her palms along my back. "And you feel wonderful. This is just a warmup, darling. We need privacy." She jerked her head toward the door, and I heard a faint murmur of voices beyond, talking about an IV drip.

"Ten? Be there, Jordy, you won't regret it." She gave me a quick, decorous kiss. "Now I'm going to walk out. You walk out about a minute later. I don't want my co-workers to gossip about me." She turned and walked out, leaving me alone in the darkness. I stood there, counting to sixty, then walked out into the brightness of the hallway. Ruth stood at the far end of the hall at the nurses' station, talking over a chart with a young nurse. I turned and walked the opposite way.

I sat in my Blazer for a few minutes. Ruth sure liked to dangle carrots in front of your face, hoping you'd take a bite. She knew from my response that I was attracted to her. I was, physically. But I didn't care much for this secretiveness. If she thought it was alluring, she was wrong. I wiped her lipstick from my face with my handkerchief. I wasn't sure that I would go see her at ten.

I started up the engine, but I didn't particularly feel like heading back to the library and seeing Candace. I didn't feel guilty per se, but I wasn't comfortable about talking to Candace right after I'd been kissing another woman. And I hadn't even kissed Candace. Go figure.

Instead of heading back to the library, I drove in the direction of Bob Don Goertz's house. I'd meant to get back to see him, but I hadn't had a chance. Seeing Ruth reminded me about the fight she claimed to have witnessed between Beta and Bob Don. I thought it was high time I found out a little more about that particular incident. Odd the whims that take us, and forever change our lives.

CHAPTER THIRTEEN

I HEARD GLASS SHATTER AS I WALKED UP TO the Goertzes' front door. The door was made of thick wood and beveled, frosted panes that you couldn't see through. My first thought was that someone had dropped a glass in the kitchen, but my finger hesitated above the doorbell. I wasn't even sure what I'd heard. I stepped back from the door and looked up at the sprawling colonial home. The car business didn't seem to be hurting too badly, I thought. I put my head back to the door, leaning my forehead against it, strangely reluctant to ring the bell. I heard voices raised, Bob Don's among them, pleading. I pressed the button and the bell rang, echoing inside the home. I heard a shouted "No!" and stepped away from the door, thinking this was not the time for a social call.

I'd made about three backward steps when the porch light snapped on and the door opened. It wasn't just an entrance; it was a crutch. A woman I recognized from the framed photos in Bob Don's office leaned against the door; she would have fallen if the door hadn't been there. In the pictures in her husband's office she looked like a typically meek, quiet small-town housewife. Now she looked like a street-worn harridan. The hair-sprayed halo in her pictures was gone; a lank length of graying dark hair hung past her shoulder. She was in a rumpled pink housecoat that looked as if she'd slept in it. Her eyes, dulled as dusty marbles, blearily blinked and found me in the porch light.

"Mrs. Goertz—" I began, ready to beat a hasty retreat. I wanted no part of a drunken scene. Sister was right; I could smell the whiskey on Gretchen Goertz like she'd bathed in it.

"Well, here you are. I know you. I know you." Her voice sounded like a thumb scraping a dry, empty bottle. I couldn't remember that I'd had the formal pleasure of meeting Mrs. Goertz; Lord knows she would have made an impression on pert' near anybody.

"Mrs. Goertz—" I tried again, taking another step back.

"You come in here. You come in here and watch me kill him," she rasped. I stopped moving backward. She swayed in the doorway like a snake and I decided to try charm. I'd talked a drunken high-school friend down from the water tower when I was a teenager; I could handle a wasted Gretchen Goertz.

"You doing okay, Mrs. Goertz? You feeling all right?" I said in my most syrupy, friendly good-ol'-boy voice.

"Fuck you," she said in clear, ladylike enunciation. "I told you to come on in here and watch me kill him."

"Now, you're not wanting to kill anyone, are you, Mrs. Goertz?" I wheedled. God, no wonder Bob Don smoked heavy and kept a pint at work, if this was his domestic life. She was scaring me, and now I wondered what might happen to Bob Don if I didn't check on him and get her sobered up. He hadn't come to the door, and I didn't think most men would let their wives hold drunken tête-à-têtes with the neighborhood.

I moved back onto the porch, and she flung the door wide open. In better light she looked worse. "C'mon in, kid. C'mon in and see all the hell you've caused me."

I was firmly of the opinion her hell was a private

matter between her and Jack Daniel's. I went into the entry hall, moving past her, not looking at her. I saw a living room ahead and headed for that.

The living room was blasted with light. It was oblong, with a fireplace in the middle, pale and uninspired furniture on each end, and a wet bar on the side of the living room that led toward the kitchen. The carpet was a light beige and I wagered it was well worn by Gretchen's slippers as you got closer to the bar. An oil painting of Gretchen Goertz hung above the cold fireplace, where a shattered glass sparkled. Broad swipes of paint made the portrait look better than the model.

Bob Don huddled on the couch, his broad face in his hands. He was crying. It was not a hysterical kind of sobbing, but a slow, methodical weeping, like he was cleaning out the closet of his soul. I could see the mark of fingernails cutting across his cheek, bisecting one of his long sideburns.

I stepped to his side. "Bob Don? You okay?"

He looked up at me, not registering me for a moment. He blinked tears from his reddened eyes. "Oh, Christ!" he said, his usual heartiness gone. "Oh, mother of Christ! You got to leave, Jordy. Just leave."

I knelt by him. "Listen, Bob Don. Gretchen's drunk and saying she's going to kill you. Why don't I help you get her settled if you want, and—"

"You have to leave!" Bob Don screamed. He jumped to his feet, nearly knocking me over. I balanced myself, putting a hand out to the carpet. He leaned down and seized my shoulders in his beefy hands. He yanked me to my feet.

"Get out, get out, get out," he kept crying, not demanding, but begging.

Major-league domestic problem, I decided, congratulating myself on my quick and reliable insight. I thought:

none of my concern. He's not dead so she hasn't carried out her threats and she's too drunk to hurt him. Goodbye, Mr. and Mrs. Goertz, and have a lovely evening.

Bob Don hustled me to the entrance like I was a steer straying from the herd, but Gretchen cut us off. She pressed wet, liquor-reeking hands against my chest while Bob Don tried to push from behind. I jerked away from them both. Gretchen slammed the front door shut.

"Don't leave, Jordy. Don't leave," she whispered. Stepping toward me, she looked horrible. I could see now that makeup was smeared across her face, as though she'd tried fixing herself up long after the daily bottle was opened.

"Jordy has to go now, Gretchen," Bob Don insisted, trying to pull me away from her. "Just go out the back, Jordy, and I'll call you tomorrow about that truck you wanted—"

"You are not ... selling him ... any damn car!" Gretchen Goertz screamed. I will never forget that scream as long as I live. It sounded the way you might scream if you were dead and buried for a year, and then God let you have feeling and voice back. Her voice scraped down my spine. Bob Don wasn't pulling me anymore. I was moving on my own accord.

"Quit pretending!" she said, more hoarsely. "Don't you leave this house, you little bastard. Not after all the trouble you've caused me. Don't you walk out, Jordan Poteet," she spat out my name like it was phlegm. "Not after you've ruined my life, you little shit."

I stopped back in the living room. She followed me in. "You're drunk, Mrs. Goertz, so I'm not going to pay heed to anything you say. I suggest you go to bed and get some rest." I steadied my voice. "You're upset and you've upset Bob Don. I don't know what I've done to hurt you, but I won't trouble you further. I'm leaving."

With what dignity I could muster, I turned my back on her and headed for the kitchen. I figured there'd be a back door and I could get out.

"You stay, you stay, you stay," she sobbed at my retreating back. "I'll leave, and you stay."

I paused and heard Bob Don behind me say, "Gretchen, listen—"

"Shut up!" she howled at him. Sobs racked her. "Shut up! He can stay, and I'll leave! That way you'll have some quality time with your precious bastard son!"

I stopped in my tracks in the darkened kitchen, as though her words were glue sticking me to the floor. I heard a body hit the floor and over my shoulder, I saw Gretchen crumpled on the carpet, weeping uncontrollably.

Air felt thick in my throat, as though it was something alien and vaguely threatening. She's drunk, I told myself, and she's deluded. Bob Don collapsed to his knees, cradling Gretchen in his arms. My legs didn't want to respond to the instructions my brain sent, but finally they moved and they didn't head to the back door. I stared down at Bob Don.

"What did she mean by that? Gretchen, you better explain—" I started, but Gretchen wrestled free from Bob Don. She staggered to the other end of the living room into a hallway that presumably led to bedrooms. She turned back to us, her eyes trying to focus.

"Leave here, Bob Don, and take him with you. I changed my mind. I ain't leaving my house. Take your things and your bastard boy with you. I don't ever want to see you again." She fled down the hallway, running along the side. I could hear her body scraping the wall. A door slammed down the hall.

Bob Don stared at the floor. Anger burst out of me, unexpected and reckless.

"Goddamn it, look at me! What the holy hell is going

on here? What's wrong with her? Why is she saying this shit?"

He looked at me, looking older and more tired than I'd ever seen anyone look. "Forgive me, Jordy. God, God, please forgive me."

"Forgive you? It's your wife that's damned crazy." My voice cracked in fear. "What the hell do I have to forgive you for?" He didn't answer and the silence fell hard. I stepped away from him, but not to leave. "You better tell me what's going on here, Bob Don. I want an explanation." My voice was hoarse and shaking.

"I—" he started, and his voice broke in pain. Slowly, he rose to his feet and faced me. "I am your father."

"You're lying," I said when I found my voice. It didn't sound like my voice, but a boy's. My throat felt like ice. "Why are you doing this? Why?"

His eyes met mine and he blinked them clear of his tears. There was a thin line of blood down his cheek where his wife had raked him.

"No, I am not lying to you. I'm your father. I'm sorry, but it's true."

"You're as drunk as your wife, obviously," The ice in my throat moved to my voice. "My father is Lloyd Poteet. And I don't appreciate the slur, against my dead daddy or my mother. I was starting to regard you as a decent person, but you're not. I suggest you and your wife both get professional help. If you like, I'll help you by pouring out all the liquor in your house. And I suggest you bandage up your face 'cause you're bleeding all over yourself. Good night." I turned to leave.

"You can't walk away from me. You just asked for an explanation and goddamn it, you're going to listen to one." He grabbed my arm and shoved me down onto the couch. It stunk of whiskey.

"I'm not staying—" I began, but he pushed me back

down and leaned hard on my arms. I twisted my face away from his.

"Do me the courtesy of listening to me, Jordan Michael Poteet," he hissed, and I sat there, thinking: I am not going to sit here and listen to a bunch of goddamn lies. I tried to move away, but my muscles felt like jelly. I stared into his face.

"Listen to me, please." Bob Don didn't ease the pressure of his hands on my arms but his tone softened. "This isn't pleasant, but it's true. And goddamn it, you're going to hear it from me."

"Well, get your lies over with," I retorted. "I have places to go and people to see."

"I was friends with your mama and your daddy. They were my closest friends. They were damned good to me. But then they had a baby—your sister—and sometimes couples go through a rough time when a child comes along and they're not quite ready for it. I tried to be there for both of them, but I ended mostly on your mama's side in the disagreements. I cared about your mama and she cared about me, and we weren't strong when we were together."

"You're sick! My mother never even looked at you! She loved my father!"

"God, yes, she did. She told me she'd have to go back to him, that she'd have to make it work with him. So she did go back to him, but not without you. I gave her you." He looked hard into my eyes, unwavering.

"Shut up! Don't you talk about my mama like that, you piece of trash!"

He didn't even blink. "Lloyd took her back, and she took him back. He loved you like you were his own, and I don't know that he knew. He must've, though, but he loved you anyway. Anne made me promise I'd stay away from them and away from you. So I met Gretchen right off and married her, to try and heal the pain." He eased up his weight from me and the couch, letting me move, his story told. "And it didn't heal. God, it never healed. I had to sit back and watch you grow up, and never tell you all the things I wanted to say."

I stood, stumbling against the coffee table, rubbing my wrists where he'd squeezed hard. I made my lips stop trembling. "Why are you making this up? What did my folks ever do to you, that you would say such horrible things about them?"

"Your folks," he rasped, "were decent, caring people with just as many flaws and shortcomings as you got. You'd do well to remember that and not keep them on such a high pedestal."

"I suppose you think this is some joke you can play," I said slowly. "Do you just prey on women, Bob Don? You've turned your wife into a drunk and now you're attacking a woman who's got Alzheimer's and can't even answer your slander. Some damned gentleman you are."

"First of all," Bob Don glared, his anger showing, "it breaks my heart that your mama's sick. And second, it is not a damned joke. I didn't view it that way and neither did Beta Harcher."

I didn't want to register that last part. I had to. "What did you say? Beta Harcher?"

"Yes, Beta Harcher. She knew. She knew I was your father."

"Quit saying that!"

"No, Jordy, I don't believe I will. Just because you don't want it to be so doesn't change a blessed thing. God, I've been saving up stuff to say to you for thirty years, so don't you tell me to be quiet!"

Beta Harcher. I shut my eyes and covered my face. The list. Mother of God. Bob Don's quote talked about dividing prey—a damsel or two to every man. Gretchen and my mother, oh my God, I thought. And the quote beside my mother's name, from Genesis: *In sorrow thou shalt bring forth children.* Oh, God, I was a child of sorrow. Of sin.

"If this is true," I whispered, waving a finger at him, "then how would Beta Harcher know about this? How would she have any proof? Where's your proof?"

"When your mother went back to your father, I left Mirabeau for a while. I went to Houston, 'cause it hurt too much to be so near her. So your mother didn't ask me to stay away from you in person. She wrote me letters. I kept them, not to hurt her with later or to try to claim you, but because they mattered to me. To me!" Bob Don pounded his thick chest with his fist. "They were my private possessions. Mine!"

I thought of another letter I'd seen today, belonging to Eula Mae, and I felt suddenly cold.

"I kept the letters from your mama in a lockbox, stored in the attic. Gretchen found them a few years back, but I didn't know. She drinks because she knows that . . . someone else mattered more to me than she does. She's known that for years. She heard me arguing on the phone with Beta; Beta was trying to get me to restart the censorship fight since I'd replaced her on the board. I told her she wasn't going to do anything to hurt you. Gretchen got mad, and she gave the letters to Beta. Gretchen only knows how to torture herself; she ain't good at torturing other folks. I guess she figured that Beta could cause me more grief in town than anyone else." He shook his head. "It was like putting venom in the snake. Beta made my life a living hell."

"I don't believe this," I said to him and to myself. I needed to keep saying it to myself.

"Beta wanted money from me not to show them to

you. I told her to get the hell out of my office, I don't pay money to goddamned blackmailers."

I steadied myself. "This . . . this is what you argued about with her Saturday?"

He nodded, not wondering how I knew about that. "She said if I didn't pay, she'd hurt you and your mama. She said y'all would really pay, if I didn't. But I told her I wasn't gonna pay no damn extortionist."

"But you did," I said faintly. "You paid her $25,000."

Bob Don shook his head. "No, I didn't. I didn't want that bitch having money from me. I saw her the day she died and told her there was no point in keeping the secret."

"No point?"

"Listen to me, Jordy. Listen good. This is the truth. Just think about it. Lloyd—your daddy that raised you—is dead. He was a fine man, but he's gone. Your mama's sick. She needs us both. She can't object to us having a relationship. My marriage with Gretchen has run its course. And you've come home to Mirabeau. There's no reason you and I can't have a relationship as father and son now, like I've prayed for, like I've always wanted—"

"What?" I whispered. "You can't be serious. You lay this on me, with no proof, and want me to hug you and call you Dad? I don't think so, Bob Don." I was shaking and something was on my face. The back of my hand told me they were tears. "I mean, what do you even know about me? What do I know about you?"

"I know a lot about you," Bob Don answered, his voice softening like he was speaking to a frightened child. "Your Little League number was seventeen, and you liked to play shortstop. You hit your first home run on June 13, 1975, a little late but it still counts. You hated math from first grade on, and you never liked to study it. Your first girlfriend was a little redhead in the third grade and her name was Leslie Minter. The other boys teased you for being sweet on her but you paid them no heed. You got 1210 on your SATs. Your GPA at Rice was 3.4, and it would've been higher except you didn't do good in economics—you hated it and didn't want to study it, just like math. Just like your mama, you only wanted to work at what you like." He paused and took a step toward me. "But I don't know if you're a happy person, Jordy. I don't know if you've ever really been in love. I don't know what you want from your life—"

"Just shut up!" I said. "Just be quiet a minute, please." I felt sick and dizzy and angry and betrayed. How did he know all that? Was he watching me my whole life, some distant shadow that followed me wherever I went? A lie. My whole life was a fat, ugly lie.

"Okay, you need time. This is a shock, I understand that, Jordy." He wiped the drying blood from his cheek where his wife had scored him. "And proof. I don't have that, Beta does. Or did. She had the letters."

"Oh, God," I swayed. Shannon, lying shot amidst the wreckage of Beta's living room. "You didn't. Tell me you didn't—"

"Didn't what?"

"Someone tore apart Beta's house today. They shot her niece. In the face. She may not live." I stared at this man who'd destroyed my world. "Did you do that? Did you kill Beta to keep her from talking and then shoot Shannon when you were looking for those letters? Just what would you have done to get your proof back, Bob Don?"

"I didn't. I didn't hurt anybody, Jordy!" he exclaimed. "I didn't!"

"I hope you didn't," I said. "I'm not worth killing over, I'm not, I'm not." It was too much, too much said in this room in the past few minutes and too much unsaid the thirty years before. I ran from the room, I ran from the house, hardly hearing Bob Don Goertz calling after me.

Emotional autopilot steered me away from home. I couldn't even look at Mama. I couldn't ask her if Bob Don was telling the truth and I couldn't stand the thought of seeing her without asking. How do you ask? "Gosh, Mama, this fellow claims I'm his son. Any truth to that?" Asking Mama anything was as futile as getting a running start to jump across the Colorado.

Instinct brought me to the library, where a light still shone inside. The door was locked and the CLOSED sign was up, but I managed to jab my key in the lock and practically fall into the building. I got up, locked the door behind me, and staggered to the checkout counter. Candace was still there, gluing date-due slips into new books.

She paled when she saw my face. I tottered, taking deep, hard breaths, trying to get my emotions under control. I failed. I cried in front of her, I cried like a baby, and she came to me, wrapping me in her arms, letting my face dampen her shoulder.

When that was over, I turned away from her, suddenly and deeply ashamed. I'd never wept in front of a woman. The last time I'd cried was when Sister broke the news to me over the phone that the doctors were pretty sure Mama had Alzheimer's. I'd been alone with my grief, as most men prefer to be. I guess I could have driven down to the river that night, or into the woods, but I needed company. I needed Candace. I brokenly told her what had happened at Bob Don's.

She steered me to the couch by the coffee table where we kept the daily newspapers. "You don't have any proof this is true, Jordy," she said softly.

"Then why would he make up such a lie? What's his reason for telling me this?"

"Okay," she said softly. "Maybe he did love your mother. But maybe you're not his, and he always wished that you were."

"Do I even look like Bob Don, Candace?"

"No," she admitted. "Your looks are your mother's. But your daddy wasn't a big man, and you are." She studied my face, as though seeing it for the first time. "Listen, Jordy, looking at profiles isn't going to resolve this. You need to find those letters he says Beta took."

"I know." I thought of Beta's living room. "Maybe the person who shot Shannon, when they were looking for whatever they were, maybe they found the letters and took them—"

"Or maybe they're still in her house," Candace added. "Hidden there somewhere. Or maybe, someone else has them now and has destroyed them. To keep Beta's mischief from hurting anyone else."

"I have to find those letters," I muttered to myself. "God, it's even more important now to find who killed Beta." I shook my head. "Beta, goddamn her! She was going to blackmail Bob Don and maybe even my mother. That must've been why she checked out that book on Alzheimer's. Maybe she wanted to figure out how advanced Mama's condition was and what she could get out of Mama to keep quiet. To fund that damned church of hers."

"Listen, Jordy. I know you're horribly upset right now. But you need to think straight. You need those letters, but they could also be evidence in a murder trial. You need to call Junebug, call your uncle Bid—"

"No way," I interrupted. "I don't want anyone to know about this who doesn't have to. For God's sake, you think I want it going around Mirabeau that Mama might've had an affair? That I'm Bob Don's bastard? And tell Uncle Bid, no thanks, he already hates my guts."

"Maybe you know why now," Candace said softly.

I thought about it. The years of dislike Bid had shown me, the utter disinterest in his sister-in-law, the warning he'd given me in Mama's kitchen to stay away from that lying Bob Don. Maybe Uncle Bid already knew about this. The only bright spot was that if Bob Don was telling the truth, I was no blood kin to Bidwell J. Poteet. There was a silver lining, after all.

I put my face in my hands. "You know, I always prided myself on being strong. On not letting the rough stuff in life get me down. Right now I feel as weak as a hundred-year-old man."

"You are strong, Jordy, you are." Candace rubbed my shoulder. "You're the strongest man I know. You gave up your career, your independence to come home to help your family. I couldn't be so brave."

"My family," I snorted. "I'm not even sure who my family is." Hot anger flashed in me as I thought of my sacrifices. "Damn her, Candace! I gave up my life, my career, to take care of that woman, and what if she never bothered to tell me the truth about who I am? How could they do that to me?" I thought of my father, Lloyd Poteet. Of his love, his kindness to me, his pride in my accomplishments, his gentle hands on my shoulders, letting me know he was there for me. Had he known? If he had, I marveled at the depth of his unconditional love. Not every man would have so willingly raised another's child as his own. I missed him fiercely.

"Jordy, please, quit beating yourself up over this."

"And if it's true, Beta Harcher knew?" I didn't listen to Candace. "Let's face it, that witch was my worst enemy. That she knew, and I didn't! God, that makes me sick!"

"Jordy!" Candace snapped. "Shut up for a minute

and listen to me. Quit wallowing in self-pity. It's just not like you."

I shut up.

"I'm going to tell you a bit of wisdom here, babe," Candace brought her face close to mine and her voice fell to a whisper. "Do me the courtesy of not interrupting. It really doesn't matter if you're a Poteet or a Goertz or if you're sired by a man from Mars. What matters is the kind of person that you are, you sweet little idiot. You're a good person. Now Lloyd Poteet raised you and loved you. Even if he didn't make you, that doesn't mean he's not your daddy for all intents and purposes. It just doesn't matter."

It did matter, but I stayed quiet till I sensed she was done speaking. I laughed bitterly. "Southerners are always so concerned about the families they come from. My friends up North used to tease me about being one of the Poteets of Mirabeau because I made such a big deal about my family. And now I don't even know who I am anymore." I sagged against the couch. "I feel like a nobody."

"You are somebody," Candace whispered, and she kissed me. Her mouth didn't taste of chocolate like Ruth Wills's, but the kiss was far sweeter. I lost myself in her. I vaguely remembered my arm going around her shoulders, her fingers locking in my hair, passion and heat rising between us like close campfires. Her fingertips traced delicious patterns on my face, my chest, my stomach. Wanting her burned away the old miasma of death that Beta Harcher had left on the library. And as we made love, shuddering together on that old couch, the deepest part of myself came through, telling me that Jordy Poteet was still alive.

CHAPTER FOURTEEN

I WASN'T ABOUT TO CASTIGATE HALF MY FAMily tree for all the lying that they might've done to me over my lifetime and then lie to Candace. Especially not after making love. I don't imagine either of us had thought we'd consummate our relationship, if we ever had one, on the library couch where Old Man Renfro read the Houston papers every morning. So, with Candace lying against me, her warm back against my chest, I told her about Ruth's advances to me, and her request that I meet her later this evening.

"Are you going?" Candace asked, looking at the floor as though there was an object of monumental interest on the carpet.

"No, I don't believe so," I said, stroking Candace's hair. "I'm not going to pretend that Ruth isn't sexy, but she's not real attractive to me. You know the difference."

"I wonder what she meant, though. Saying she could help you be sure that your mama was never in a home."

I rolled my eyes. "Probably just a coy lure to get me over there. I am, of course, above such common ploys."

"Maybe she was going to offer you money for your services." Candace giggled, now that Ruth was swept under the rug. "She certainly seems to do well for a nurse in a small town."

"Doesn't she, though? Nice jewelry, new Miata."

"Kept woman," Candace guessed. "She'd fit the bill."

"Kept by whom?" I said, kissing her ear. "Maybe that's an angle we haven't considered."

Candace considered. "There's any number of candidates in town, but that'd be a damned hard secret to keep."

"I'm starting to think that adage about no secrets in a small town is a load of crap," I answered. "We seem to be unearthing them left and right."

"Adam Hufnagel," Candace said. "That'd be my guess. He's smooth but sometimes I swear he's got his mind elsewhere. Like maybe on a sweet young thang for a mistress."

"Your ability to see scandal everywhere," I laughed, hugging her, "is one of your most attractive traits." I hadn't expected to smile or laugh anytime soon, considering the past two hours. Candace was good for me.

"You're smiling," she said, glancing up at me.

"You put it there."

It was she who smiled this time. "Look, about Bob Don—"

"Honey, if I dwell on that I'm going to go crazy. I have to deal with it, no doubt. But I want to finish what I started. I want to find out who killed Beta and shot Shannon. I want the suffering that crazy bitch caused people to stop. And I want to find those letters." I paused. "Anyhow, if Ruth is a kept woman, how could she say she'd help me? That would only work if the money was hers. I don't think her lover would take too kindly to underwriting her affairs."

"I don't think you should pursue this anymore, Jordy," Candace said carefully, turning in my arms to face me. She snuggled to me, kissing my cheek with small nibbles. It felt so good I held my breath. "You've gone through enough in the past few days. Just tell Junebug what you've learned and let him do it."

"No," I said. "I'm not going to have Mama's possible indiscretions broadcast around town as part of a murder investigation. I already know that Beta blackmailed Eula Mae and tried to blackmail Bob Don and might've tried to get money out of my mother, if she thought she could. That list of Beta's must be a blackmail list, some way she thought she was going to get money out of folks for their sins so she could build her damned Holy-Roller church. I still don't believe that Eula Mae could've killed her. I can't let her rot in jail."

"So what was she trying to blackmail folks over? Aside from those rather vague quotes, you don't have a clue."

"No, there's more." I reminded Candace about the books Beta had checked out and Shannon had returned to me. "She got that book on video technology and on a trip she's on with Hally Schneider, his camcorder disappears. She had a book on book publishing and she'd squeezed ten grand out of Eula Mae. She'd gotten a book on Alzheimer's, maybe to bone up on whether my mother could remember enough of her past to be blackmailed."

"There's that book on drugs," Candace said.

"Yes, there is, isn't there? And I didn't mention this before, but Matt Blalock had been smoking a joint when I went out to see him. I'm wondering if there's a connection between that drug-abuse book and Matt being on her list."

"Big whoop," Candace huffed. "Everybody knows those guys in Vietnam tried it. I don't think that would terribly surprise anyone that Matt might smoke marijuana." She eyed me. "You don't do that, do you?"

"Not anymore," I said. "I tried it in college once, but I'd rather smoke tobacco."

"I wonder. Maybe Hally's the one doing the drugs. You hear about how bad it is in the high schools."

"Maybe, but Hally really doesn't seem to be into that. I don't think he could sneak it too easily around his Stepford battle-ax mother."

"Gaston said Beta's car was out late at night by the Blalocks' last week," Candace said.

I stood. "Wait a minute. Let's say she was out there sneaking around, 'cause she suspected drug-type activities were going on at Matt's. What would you wear?"

"I don't know what DEA agents currently find fashionable," Candace sniffed.

"Maybe black? I'll bet that old toot was out sneaking on their farm at night, dressed in black so she couldn't be seen. And out back on Matt's farm, the overgrowth is as dense as the day Mirabeau was founded. Perfect to hide a marijuana crop. It might stay muddy back there, even if we hadn't had rain for a few days. Remember that tarry-black mud on Beta's shoes?"

Candace licked her lips. "I think you might have a point. Call Junebug and tell him about it."

"He couldn't do anything. We don't have a shred of proof." I pulled on my pants and fumbled in my pockets for my keys. "I think I should go out there and take a look."

"If Matt Blalock's growing pot in the forest, there's no need for you to go stomping around out there," Candace insisted.

"If Bob Don's telling the truth, he didn't give Beta a cent. Now there's $25,000 in Beta's account that she got recently. If I can find who else paid off Beta, I can kill me several birds with one stone. I can maybe get suspicion off Eula Mae, find out if Bob Don is remotely telling the truth, and maybe see who might have torn apart Beta's house and shot Shannon." I jingled my keys. "Now I'm going out there and see if ol' Matt had anything worth being blackmailed over."

"Fine. I'm coming with you." Candace stood.

"No, you're not. It might be dangerous."

"I am too coming with you."

"No, you're not."

Candace and I were obviously on the accelerated course for relationships. We'd made love and had our first fight in pert' near record time. And guess who won?

Candace insisted that we eat before going out to the Blalock property. It was close to nine and I desultorily ate a cheeseburger and fries at the Dairy Queen. Candace picked at a basket of chicken fingers, Texas toast, and peppered cream gravy. We sat on the same side of the booth (sure to fuel gossip) and when I pushed my food away, Candace took my hand.

"I expected you to have more of an appetite, Jordy." She smiled.

"Sorry, I just—"

"Hey, Mr. Poteet. How you?" One of the high-school boys who I'd helped in the library once in researching a paper passed by, cleaning off the next table.

"Fine, Mike. How are you?"

"Fair to middlin'." He finished bussing the table and moved on.

"Mr. Poteet," I said. "Notice I didn't correct that young man. I'll just have to get those letters and get Bob Don to give me a little blood for a test. Gretchen had already bloodied him, so maybe I should have just asked him for some then."

"Don't sound bitter. We're going to find out the truth."

I slapped my head. "God, I haven't called Sister. I haven't told them where I am."

Candace fished a quarter from her purse. "Take my advice, you're in no shape to chat with them right now. Let me." I did. She came back from the pay phone with a faint smile. "Your nephew is holding down the fort. I made up a story that we had to stay late at the library to catch up on work from being closed."

"Thanks." I squeezed her hands and she squeezed back. I looked down at the ruins of my hamburger. "I don't have much stomach for this. Let's go."

We made a quick stop at Candace's for her to change into a dark sweatshirt, jeans, and sneakers. I was already in a chambray shirt, jeans, and boots, so I figured I was camouflaged enough. She came back to the truck quickly, with a heavy dark flashlight in her hand. I hadn't even thought that far ahead. I was glad she was being the brains; mine felt too fried.

She modeled her black sneakers for me. They were expensive looking and I'm sure would make Candace look like a badass on the aerobics floor.

"Aren't they cute?" she said. "I got 'em for the ladies' soccer league over in Bavary."

"Charming," I murmured. "Just what every aspiring Nancy Drew needs."

She huffed and handed me an old dark windbreaker and an Astros baseball cap, dark navy with an orange *A* stitched in the middle. "Cover up that blond hair of yours, smarty." I bowed and pulled the cap low on my head.

The drive out to the farm-to-market road that eventually curved away from Mirabeau and into the east side of Bavary was brief and uneventful. The night hung above us, heavy with clouds. The moon peeked through occasionally, like a flirtatious girl. I could hardly see any stars and I wanted to. My daddy had always told me wishes on stars were the best kind to make.

I parked the Blazer far off the road, on the side opposite the Blalock property. We shut the door softly, both of us suddenly aware of how far sound travelled in the hush of night. Crickets chirped busily, as though gossiping about our errand. The air felt cool; the heat of spring had temporarily fled. I shivered in the navy windbreaker, walked around to the passenger side of the Blazer, and hugged Candace close.

"We'll have to be very quiet," I told her. "No talking. Let me have the flashlight and stick close to me." She nodded and took my hand. Her palm felt good against mine. We dashed across a weed-eaten field, across the farm-to-market road, and then began our careers as trespassers.

We crept into the deepening gloom of the overgrowth. I kept the spot of light moving low on the ground. Shadows blurred together as trees grew closer. In this part of Texas we have trees called lost pines, and there were a lot of them to be found in these woods. They're called lost because you have to get farther east, toward Arkansas and Louisiana to hit real heavy Texas pine forests. These pines had gotten separated from their eastern brothers and taken root here. The idea of wandering trees made me think of the last scene of *Macbeth*, unluckiest of plays. Thin and soaring, the lost pines bunched around us, forming nature's own maze. My shoulders kept bumping against their trunks, and I could feel an occasional needle fall against me.

We wandered for at least thirty minutes, moving in a widening circle. I didn't know the legal boundaries of the Blalock property but I was willing to guess that we'd crossed them long ago. We didn't speak. I kept playing the light across the needle-strewn dirt and Candace kept her fingers dug into my belt, freeing my hands.

I played the light a little higher and she saw them before I did, silently guiding my arm back to where I'd shined the light. Fronds of five, poking up in fairly even rows. There were a lot of rows; a lot of money. I bit my lip, thinking.

"Those are pot plants!" Candace whispered in my ear. She disengaged her fingers from my belt. "What should we do now? We've got some proof; let's get the hell out and call Junebug."

"Let me think a second," I mumbled back. I played the light a little higher, above the fronds, and that's when I saw it. A small box, fastened to a tree not four feet away from us. My arm lashed out and I grabbed Candace in an iron grip.

"Don't move," I said in a normal tone of voice. "Booby trap."

She froze like Lot's wife. Her arm muscles bunched and tensed under my fingers. Slowly and deliberately, I played the light directly around our feet. About three inches from Candace's left foot there was a wire. I kept the light on it and squeezed her arm twice.

"Jordy—" she hissed.

"That's the trigger, by your foot. I'll move first, okay? I'm going to step to your right, then I want you to follow me exactly. Exactly, Candace. Do you understand?"

I sensed her nod in the darkness.

"You don't step where I haven't already stepped. You hit a wire and those boxes blow buckshot in your face. They blow off your head. You understand me?"

"Yes." Her voice was frightened but steady.

"Okay. I'm moving now." I pressed the light down on the ground, shuffling my feet slowly to her right. I put my back to her and she looped fingers in my belt again. Keeping the light tightly focused on the dark earth, I moved forward, away from the wire. Candace stuck to me like ugly on an ape. God only knew how many other wires we might have passed by. I didn't think we could have made it unawares passing many; no one's luck was that strong. If they'd strung wires higher than our feet we would have hit them, but from what I'd heard about such traps I didn't think it likely they were strung that way. We shuffled along for several minutes at an agonizingly slow pace. Every movement made me wonder if hot lead would pepper our bodies. The clouds parted and the moon glanced through, casting a little more light through the arching pines. We'd gotten a fair distance away and I felt Candace sag against me.

"Are we clear of them?" she breathed.

"I'm not sure. We'll take it slow for a while longer." We scraped our shoes along.

We hadn't gone too much farther when Candace gave a gasp and, reaching around me, snapped off the flashlight. I didn't make a noise and I whirled. Two other lights fanned through the trees, searching, less than thirty feet away. My heart, exercised enough over the course of this unforgettable evening, jumped back into my mouth, where it felt right at home.

"Here's their track!" a course male voice hissed in darkness. His light played along where we'd been dragging our feet, trenching out a nice little path in the forest for homicidal drug dealers to follow. I seized Candace's arm and ran, tearing through the brush. If we didn't move, they'd track us easy. I'd rather risk hitting a wire than begging for my life from a pot harvester.

Bullets whined above our heads and Candace yelped.

I didn't think she was hit 'cause she started running
harder than me. You just don't know the adrenal surge
you get when someone's shooting at you. I couldn't
imagine the high was any less than what you got from
the plants these folks guarded. Another bullet thundered
and bark exploded from a trunk a few feet left of my
head. I yanked Candace to the right and barreled into
the bushes. We ran for several more feet, and then hunkered down. She pressed her face against my back, not
wanting to look up.

I heard footsteps running along past us, and I kept as
still as stone. The moon flirted again, hiding behind one
of the long, thready clouds that streaked the night sky.
I cursed myself for my stupidity. I should have brought
a gun, I shouldn't have brought Candace, I shouldn't
have come up here myself. My own stubbornness might
get us killed. Candace's fingers twined with mine in
the silence and the darkness. We crouched there in the
bushes, letting minutes pass.

I heard footsteps coming back along the forest floor,
and I risked a peek through the foliage. I saw a dark
form striding along, a shotgun nestled under one arm.
Faint moonlight gave a profile I knew. Hair pulled back,
high cheekbones, confident body. The eyes I couldn't
see, but I had looked into them enough to know they
were intelligent and catlike. Ruth Wills.

I held my breath as she passed within ten feet of us.
Candace kept her eyes buried in the side of her arm.
Ruth went by and I heard a man's voice, unfamiliar and
tinged with a Spanish accent, call to her in the distance.
I didn't hear her answer.

I hunkered back down and counted to two hundred. I
wasn't sure it was enough, but I wanted the hell out of
there. Slowly, Candace and I crept along the forest
floor, not using the flashlight, stopping in the pitch

blackness and waiting for the moon to be kind and dimly light our way. Eventually the forest spat us out on a stretch of the farm-to-market road. I got my bearings and figured we were about a mile from the car. We hiked back, keeping a ways off the road, without flashlight. One pickup passed and we hid in a ditch, waiting for the truck to disgorge Jamaicans with Uzis. The truck whizzed past, only tossing out a Clint Black tune from a cranked radio.

We made it back to the Blazer. The tires weren't slashed and no one lay in wait for us. We got in the car, I started the engine with a minimum of noise and, keeping the lights out, shot down the road.

"God in Heaven!" Candace yelled at the top of her lungs. Apparently I hadn't heard her entire decibel range. "We could have gotten killed! Jesus Christ, Jordy!"

"Okay, so now we have proof," I said placatingly. "Assuming they don't torch the crop and clear out because they think someone's onto them. They might've thought we were just deer."

"Deer don't drag their feet for half an acre, babe. They saw our tracks," she fumed.

"Okay. Here's the plan. I'll drop you at home, and you go straight to bed. I will go and call Junebug and—"

"No, Jordy, here's the plan. We go straight to the police station, right this minute. And we tell Junebug everything, damn it! Everything!"

I, unfortunately for Candace, still had control of the steering wheel. I pulled up a few minutes later in front of her house.

"To the station!" she barked.

"Can I use your phone?" I asked sweetly.

Since the phone was already closer, I won. Candace

stood there while I called the police station. Junebug was at home, but I got his deputy. I explained what had happened and he told me to stay put, and he and Junebug would be over shortly. I hung up quickly so I couldn't claim I'd heard him.

"They'll be over shortly," I informed Candace.

"Fine. I look a wreck." Candace stormed off to the bathroom. She shut the door and I bolted, easing her front door shut behind me. I had decided to keep my appointment with Ruth. I wanted to see if she'd show up.

I was late and so was she. I made sure that I cleaned off any pine needles from my person. I was certain she hadn't seen me, but I didn't want to give her any clues as to where I'd been spending my evening.

I parked in front of Ruth's modest little home and she wheeled into her driveway a few minutes later. She pulled herself out of the Miata, dirty in jeans and a black windbreaker. I saw her glance at her watch, then wiggle fingers at me. I wondered if those fingers had pulled the trigger that had nearly blasted my head off. I steadied my nerves and my anger and put a smile on my face. Mama always said to smile in adversity, and I was grinning from ear to ear.

"I'm a wreck," she purred, not too differently from Candace. "Sorry I'm late, come on in." She unlocked her door and I followed her into her den.

Contemporary, Danish-style furniture decorated her home. Travel posters of faraway places covered the walls: Prague, London, Beijing, Calcutta. I didn't see Peru represented but maybe she didn't want to advertise the competition. She stopped and I nearly bumped into her. She turned into my arms and kissed me hard. I forced myself to respond, but even as beautiful as she was, I'd rather have bit into an overripe lemon.

"I could use a shower," she murmured against my throat. "How about joining me?"

"Business first, sweetheart," I said cordially, pulling her arms from my shoulders. "I believe you have a proposition for me?"

"Business before pleasure," she laughed. "I like that in a man."

"I need to get back home, Ruth, and I don't like to beat around the bushes." No, I preferred running through them to avoid getting shot. I swallowed. "You didn't ask me to come over here for just a roll in the hay, did you?"

"No. What's your financial situation, Jordy dearest?"

"I'm totally broke."

"Really?" She stared into my eyes.

"I'm sure everyone thinks I'm keeping Mama at home out of nobility. It started that way, but now it's necessity. I don't have the money to put her in a decent place and I doubt I ever will on a librarian's salary." I leaned down and kissed her roughly. She responded and I broke the embrace. "So what's this proposition? You going to show me the pot of gold or you just gonna share a winning lottery ticket?"

Her lovely, lying face studied mine for a long while. I made myself think of how little money I actually had left. I hoped I looked a little amoral and desperate. Considering my position, I probably put on a good show.

I wasn't found wanting on whatever internal scale she used. "I need you, Jordy. The same way I need Matt. He was in dire straits, too, you know. His family's farm sure wasn't paying for itself and his computer work wasn't steady enough to help."

"Matt? I don't understand," I lied. "What does he have to do with this?"

"You were there when he was smoking some dope, and you didn't blab on him to your buddy the chief of police. Why?"

"Matt talks to you, obviously." I smiled and made myself ruffle her hair. "I figured what Matt does is his own business. Not mine. Anyway, drugs aren't such a big deal. I knew plenty of folks who did coke and such up in Boston. Pot was a little too pedestrian for them."

"It's not too pedestrian for the simple, hearty folks of Bonaparte County." She laughed. "It's a booming business." She watched my face, and I inched up one corner of my mouth in a half-smile.

"I'm glad to hear business is good. The local economy needs a boost. And so does my own pocketbook."

"Good," she said. "Here's the deal. I run the operation. You take orders from me. I hope being something of a good ol' boy, you don't have a problem with that."

"No, ma'am," I drawled.

"Matt Blalock provides the land and two of the vets from his support group farm it and distribute it. Actually, you're already somewhat involved—they've been using their support group meetings for a distribution time for several months now."

Blood rushed to my face and she saw it. Using my library for this? "I—I'm surprised," I heard myself say.

She shrugged. "We're careful. I've got plots scattered all over Bonaparte and Bastrop counties. We mostly sell into Austin, but we're selling more here, too. I thought you might help us, since so many young folks use the library for school papers and such. You'd be a good contact for them."

I made myself smile. "Get a joint with their Joyce?"

"That's the idea. You catch on fast, Jordy. I knew you'd be a natural at this."

I tried not to bristle at the compliment. "Just how secure is this operation? Aren't you worried about getting caught?"

"We move the planting sites around. We protect them with booby traps . . ."

"So if someone stumbles across your crop and gets killed, you don't get the cops coming in," I said dryly.

"We can move quickly, if we have to. I've done this for quite a while, Jordy." She sat on the couch. "And we've got a friend in a high place."

I thought, and the answer came to me in inspiration. "Let me guess. Reverend Hufnagel."

It was her turn to be surprised. I shrugged, as though my deduction was no big deal. "I saw him and Matt talking. Brother Adam claimed Matt wanted the church for a vets' meeting. I just didn't quite buy it." I didn't mention my trick phone call to Matt where he'd said there was no vets' meeting for the week.

"Well, cancer and chemotherapy's one of our best business references." Ruth laughed. God, she was cruel. I wanted to wipe her kiss from my mouth. "Poor Reverend Hufnagel's chemo last year was real hard on his body. I was his nurse. His pain got so bad I kidded him about trying pot to relieve it and he took me up on it. You could have knocked me over with a straw, but he was dead serious. He's a real weakling about pain." I couldn't imagine the agony of chemotherapy and didn't particularly want to try. "He developed a quick liking for it. Of course, he couldn't let anyone know; he'd lose his church. So now, he just hooks up with Matt every few nights and smokes a joint before bed. I don't think that priss-assed little wife of his knows."

I sat down next to her, quietly. "Beta put you on her

list of sinners. 'There is death in the pot.' I thought her quote for you was about when she thought you tried to poison her. I see now the operative word there was *pot*."

"Just a coincidence," Ruth said easily.

"I don't think so, Ruth. She was all in black when she was killed, and there was a lot of mud on her shoes. I'm thinking she was out traipsing around in the dark somewhere, maybe checking out one of your little secret plantations. Maybe she got some proof on you and Matt." I paused. "Maybe you killed her, and then shot Shannon when you were trying to find that evidence."

Ruth frowned. "I offer you a business proposition and you accuse me of murder. And here I thought you were a gentleman." She stood, went into the kitchen, and poured herself some water. "I didn't have anything to do with Beta's death or Shannon's shooting. Beta didn't know anything about my sideline. When she was in the hospital, I just pretended I was going to poison her to scare her. I knew no one'd believe her, and I wasn't going to hurt her. I just wanted to put the fear of God in the old girl."

"Your professional ethics are charming." I smiled.

She took it as humor, not as an insult. "So are you in?"

"You've told me a lot; do I even have a choice?"

"Sure you do. If you don't want in, just keep your mouth shut. I mean, you wouldn't want anything to happen to that sweet mama of yours, would you? Or maybe your sister, or her boy?"

"I'm in," I lied easily enough. "As long as you had nothing to do with Beta's murder. I want no part of that."

"I didn't kill her. Matt and Reverend Hufnagel, them I don't know about." She put down her water glass and came to me, wrapping her windbreakered arms around

me. "How about we seal the contract the right way?"
She kissed me, hard and demanding.

"Is this how you conduct all your negotiations?" I
asked a moment later.

"Yes," she smiled. "Even with our friend Matt. Of
course he had certain limitations, but I do admire initiative and enthusiasm."

"I can tell." I pulled away from her. "We'll seal our
deal later—when we've agreed on my percentage. Shall
I call you tomorrow?"

"I don't like being turned down twice, Jordy," she
snapped. An unpleasant gleam showed in her eyes.

"Not turned down—just delayed. I have to get back
home, or they'll think something's wrong. You don't
want me attracting undue attention, do you?"

Sense made her relent. "All right. I'm working the
day shift, but I'll be off at three."

I told her I'd call her then. I stumbled out into the
night to my car. I felt dirtier than after I'd run through
the brambles. I took a long, hard drink of air and started
the engine. I was about halfway down the long street
she lived on when a Mirabeau police car shot past me.
I saw it slow in front of her house.

I had the strongest feeling that Junebug'd paid a visit
to Matt Blalock and he'd turned in his boss. I wondered
if Ruth would look as good in Bonaparte County Jail
orange as she did in hospital white.

CHAPTER FIFTEEN

BETA HARCHER'S HOUSE STOOD DARK AND foreboding in the faint moonlight. I tried not to think of it as the scene of bitter blackmail, attempted murder, or even as the lair of the woman who should have been voted Most Likely to Cause Suffering. I just tried to think of it as a house I needed to break into.

I'd thought that if Junebug had indeed descended on Matt Blalock's farm (and not to do so immediately wouldn't be politically advantageous—most citizenry didn't view drug crimes favorably), he'd gone in with force. Quite possibly there was no longer a guard at Beta's home. There wasn't.

I parked several houses down and checked the flashlight Candace had left in my car. I tried to walk nonchalantly down the street at this late hour, but no one really ambles in Mirabeau past eleven at night if they're not staggering home drunk. I gave it up and jogged over to the back of Beta's house. Like I said before, most yards in town don't have fences, and Beta's backyard tumbled down to the shores of the Colorado. I snuck around to the back, keeping an eye on the neighboring homes. They stayed dark in slumber.

The back door was still locked, and so were all the windows I tried. The window that Shannon's attacker broke in through was efficiently boarded shut. I

weighed the choices in my mind. I needed those letters
Mama had written Bob Don. After an evening of having
a near stranger claim paternity of me, getting shot at,
and being offered gainful employment by our local drug
czarina, a little breaking and entering seemed mild. If I
got in trouble, I got in trouble, and I'd explain it to
Junebug later.

I wrapped my dark windbreaker around my hand.
Popping out a pane of glass in Beta's back door
sounded deafening, but there was no neighborhood call
to arms. Maybe the constant murmur of the river inured
the folks to sound. I slipped inside.

I kept the flashlight off and eased to the front windows. The drapes had been closed. Good. I didn't want
anyone to see my light. I made a quick pass upstairs,
just in case there was a room labeled HERE'S WHAT
YOU'RE LOOKING FOR. No such luck. There was a small
bedroom, a dusty guest bedroom that smelled stalely of
disuse, and another smaller bedroom with Shannon's
luggage still sitting in it. The poor girl hadn't even had
a chance to unpack.

I went back downstairs to the den. The police hadn't
tidied up after Shannon's attacker. Books and broken
bric-a-brac covered the floor. My light played along the
carpet and found a stain of gore. Shannon's blood. I reminded myself I was dealing with someone who had
few compunctions about killing.

I played the light along the room and it caught the
Bible that Junebug had pulled Patty Quiff's yellowing
letter from. I remembered he'd opened the Bible to the
letter, then set the Good Book on the side table. I examined the Bible; it was open at the Book of Job, who
could have only suffered more if he'd lived in Mirabeau
and gotten on Beta's bad side. Eula Mae's quote, about
your enemy writing a book, came from Job. I straight-

ened up and cast the beam across the other shelves and the floor. Lots and lots of Bibles, some still on the uppermost shelf.

I dragged a chair over to the big built-in bookshelf and climbed on it. I opened one, and let the pages flip past my thumb until I got to a piece of paper that wasn't covered with holy scripture. The book of Isaiah, where my quote had come from. I turned the light on the page.

A picture of me stared back at me. It was a photo that'd been on the front page of the local newspaper, *The Mirabeau Mirror*, when I'd gotten the librarian job. That'd been the biggest civic news in town that week. In the picture I looked a little startled, as though getting the library job was an honor I hadn't expected. Across the picture of my face, written in heavy red ink, were the words: FIRE PURIFIES. My throat felt thick and I swallowed. I wondered for one moment if the library had been her only intended target for arson; maybe she'd have burned my house down, with me and my family inside, and hummed a little hymn for our sinning souls. I dropped the Bible and the newspaper clipping on the floor.

The next two Bibles apparently weren't being used in Beta's odd filing system. The third one I checked fell open at the beginning, in the book of Genesis. Mama's quote about bearing children in sorrow came from there. I let the Bible fall noisily to the floor and pulled three letters, yellowed and crackling with age, out of a small manila envelope.

Mama had loved the man she wrote them to, and she'd written them to Bob Don Goertz. I tried to remember to breathe as I read through them. Mama had always been sentimental to a point, but I'd never heard her speak to Daddy with such tender emotion. For her privacy I won't record them here. But the last one was the hardest to read, because she asked Bob Don to stay out of her life and her unborn baby's. She begged him, if she loved her and their child, to follow her wishes. She could not hurt Lloyd—she loved him, too—and there was little Arlene to consider. I read the last one through three times.

I switched off the flashlight and leaned against the dusty bookshelf. "Oh, Mama," I finally said. "Why didn't you ever tell me? I should have heard this from you." I put the letters in my jacket pocket, feeling cold anger that Beta Harcher had touched them, read them, kept them here to hurt me and my mother. I tried to think about Bob Don but he just appeared in my mind as sort of a shapeless blob that I couldn't picture as my father.

I was putting back the Bible that contained Mama's letters when some paper slipped out the back. A photo, and another letter. I stared at that photo a long while, feeling cold in my veins. A much younger Uncle Bid and Beta Harcher smiled at me from the picture, looking merry under a Ferris wheel. The letter was to Beta from a woman whose name I didn't recognize and mentioned Uncle Bid's name. The postmark was from Norway. I put the letter and the photo with Mama's letters.

Some Bibles remained and I flipped through the rest of them. They were empty except for one notable exception. I guess Beta felt she had holy words to spare, because she'd scooped out most of them from this particular volume. The pages had been cut away, so you could hide something in the closed Bible. The something there was a videotape. According to Gaston, Hally Schneider had a camcorder stolen on a trip Beta chaperoned. She'd checked out a book on how to operate a camcorder. If my guess was right, the proof Beta had gotten on Matt and Ruth's drug operation was on this tape. I tapped the tape against my forehead, thinking, and let the scarred Bible tumble to the floor. I tucked the cassette into my jacket, deciding I needed to get to the nearest VCR possible and see this tape.

I snuck back out of the house into the cool spring night. Clouds hid the stars now and the breeze was brisk, strong with the woody scent of river. I eased around the corner of Beta's house, glad that the moonlight seemed to be gone. I was about halfway across her yard when a twig snapped and I froze. I glanced around, didn't see anything, didn't hear anything. Probably a raccoon, I told myself. I ran on to the car and headed home.

The den lights blazed when I opened the front door, even though it was near midnight. Mark and Mama sat watching a talk show. I found it real hard to look at Mama, but I made myself. She stared at the TV screen, not laughing at the jokes. Somewhere in that muddled mass of neurons that was her brain, there were memories of Bob Don and the truth she'd never bothered to tell me. I felt incredibly angry with her, but I knew chewing her out would do only me good. Not the time or the place. I swallowed the fury I felt and let it start to burn an ulcer in my gut.

Mark bolted up from the couch. Now he didn't look like a wisecracking thirteen-year-old, but more like a worried little boy. "Have you heard anything about Shannon?"

My news on her was hours old. I hoped it was still current. I told him what Ruth had told me when I'd seen her at the hospital. His face pinched with concern.

"Mark, why isn't Mama in bed?" I asked, pulling the videotape out of my jacket. Alzheimer's patients can be notoriously active at night, much to the annoyance of caregivers. We'd tried to control Mama's nocturnal activities as much as possible, but Mark was a lax Mamasitter.

"She wanted to watch TV." Mark shrugged.

"I'll bet." I looked at the television. The VCR had taken flight. "Where the hell is the VCR?"

"Oh, it's hooked up in your room. Sorry, I forgot. I'll go get it—"

"Never mind. You and Mama watch TV down here." I ran up the stairs.

"Junebug called, he wants you to call him as soon as you get home," Mark yelled after me. I made a noise of acknowledgment, shut my door, and slid the tape into the VCR.

I'd half expected the tape to show an unsteady walk through the Blalock property, like a press escort of a drug raid with narration: "And here we have some actual cannabis, grown by the alleged perpetrators. . . ." This wasn't it. The scene that unfolded was a nature hike of sorts, but more along the paths of biology than botany.

It started slow, an empty bedroom, spartan and unadorned, like you might find in a cabin. I pressed the fast forward button, with great haste Tamma Hufnagel and Hally Schneider walked into view. It looked like the camcorder was somewhere above them, possibly on a tall bureau or bookshelf. I let go of the fast-forward. Tamma and Hally hugged, kissed, and disrobed with still a fair amount of speed, even without help from the VCR.

"Oh, shit!" I said, half laughing with shock. They were not much into foreplay; it wasn't long before they were sweatily making love. It appeared that they were not strangers; they handled each other with graceful familiarity. Tamma cooed his name a lot; Hally didn't say much. Her mousiness had faded; she barked out sexual orders to him with the ease of command.

I heard the doorbell ring and thought: Junebug is going to find this fascinating. I pushed the fast-forward button, to see if there was anything else on the tape. I hadn't gotten too much further when there was a crash and a scream from downstairs.

I flung the door open and ran down the stairs, nearly tumbling down them in my haste. My eyes took the scene in one glance: Mark lying on the floor, not moving, with blood welling from the side of his head; Mama cowering on the couch, crying; and Tamma Hufnagel, standing in the middle of the room, steadily holding a gun aimed at my mother. That gun swung around and the black eye of its barrel stared into my face.

"Hands on your head, Jordy," Tamma said with that same wavery voice of innocence she'd used with me when I talked to her at the church announcement board. I obeyed.

"What's this all about, Tamma?" I said. I was halfway down the stairs, and wondered if she wanted me to come the rest of the way down. I decided to wait for an invitation. I kept looking at Mark and his bloodied head. I saw his back heave the shallow motion of breath. Thank God.

"You have something I want, Jordy," Tamma insisted. Mousy brown eyes glared into mine. She didn't exactly look a threatening figure in a dark sweatshirt with painted bluebonnets on it, jeans, sneakers, and a long denim jacket.

"I don't know what you mean," I answered. "But that gun isn't going to solve any problems. Put it down and let's talk."

"No, thank you. Just give me the videotape that you took from Beta's house."

"I told you I don't know what you're talking about."

"Look, you don't have a lot of time for this," she said, which I thought didn't bode well for me. "You beat me into Beta's house tonight. I peeked in the windows and saw you searching. After you left, I went into her house and found that carved-up Bible. It's not hard to figure out what she hid there. I'd like it, please." I opened my mouth and she saw the protest coming.

"Don't make me shoot your mother in front of you, Jordy." The gun stayed on me, but Tamma's eyes flicked to Mama. I didn't see much Christian mercy in them.

"Okay, okay," I yelled. "I'll give you the tape. It's upstairs. I'll get it." I turned and took one step up before she shouted at me.

"No! You do what I say. You step on a crack, Jordy, and I'll break your mother's back. That's how this works. You understand me?"

"Yes."

She went over and pulled Mama to her feet. Mama went unprotestingly. Tamma took Mama's arm and pressed the gun to Mama's head. The barrel made a neat circle in her temple.

"You see where this is, Jordy?" Tamma demanded. "We understand each other?"

"We understand each other perfectly," I answered calmly, and I thought: But just wait till I get that gun away from you, you bitch.

I stayed put, and she and Mama came up the stairs behind me, the gun still pressed into Mama's head.

"Okay, Jordy. March. You don't turn a corner till I say so. You make any sudden moves and she's dead."

"Yes, I understand. Can I start up the stairs now?"

"Yes." It was like a game of Simon Says, I thought.

"Talk, Jordy. What do you know?" Tamma demanded.

"I don't know anything," I answered, starting to walk slowly up the stairs. I could hear Mama whimpering a little bit as Tamma hauled her up after me. "I'm going to guess that Adam wasn't at home the night Beta died. Maybe he was over at his buddy Matt's, toking up some gange. I'm sure the ladies' church auxiliary just wouldn't understand that. You were with Beta. You went with her to the library; she never had to steal a key. You were there because she was blackmailing you. Now since you don't have much money, I'm going to guess that you were going to help her to burn down the library as your payment. She'd made a tape of you and Hally making love on that youth-group trip. She'd taken Hally's camcorder and caught y'all red-handed."

"Not quite it, Jordy. Hally made the tape for fun. Beta found the tape during the trip, so she stole it and the camcorder."

I'd reached the top of the stairs and didn't move till they were on the second floor with me. I walked slowly down the hall toward my room, with a killer and my mother in tow.

"Look, Tamma," I said, "this just isn't necessary. If she was blackmailing you, maybe you could get off with a lesser charge—"

She didn't appreciate negotiation. Mama squealed and I guess Tamma jabbed her hard with the gun. I shut my mouth. We were at my room. Tamma and Mama stopped in the doorway. The tape was still playing on the VCR; Hally was lying back on the bed and Tamma lay between his legs. Tamma saw the screen and her face turned a sullen, angry red. Her eyes smouldered, looking at mine.

"You son of a bitch. You watched it." Her voice was killing cold.

"I thought it was . . . of someone else. I thought Beta had taped—"

"Never mind!" she screamed. "Turn the TV off and give me that tape!" I obeyed, sliding the tape out of the machine and gingerly handing it to her. She'd gotten upset and she'd taken the gun away from Mama's head. I tensed.

She took the tape and stepped back. Watching her, I said, "Well, Beta's quotes about y'all were right. She said Hally and other fools 'make a mock of sin' and she said 'your sin will find you out.' Ol' Beta was pretty perceptive."

"Shut up. Infatuated boys do incredibly stupid things." She'd had to let go of Mama's arm to take the tape. Tamma stuck the tape in a jacket pocket. The gun swung back to Mama's temple.

"I see you've involved my cousin in all kinds of depravity," I murmured, watching the gun at Mama's head. Mama's eyes watered in her confusion and a big tear ran down her cheek.

"Hally had nothing to do with all this."

"Really? Then why'd he go through with a last-minute convenience date with Chelsea Hart? So he could have an alibi, that's why. Did he hold Beta while you hit her with the bat?"

Tamma snarled at me. "Forget about baiting me, you moron. He didn't have anything to do with Beta's murder. I just told him he couldn't be with me and to be sure he was with someone that night. He didn't know what I was planning."

"But he could guess," I said quietly. "That's why he's so nervous, why he tried to put blame on Eula Mae. He knows you did it." I jerked my head at the silent TV.

"You think he's still going to be infatuated with you, knowing that you're a killer?"

"He doesn't know that," she responded, then screamed, "Stay still!" at Mama, who had dared to move slightly. Mama closed her eyes. My hands curled into fists.

"Don't even think of trying something, Jordy," Tamma snapped. "Get downstairs. Now!" She jerked the gun away from Mama and pointed it at my heart.

"Are you going to kill us all, Tamma?" I asked quietly. "That's three more deaths on your conscience. Then what? Kill Shannon so she doesn't wake up someday and identify you? Is that tape worth five lives?"

"That tape was worth one life. Beta's. Avoiding prison for her murder is worth as many lives as I decide. Downstairs." Her calm was eerie. She put the gun back on Mama's head and stepped away from the door. "Just like before, Jordy. You go down the stairs first, and your mother and I follow."

We walked slowly down the stairs, and I started counting the number of steps I had left in my life. There seemed to be one for each heartbeat.

"I'm sorry, Mama," I managed to croak out. Mama didn't answer me. I'd reached the living room. Mark stirred, very slowly.

"Look." I turned to Tamma as she pushed Mama toward me. Catching Mama, I set her on the couch. "Let them go. Mama can't possibly testify against you or identify you. She just isn't aware of what's going on. And Mark, he's just a little boy. I can't believe you want to kill a little boy."

Her eyes said, no, she didn't want to kill a little boy but what she wanted wasn't relevant. "I'm really sorry, Jordy, but this is all your fault. If you hadn't interfered, if you'd left things alone, Mark and your mama wouldn't be in this mess. I'm sorry, but—"

She didn't get a chance to finish, either her sentence or us. A pounding swelled on the front door, accompanied by a nonstop ringing doorbell.

"Jordy! Anne!" Bob Don's voice bellowed. "Goddamn it, open up!"

Tamma's head jerked toward the door. Bob Don sounded like a one-man SWAT team.

"They know you're here, Tamma," I said, trying to sound mild. "You better surrender." I bit my lip.

"Jordy! Jordy! Goddamn it! Open up!" Bob Don bellowed. The door vibrated in its frame.

"He's not going to go away, trust me," I said. "Give it up, Tamma."

She licked her lips, tongue darting like a rattler. "On the floor, both of you." She pushed Mama down from the couch. "You too, Jordy. Or I shoot her."

"Jordy! Jordy! Anne, darlin'!" Bob Don's words slurred together.

I watched the gun pointed down at my mother's head. I got on the floor, pressing my palms to the carpet. Mama took that moment to let everyone know she was damned tired of having a gun pointed at her, rude visitors, pounding on her door, and lying on the floor. She screamed, and she screamed loud.

Tamma shrieked, "Shut up!" and I jumped on top of Mama, pressing my body over hers. I was sure Tamma would shoot her.

The scream pierced my ears for about three seconds when the front door caved in. Bob Don swayed in the doorway and staggered in, taking in the scene.

"Goddamn!" he exclaimed. "What the hell—"

"Get back, Bob Don," Tamma demanded.

From my position on the floor, with Mama still yelling underneath me, I couldn't see Bob Don's face. I looked up and saw Tamma still had the gun leveled at us.

"What the hell you doin', little girl? Give me that," I heard Bob Don roar and Tamma whirled the gun up, in the direction of his voice, and she fired. Bob Don cried out and I heard a heavy fall.

I kicked out Tamma's legs, and she hollered and fell on her back, near my feet. The gun was still in her hand and she struggled to get it pointed in my direction. Her chest was the closest part of her to my feet and I kicked out hard, catching her in the right breast and the arm. She screamed and let go of the gun. It landed a few feet away.

I scrambled across the floor for it and she did too. I nearly closed my fingers around it, but she fell on me, biting and kicking. I squirmed and booted the gun out of her reach as we fought. It slid across the room and under Mama's easy chair.

I tried to get a grip on her shoulders, but as I did she kneed me in the groin. Yelping, I let go. She broke free from me and scrabbled like a crab toward the chair, panting. I chased her, stumbling to my feet in pain, trying to run without using my molten legs. Seeing me coming after her, she grabbed one of Mama's heavy antique candlesticks and swung it at my head. I was a harder target than Beta Harcher. I ducked but felt the whoosh of air as the heavy brass passed near my hair. The second swing around, I grabbed the candlestick and wrestled it out of her hands, tossing it aside. I completely forgot all the gentlemanly manners that Mama and Daddy ever taught me, and I punched Tamma Hufnagel in the jaw. Hard. I got a grip on her shoulder and she was still conscious, adrenaline fueling her, spitting at me. I belted her again and her eyes rolled white. I let go of her and she crumpled to the floor.

I staggered around for a second, breathing, glad to be alive.

"Jordy!" It was Junebug and another officer, coming in with service revolvers drawn.

"She did it. She killed Beta. She tried to kill us," I managed to gasp, standing over Tamma and pointing at her. "Would you please arrest her?"

Junebug rushed over to Tamma, keeping the gun aimed at her, pulling out handcuffs. Mama lay sobbing on the floor, while Mark murmured in a broken voice for his mother. I stood. Oh, God, oh my God!

I stumbled past the couch and the coffee table, toward the busted door. Bob Don lay behind the couch, still, a red stain spreading across his shirt.

"Oh, God!" I screamed, kneeling beside him. "Somebody call an ambulance!"

CHAPTER SIXTEEN

THE NEXT MORNING, CANDACE FOUND ME IN the waiting room outside of the intensive care unit. I had abandoned conversation with a prim, elderly lady whose husband was undergoing arterial surgery. She'd asked who I was there for and I didn't know what to say. A near stranger? My friend? My father? I fumbled on my own words so badly I'm sure she thought I had a speech impediment. I finally had mumbled something about a friend getting shot and she turned up her nose to me, probably thinking I frequented cheap honky-tonks with a dangerous crowd. I wasn't drunk with liquor, but with exhaustion. I'd stayed up all night, pacing the waiting room, then talking on the phone with Junebug after Tamma's confession, and then wearing out a new track of carpet while I waited for a doctor to tell me whether or not Bob Don would live or die.

Candace sat by me on the couch, handing me a cup of coffee, winking and trying gentle teasing to raise my spirits. "You better look out, Jordy. You know us and couches. I may have to take you right here."

The prim lady gathered up her knitting and fled to a remote corner of the room, not wanting to hear about us and acrobatics on furniture.

Candace gave me a timid kiss and I kissed back. "Hell of a night," she said, rubbing my neck.

"One way of putting it," I agreed wearily. "I feel like I could sleep for a week. How are you?"

"I'm fine. I was just down seeing Mark. Arlene's with him still. She said Dr. Meyers said y'all can take him home today."

"Good," I said. "I'm sure he can't wait to tell all his friends how his Uncle Jordy nearly got him killed."

Candace ignored that jab of self-recrimination. "And they released Eula Mae last night, of course. She volunteered to stay with Anne this morning while we're all down here. She said she can't wait to talk to you."

"So she can pirate all this for her next novel," I guessed.

Candace looked hard into my eyes. "You can quit with the jokes. You don't fool me a bit. You going to stay here awhile?"

"I can't leave him, Candace. Not till I know he's going to be okay. I mean, I don't think of him as my father, but he got shot trying to help me."

"I know, babe," she said, patting my hand. "You know, Bob Don's pretty special. I know you already got a man in your heart that you think of as your daddy, but you got a big heart, Jordy. Could be room in there for two, y'know."

"Junebug told me they arrested Ruth and Matt," I offered, changing the subject and getting myself in trouble. Candace's eyes hardened.

"They did. They found another videotape in Beta's house, this one with footage of the pot crop. She must've taken that camcorder she stole from Hally and taped the field for evidence. I guess she planned on hitting them up for money, too." She coughed. "You know, I did not appreciate you running out on me like that."

"I didn't want to involve you any more."

"Doofus. Could have gotten yourself killed." She

sniffed, and that was the extent of the fight. At least for the moment. She cleared her throat and continued: "I talked with Arlene. She said the police are talking to Hally, but they don't think he had anything to do with killing Beta. And I heard Billy Ray offered Adam Hufnagel a plea bargain to testify against Ruth and Matt. I imagine he'll take it. He seems to be in deep shock that Tamma did all this."

"He should be. She very nearly got away with it."

"How, for God's sake? And why resort to murder?" Candace asked.

I leaned back on the couch. "She was a lot smarter than anyone gave her credit for. When Beta found out that Tamma and Hally were lovers—and how she did, who knows, but she did and she found that tape of them—Beta made Tamma start giving her more control over church functions. And therefore church money. Tamma couldn't do a thing out of fear that Beta would show the tape. So she had to agree to whatever Beta suggested."

"So," Candace pursed her lips, "the afternoon that Bob Don saw Tamma leaving Beta's looking so scared and upset—"

"Beta had given her the penance to get the tape back. Burning down the library that night. And that's when Tamma decided to put a stop to the threats. She realized that if it looked as though Beta planned to burn down the library but was killed before she could light the matches, so to speak, I'd be a real big suspect. She decided to frame me for Beta's murder."

"Bitch," Candace said tonelessly. She hugged me hard.

"She put out the bat on the path to the library, already wiped clean of prints. She watched and made sure that I'd picked up the bat and then took it inside with me.

Perhaps Beta had told her already about threatening me with closing the library, and Tamma made sure she was there to see Beta assault me. She was the one who told Junebug and Billy Ray that I'd said, in anger, that I could've killed Beta."

"You do have a mouth on you," Candace agreed. "So Tamma met Beta at the library and killed her."

"Yeah. According to Tamma's confession, Beta wanted to pray before they torched it, like the library was going to be some burnt offering before God. Tamma said she put on her gloves and hit Beta halfway through the Lord's Prayer." I shivered.

"Then she planted the key on Beta's body. That I don't get," Candace said.

"She wanted it to look like Beta had managed to get her own key somehow. If she had a key, she didn't need anyone on the library board to let her in. The story about Beta swiping Adam's key was pure fluff."

"Beta's little list, though, put attention on other people besides you."

"That's right, sugar. Tamma didn't know about that list. She did tell Junebug though, that Beta had bragged to her that when her church was built, she was going to have pews in it with contributors' names plaqued on them, along with an appropriate Bible verse. Sick, isn't it?"

"But how did Tamma know you'd be at the library around the time of the murder?" Candace asked.

"She didn't. That was bad luck on my part. Tamma told Junebug that I'd scared the hell out of her; she had just killed Beta not a minute before I walked in. After I left, Tamma went home and got there before Adam got back from having his therapeutic joint with Matt Blalock. When the police started asking for alibis, Adam made up the story that they'd both been home watching an old John Wayne movie. He never dreamed his wife needed an alibi worse than he did. He was only worried about someone finding out about his smoking dope."

"Tamma must've been searching for that videotape when Shannon surprised her," Candace said.

"Tamma claims they fought for the gun and it went off by accident. Of course, it went off in a closed room and nearly deafened Tamma. When I called the Hufnagels to tell them about Shannon being shot, I thought Tamma sounded funny, like she had a cold, and I had to repeat myself for her to hear me. It was from the shock of the gunshot."

"How's Shannon doing?" Candace asked.

She'd gotten out of surgery an hour or so before Bob Don was rushed in. "They're very hopeful. God, that poor girl."

Candace snuggled next to me. It felt great. "Lord, all this suffering that Beta and Tamma caused."

I grunted in agreement and hugged her close.

Candace murmured, "One of Junebug's deputies went by the Goertzes', to see about getting Gretchen to come to the hospital. They found her passed out in bed. She won't be coming down today, at least."

"I'm not sure Gretchen would come anyway, Candace. I think she hates him now. Maybe it's for the best, 'cause I don't think he ever loved her."

A runty figure lounged in the doorway, watching me. I let Candace go. "Sugar, would you excuse me? I'd like to talk to Uncle Bid in private, please."

Candace rose and left, murmuring a hello to Bid. He didn't answer, he just kept staring those glassy dark eyes at me. He lit up a cigarillo. The knitting lady, fuming worse than the smoke, gathered up her yarn and fled.

"I see you survived the night," Bid drawled at me. "From all accounts, that's something of a miracle. Perhaps Six Flags Over Texas will design a stunt show after your adventures." He snickered.

I stood and smiled down at him. "Cut the crap with me, Bid. I know what you are, and although I didn't think it possible, I dislike you more than ever."

He squinted through smoke with his intimidate-the-prosecution eyes. "Whatever do you mean?"

"That extra $25,000 in Beta's savings account, that I thought for a while either Ruth Wills or Bob Don had paid off Beta with. That's your money."

"I don't know what you mean, Jordy."

I pulled the photo and letter I'd found at the back of the Bible in Beta's house last night. I'd kept them in my back pocket, as close to my heart as a picture of Uncle Bid would ever get. "Not really a good likeness of you, Bidwell. You had a lot of hair then." I dangled the photo in front of his face, watching his shock, then admired the snapshot myself. It was an old photo, black and white, in a sleeve with a State Fair of Texas border around it, 1960. A younger Beta and a younger Bid, smiling, arms around each other. Beta had a wisp of the famous State Fair cotton candy in the corner of her mouth and she looked like a fun-loving kid.

"You'd said you never dated her, that she was too wild for you. But you lied. You got her pregnant and you paid for her to go to Mexico for a quiet little abortion. Then you dumped her. She turned to religion for solace like a drunk turns to the bottle."

"That's an ugly lie, Jordy," Bid observed mildly, puffing on his foul little cigar.

"You thought she didn't have any friends she could dare confide in here, so you were safe. You were wrong. She had a special friend." I held up the letter that had been with the photo. "She'd confided in letters to her pen pal, Kirsten Koss of Stavenger, Norway. Old Man Renfro told me he remembered Beta having a Scandinavian pen pal. Kirsten wrote this very supportive letter to Beta, calling you by name and telling Beta that she could make it past having an abortion, that it wouldn't ruin her life." I eyed the letter. "Kirsten says for Beta to get away from you. Sounds like good advice."

"Give me that letter!" he snapped, trying to grab for it. I used my Goertz height to keep it from his Poteet hands.

"Naughty, naughty, Bid. So she finally came to you for money, after all these years."

"She came to me," he spat harshly, "because she knew you were nothing but a common bastard. And she knew I'd want to protect my brother's good name."

"Spare me," I interjected. "You never gave a crap about your brother. So you knew, didn't you? All these years, you knew."

"I told Lloyd he'd be better off without that—" He saw my eyes gleam and he didn't use a pejorative. "—without Anne, but he didn't listen to me. The fool, raising you like you were his own."

"It's called love, but don't worry, Bid. You'll never be inconvenienced by it."

"I don't know why I wasted money on that woman to protect a bastard like you," he hissed.

"You didn't protect a soul, you heartless shit. You treated Beta Harcher like crap and she molded herself into the bitterest person alive. You knew the truth about me and you didn't tell me because you didn't want shame on your precious Poteet name. You knew Beta was a blackmailer and you stayed silent. And worst of all, you've hated me for years for something that's be-

yond my control—my parentage." I turned my back on
him. "Get out of here." I half expected a burning cigarillo extinguished on the back of my neck, but Bid beat
an honorable retreat.

I sagged back into the chair and waited some more.
Finally a nurse came into the waiting room. "You Mr.
Goertz's son? He's been asking for you. You can see
him now." I mumbled a vague assent and followed her
into intensive care. The rooms were more like patios,
with an open wall that faced out onto the nurses' station
so they could see the patients at all times.

Wires made him look like a Christmas tree without
lights. There were wires to his heart, his guts, his arms.
Calm agreed with Bob Don. His eyes were shut and I
stood next to the bed for a long time, studying his face.

"Hey," I finally said.

He opened those big blue eyes and blinked at me.
"Hey there, Jordy. How you?"

"Better than you, Bob Don."

He grinned and I saw it hurt him. They'd taken the
bullet out from near his heart last night and mirth didn't
make him feel happy.

"But don't get me wrong," I said. "You're going to
be okay."

"Anne? Mark?" he whispered.

"Fine, both fine."

He eased back into the pillows. "Thank God, thank
God." He glanced to the other side of the bed. "Where's
Gretchen?"

I coughed. "Gretchen didn't feel up to coming, Bob
Don. I'm sorry. Maybe tomorrow." My face tightened.
"That was a damned brave thing you did, Bob Don."

He snorted, like a car salesman would at a ridiculous
offer. "Damned stupid. I'd been drinking a bit after you
stormed out, and I had mostly liquid courage."

"Whatever it was, it worked. You saved us."

"I don't have the right to say this to you, Jordy, but I'm gonna. I'm old and maybe I won't make it out of here. I would have died for you." He choked with emotion and he shut his eyes, leaking tears.

"Listen, Bob Don, I've been thinking." I gulped. "You know, I just can't forget my dad—you know, Lloyd. He was the man who raised me, the one I called Daddy all those years, the man who made me the man I am today. I won't ever, ever forget him and no one can replace him."

"I don't want you to forget Lloyd," Bob Don murmured. "I don't want to forget him either. I just want . . . I just want a chance to be a father to you, too." He opened his eyes, searching for the copies of them in my face. "You're a lucky fella, y'know. Not many folks get a chance to have two daddies that love 'em. I do love you, Jordy, very much. I always have and no matter how you feel about me, I always will."

I couldn't answer. My own tears flooded my eyes and I stared down at the sheets covering his wounded body.

"Excuse me, Mr. Poteet?" a nasal voice screeched. I looked up, blinking. A bone-thin nurse frowned at me, glancing between me and Bob Don. I recognized her as a regular customer from the library—she liked historical novels. "Are you supposed to be in here, Mr. Poteet?" she demanded, sounding irritated. "Are you immediate family to Mr. Goertz?"

I blinked away tears and my hand found Bob Don's. I cleared my voice before I answered. "Yes, ma'am, I am."